At Least I Know I'm Free

How Americans Could Have Lost Their Freedoms

An Alternative History of World War II

William C. Grayson

For Mike
Best wishes
Bill Grayson

Copyright © 2007 by William C. Grayson

ISBN 0-7414-4036-9

Published by:

PUBLISHING.COM

1094 New DeHaven Street, Suite 100
West Conshohocken, PA 19428-2713
Info@buybooksontheweb.com
www.buybooksontheweb.com
Toll-free (877) BUY BOOK
Local Phone (610) 941-9999
Fax (610) 941-9959

Printed in the United States of America

Printed on Recycled Paper

Published July 2007

Also by William C. Grayson:

Chicksands: A Millennium of History ISBN 0-9633208-1-5

Delaware's Ghost Towers ISBN 1-4208469-1-4

Americans and Brits without first-hand experience of the early days of World War II may not appreciate the pervasive anxiety gripping both nations that they were about to be invaded and occupied by brutal enemy forces. Neither the U.S. nor Britain was effectively prepared to repulse large invading armies and the spirit of both countries' populations teetered on the rhetoric and encouragement of Franklin Roosevelt and Winston Churchill. Both leaders, contemplating the certain ghastly consequences of modern warfare within their homelands, could have sought desperate terms with Germany and Japan that would have averted invasion. Instead, both made decisions to resist to the utmost and those decisions rallied their countrymen, who flocked to recruiting stations, defense industries, and farms.

It might have been quite different. Especially in the U.S., which was not already under heavy aerial bombardment, prominent voices urged appeasement and isolationism, some from an admiration of *Nazi* Germany, some from a blind dread of war. An FDR decision not to join a bloody fight and not to supply the war efforts of the British and the Communist Soviet Union could have had a disastrous outcome for the U.S. nonetheless. It was the conversion of U.S. industry to defense production and the rapid buildup of the armed services and their infrastructure that finally propelled the national economy out of the Great Depression. An economically weak U.S. restricted by terms dictated by the Germans and Japanese could also have become vulnerable to attacks on its moral fiber and steadfast commitment to basic freedom and civil liberties.

At Least I Know I'm Free examines the momentous events of the run-up to America's entry into World War II and suggests how the reversal of a few key decisions could have led to the loss of Americans' freedoms.

TABLE OF CONTENTS

FOREWORD and ACKNOWLEDGEMENTS

At Least I Know I'm Free seeks to describe a fictitious but plausible 1940s world scenario in which American basic rights and freedoms are lost; squandered by irresolute officials who fail to step up to great challenges with heroic action. However, Americans *really are* free and this book's message is an unequivocal assertion that all Americans owe an enormous debt that can never be repaid to the statesmen, service members, law enforcement officers, and citizens who risked and sacrificed greatly in the preservation of liberty.

Some reviewers of *At Least I Know I'm Free* have commented that, with knowledge of the actual historical record, they were unable to accept, as plausible, one or another of the book's personas uncharacteristically failing to act decisively in defense of freedom. These insightful comments directly affirm the book's thesis: irreplaceable heroic acts are knowable and deserve perpetual celebration but without them, freedoms taken for granted today could have been and could still be lost.

So, *At Least I Know I'm Free* is "what-if" or "alternative history." Readers familiar with the actual history of the period will recognize places, events, dates, and the names of some of the major players, however, the story told by the book fictionalizes the truth as a device for demonstrating how a combination of inappropriate actions or failures by the principal characters to act, when confronted by hard decisions, could have combined to result in American freedom being drastically curtailed.

I have taken the liberty of extrapolating from some of the story's historical personas and their documented political philosophies to suggest how they might have addressed the scenario I have contrived. Of course, Norman Thomas, Charles Lindbergh, Jeanette Rankin, Eugene Talmadge, the various military officers, and several of the others included were not actually confronted by the grave issues fabricated in the book but the alternative history pointedly asks: is it plausible that those characters might have actually been impelled by their personalities and politics to act out the scripts I have assigned them? Readers will note fictitious events wrapped around real history and the playful recycling of some actual historic dates but with alternative outcomes.

I was influenced by the approaches taken by other authors of alternative histories and acknowledge the challenge to readers to recognize the subtle differences in the text between the "what-if" history and the actual historical record. To enhance readability, repetitious reminders to "suppose" or "imagine" are minimized. Philip Roth, in *War Against America* (ISBN 1-40007949-7), wrote about some of the same major players in the same period of time but told a very different story. As Mr. Roth did, *At Least I Know I'm Free* also presents the "Ground Truth" historical reality at Annex C and readers are encouraged to continue through the three follow-on annexes. In particular, Annex C, the "Ground Truth" annex, demonstrates the real plausibility of historical detours suggested in the alternative history.

Several others have also written alternative histories of the period. Peter G. Tsouras' *Rising Sun Victorious* (ISBN 1-85367-466-X) and *Disaster at D-Day* (ISBN 1-85367-411-7), and Ron Fyten's *Conquest & Defeat* (ISBN 1-58721865-8) present imaginative World War II scenarios that are very different from actual history but have few parallels with *At Least I Know I'm Free*. Kim Stanley Robinson's *Lucky Strike* and Brad Linaweaver's *Moon of Ice* are also World War II alternative histories published as a collection in ISBN 0-345-43990-2.

The concept of *At Least I Know I'm Free* drew substantial inspiration from the Civil War alternative history, *Never Call Retreat*, by former Speaker Newt Gingrich and William R. Forstchen, ISBN: 0312342985.

In the closing moments of the editorial process for *At Least I Know I'm Free*, Gingrich and Forstchen announced the publication of their new alternative history of the December 7th Japanese attack on Hawaii (ISBN 1427201277). Quite independently, their new *Pearl Harbor* and my *At Least I Know I'm Free* offer remarkably similar "What if" scenarios. I am pleased by affirmation of the plausibility of my approach by two such distinguished PhD. historians.

Much valuable help was provided by friends, who read the manuscript and offered constructive suggestions. Brigadier General Grover Jackson, Colonel Vic Brown, Lt. Colonel. Ernie Short, Chief Master Sergeant Dan D'Apolito, Senior Master Sergeant Larry Tart (all USAF Retired) and Vince Wuwert, an ex-USAF Morse Intercept Operator, reviewed the fictionalized World War II intelligence aspects. Jennifer Leetz checked the book's German language content. Retired U.S. Marine Chief Warrant Officer Allan Storm and Historian Lee Jennings of the Delaware Department of Natural Resources and Environmental Control checked and helped with the account of the Coast Artillery's fictitious close encounter with the German fleet off the Delaware coast. Dr. Gary Wray provided technical support regarding the history of German World War II naval ship movements. My son, Charles W. Grayson, performed a helpful editorial check.

Photo Credits

Individual photo credits are included in the end notes for each chapter. Every effort has been made to trace copyright holders of photographs annotated by the Photographs and Prints Division of the Library of Congress "no known restrictions." If advised, the publishers will rectify any omissions at the earliest opportunity.

Going in Harm's Way

Annually on Veterans' Day at the Vietnam War Memorial in Washington, a series of distinguished speakers pays tribute to the men and women who gave their lives in Vietnam, protecting American freedoms. On this day of national observance some years ago, songwriter Lee Greenwood appeared and performed his popular song *"God Bless the USA,"* which has grown to anthem proportions among modern patriots.

"I'm proud to be an American, where at least I know I'm free
And I won't forget the men who died, who gave that right to me"

- Lee Greenwood

The words of this important song suggest some interesting questions:

- Which men, who died? When did they die?
- Which "right" is the "right" that was given? Just one right? The "right" to be free?
- Without those men who died, which rights might we now not have or no longer have?
- What if American and Allied men had chosen not to fight and risk death?
- What does *"At least I know I'm free"* actually mean?

American forces in harm's way are automatically credited with protecting our freedoms but it takes some analysis to understand which freedoms are being protected and from what or from whom. "Harm's way" is usually taken to mean being at risk of death, injury, or capture and can refer to actually being exposed to dangerous threats, such as hostile fire or serious accident during risky activities. Thus, uniformed American servicemen or women and sworn law enforcement officers would be in harm's way, if hostile fire were directed toward them (as in combat) or might be directed toward them (if armed hostiles decided to aim fire in their direction). Similarly, uniformed Americans are in harm's way when performing dangerous duties in aircraft, vessels, vehicles, and unhealthful environments, even when there is no threat of hostile fire.

The concept of "going in harm's way to protect our freedoms" is much easier to grasp in some contexts than in others. Probably the two clearest examples are the combat service of U.S. forces in the War for American Independence and then in the War of 1812. Although some might find acceptable the rights we would have today as British subjects, if American freedoms had not been gained in the War for American Independence and successfully defended in the War of 1812, it must be reckoned that, except for the combat service of U.S. forces in those early wars, those treasured uniquely American rights and freedoms would not exist.

The service performed in harm's way by American soldiers and sailors in those first two wars is irrevocably linked to the United States' democratic way of life and Americans' cherished rights and human freedoms. Definitive military service examples are provided by George Washington's Christmas Eve 1776 crossing of the Delaware River during the War for American Independence and Dwight D. Eisenhower's decision to launch the D-Day invasion on June 6, 1944, although better weather conditions might have been obtained by delaying.

Washington's was a last-ditch, all-or-nothing gamble that kept the Revolution alive and dissuaded some of the former colonies from surrender. Eisenhower's reckoned that any delay might jeopardize security and surprise and also might give the German defenders the opportunity to strengthen their coastal positions. Without General Washington's unwavering resolve and firm rejection of defeatist advice that the war was lost so the crossing should be abandoned, the Revolution would have collapsed and the American rights and freedoms proclaimed in the Declaration of Independence and the Bill of Rights would not survive in their present forms and scope. Without Eisenhower's decisive decision-making, the Germans might not have been dislodged from Europe and American freedoms may have been ultimately abridged. I have tried to explain how this could have happened in *At Least I Know I'm Free.*

"Going in harm's way to protect our freedoms" becomes murkier and much more difficultly grasped in some later conflicts. The Mexican War, various 19th Century expeditions against Indian tribes (officially catalogued as American "wars'), various minor rebellions and skirmishes, the Spanish-American War, and even World War I could be argued as not to be guarantors of American freedoms and rights as much as they assert other compelling national political or economic objectives. Certainly, the American Civil War preserved the Union but, with the exception of lifting the terrible yoke of slavery from Blacks, the Civil War example does not readily support the proposition that basic rights of the general U.S. population were being protected.

The Korean and Vietnam Wars were proxy campaigns of a larger, half century-long conflict. The "Cold War," as it is called, was waged to prevent World Communism from threatening the basic freedoms of the democratic nations as it certainly did. However, it could be reasonably argued that, while a continued stalemate in the Cold War could have had major negative impacts on some economic, social, and travel *choices* Americans might make, citizens' basic liberties probably would have continued undiminished.[1]

---

[1] If a scenario that includes military defeat and occupation of the U.S. by Communist armed forces is plausible, then a major disruption of basic liberty and freedoms would be likewise plausible.

Although a sizeable bloc of historians might not agree, the Korean and Vietnam Wars directly challenged Communist China's agenda of fomenting "wars of national liberation" elsewhere in Asia and in Africa and Latin America, as well. These two costly wars, whose tally includes continuing substantial ingratitude towards the American troops who fought them, distracted China's dream of wider dominance, buying time for the emergence of her "Cultural Revolution" and a shift in emphasis that prioritizes Chinese domestic growth.

American forces and Coalition Allies went into harm's way during the Gulf War of 1991, which liberated Kuwait and protected Saudi Arabia from Iraqi invasion. While obviously protecting the set of rights enjoyed by Kuwaitis and Saudis, the stretch necessary to see that Gulf War service in harm's way as protective of American freedoms is a long one.[2] On the other hand, the bitterly divisive political atmosphere produced by the invasion of Iraq in 2003, seriously complicates the analysis. Most Americans accept the connection between the threat to basic American rights and freedoms posed by unchecked terrorist attacks in the U.S. and the invasion of Afghanistan and its Taliban government, which abetted the 9-11 attacks.

The case is much more difficult for many Americans to accept that servicemen and women in harm's way in Iraq are protecting American freedoms. If the threat of surprise attacks on office buildings and mass transportation makes Americans fearful about simply going to work, to school, or to travel, it could be argued that at least some freedom would be lost. That is a highly complex issue needing separate, detailed examination and is not addressed

---

[2] Martin Rue, a Vietnam War disabled veteran, has an interesting perspective quoted in the April 2006 issue of the American Legion Magazine. Rue observes: "When another country wants to be free, we need to help them find that means. I feel it's our obligation to help those countries." Conversely, former President Gerald Ford wrote an opinion about the war in Iraq that he wanted kept secret until after his death: "I just don't think we should go hellfire damnation around the globe freeing people, unless it is directly related to our own national security." (Published posthumously on December 20, 2006).

here. What is clear is that the American military sacrifices in Iraq and Afghanistan have drawn Islamofascist murderers to fight *over there* instead of in the U.S. Volunteer American men and women in uniform have offered themselves as bait to distract some of the murderers from attacking civilians in the U.S and diminishing their liberties.

To the people who lived during the 1940s and were alive to see the 1990s, World War II was the most important aspect of their lifetimes and of the 20th Century. Philosophically, there does exist a close parallel between the 21st Century war against terrorism and World War II, fought against the Axis powers in the 1930s and 1940s. Muslim extremist terrorists say they want to kill as many Americans as possible and replace American rights and freedoms with fundamentalist *Sharia* law based on the Koran and enforced by a Muslim caliphate. The Axis powers, especially Germany and Japan, slaughtered as many people as possible they considered "enemies" and denied basic rights and freedoms to all the populations they conquered. In hindsight, it is relevant to examine American military service during World War II, asking whether going in harm's way against Axis forces was intended only to restore rights and freedoms to the victims of Axis aggression or if Americans' freedoms were being protected as well. It was, after all, a tenet of American doctrine and policy that broad oceans were primary defensive buffers and that invasion was unlikely.[3]

William C Grayson

Washington

---

[3] FDR's "Four Freedoms" speech, January 6, 1941 concentrated sharply on what the downfall of democratic nations might mean to the U.S.

"It is by no means necessary that a great nation should always stand at the heroic level. But no nation has the root of greatness in it unless, in time of need, it can rise to the heroic mood."

- **Theodore Roosevelt**

"Americans have a reputation for giving a fight to whoever asks for it."

- **Wesley Pruden**

PROLOGUE

HOW THE "WHAT-IF, ALTERNATIVE HISTORY" WORKS; AN EXAMPLE:

On board United Flight 93: Terrorist Attack on the U.S. Capitol; How It Might Have Happened

On September 11, 2001, after seizing control of United Flight 93, suppose terrorists Ahmed Alhaznawi and Saeed Alghamdi constantly patrolled the cabin aisle, checking the seated passengers intently. Brandishing their box cutters, still dripping flight attendants' blood, what if the hijackers made sure all seatbelts remained fastened and permitted no talking or use of telephones? Neither Todd Beamer, Jeremy Glick, CeCee Lyles, Mark Bingham, Tom Burnett nor any of the other passengers would have had a chance to stand up or learn that other hijacked planes had been crashed into buildings.

At the cockpit controls, Ziad Samir Jarrah slows the Boeing 757 to an airspeed of 300 knots and brings the aircraft into a wide left turn until the compass heading reads 135 degrees (southeast). He enters the geographic coordinates of the Pentagon, 38-86N; 77-05W, into the autopilot and switches it "on." The twin-engined Boeing will now be guided directly to the point at which Jarrah will resume manual control. The cloudless blue sky gives the hijacker a clear view of the Appalachians below and, in time, he spots the Skyline Drive running along the mountains' eastern edge. As the mountains recede from his side view, Jarrah throttles back to an airspeed of 220 knots and eases the control yoke slightly forward, beginning a gentle descent. The autopilot maintains a course of 085 degrees - almost due east. Jarrah is not distracted by any noise or movements in the passenger cabin and concentrates sharply on his flying.

In Osama bin Laden's plan, a Boeing 757, smaller than a 767, will be more maneuverable at very low altitude in downtown Washington. He is also confident that although smaller, the 757 is big enough to destroy the Capitol Dome and will not need to hit it as hard as the planes striking the World Trade Center towers and the Pentagon. A slower impact speed is planned. In less than two minutes, smoke ahead, rising from the Pentagon, rammed earlier by hijacked American Flight 77, thrills the Arab terrorists in the cockpit, who lustily exclaim, *Alahu Akhbar!* The City of Washington glistens before Jarrah in the bright morning sunshine as Flight 93 passes quickly through some of the smoke and Jarrah disables the autopilot. The U.S. Army surface-to-air missile

battery on the roof of the Pentagon is unmanned because of the fire from the earlier Flight 77 crash and does not engage Flight 93. The hijacker levels off at 500 feet.

The Potomac River rushes past below and clenched-jawed Jarrah keeps his unblinking eyes fixed on his checkpoint, the Washington Monument, coming up just to his left.

The 757 screams down Independence Avenue till alongside the 555 foot-tall obelisk, causing some pedestrians to gawk, others to drop to the ground. Jarrah's gaze switches to the Capitol, as he steers manually to center the aircraft over the Mall and point the Boeing's nose directly at the gleaming white dome.

As Flight 93 banks in its slight right turn, its starboard wing dips toward Independence Avenue, just south of the Mall. In an instant, a heat-seeking missile launched from the White House roof hits the 757's starboard wing between the fuselage and starboard engine. The wing's fuel tank explodes violently, causing the outer pieces of the wing to depart the aircraft. In the pilot's seat, Jarrah is shocked and cannot comprehend what has happened. He sits, open-mouthed and paralyzed by his confusion, as the Capitol dome looms into view but higher than and left of where he expected to see it through the windshield. Forgetting to shout his salutation to Allah, he gasps bug-eyed and dies silently in the fireball as the aircraft slams into the right side of the Reflecting Pool, carries away the fence along First Street SW and nearby trees, stopping at the end of the deep ditch it has plowed in the wide lawn surrounding the Capitol. All on board are killed but there are no injuries or building damage on the Capitol grounds.

The 757's right wing tip and starboard engine, pushed by the exploding missile and aviation fuel, travel in separate descending arcs to the right. The wing tip, still possessing aerodynamic qualities, sails in frisbee fashion through the north-facing glass façade of the Smithsonian Air and Space Museum. Miraculously, the museum's opening time is 10am and visiting school groups, just getting off buses on Independence Avenue, are not yet in the building. The wing tip comes to rest, ironically, in the museum's commercial airliners exhibit room. Two sales associates in the next-door book shop are slightly injured by flying glass. The starboard engine, however, hits and bounces off the roof of the Holiday Inn, just south of Independence Avenue on 6th Street SW, cart wheels another 300 feet, and slams into the rear of a five-story office building at 475 School Street, killing 14 employees of a government contractor at their desks.

The 9-11 Reality

Of course, the heroic decisions and acts of United 93 passengers prevented the terrorist, Ziad Samir Jarrah, from reaching Washington and his planned target. However, except for the passengers' sacrifices, the Boeing 757 would surely have caused many deaths on the ground, shocking damage, and lasting trauma not only to people who work at or visit Washington but also to the millions who would see the video coverage and replays. It must be concluded that the heroes of Flight 93 made and implemented an indispensable decision. The "what-if-they-hadn't" alternative history example emphasizes their well-deserved place in American history.

> *Plausible: Seemingly or apparently valid, likely, or acceptable; credible.*
>
> **- American Heritage Dictionary**

Dedicated to the long line of courageous, freedom-loving Americans that stretches from Colonial times through the present and into the future, who have made and will make the tough but right decisions undaunted by grave risks to which they were exposed. Immeasurable gratitude is due those who fell for freedom while in harm's way without knowing that they had contributed to victory.

1

PEARL HARBOR AND THE COLLAPSE OF AMERICAN RESOLVE

Suppose Japan's goal of preventing U.S. interference with her dominance of Asia by destroying the fleet at Pearl Harbor and attacking the West Coast frightened Americans into pressuring the government and the U.S. decided not to fight? What might have followed?

The Alternative History . . .

Following the surprise attack on Pearl Harbor and the U.S. declaration of war, the Japanese overran and dislodged U.S., British Commonwealth, Dutch and French forces in Asia and the Philippines. By mid-1942, Japan had occupied and subjugated all of eastern Asia from Burma to Manchuria plus what is now Indonesia and all the islands of Micronesia. With Japan's unopposed access to raw material riches and unlimited slave labor, she was able to strengthen her naval and air forces aggressively and deployed them strategically for protection of a greatly enlarged empire. Ranging broadly across the region, growing numbers of Japanese submarines waged unrestricted attacks on enemy naval and merchant shipping as far south as Australian waters and as far east as the U.S. west coast. Japan seized all the islands in the Aleutian Islands chain west of Adak, setting up naval and air bases. Japan "cleansed" some of the islands of their native populations by shipping them to Japan as POWs.

Beginning in mid-December 1941, Kauai, westernmost of the major Hawaiian Islands, was occasionally shelled and briefly occupied by raiding Japanese commando parties. Highly destructive sabotage was carried out during these incursions, which included brutal assassinations and the kidnappings of Hawaiians of Japanese ancestry, who were never accounted for. The FBI and Navy Department had credible reports of espionage activities and flashlight signaling from Mt. Kalelau but had apprehended no suspects. A Marine Corps detachment and its radio station on Kauai were wiped out by Japanese commandos supported by naval gunfire and were not replaced.

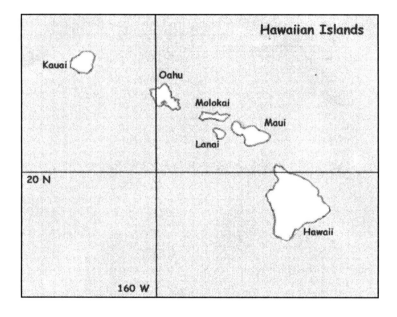

Throughout the early months of 1942, the U.S. Navy's Pacific Fleet was reduced to licking its wounds while the attempted resurrection of capital ships sunk at Pearl Harbor was repeatedly interrupted by Vice Admiral Chuichi Nagumo's carrier-launched air strikes and the shelling of coastal assets. The attacks on Hawaiian military airfields had eliminated nearly all U.S. fighter aircraft and their fuel dumps, giving the Japanese a degree of air superiority that permitted them to raid with impunity. Ship repair crews were frequently surprised by *Zero* fighters, which came in below radar coverage, suddenly strafing small boats and parties of repairmen.

Mitsubishi Zero

Night brought no respite as the Japanese pilots were skilled at machine-gunning anything in the harbor with lights, including the damaged areas of ships under repair. Between losses to strafing attacks and the growing refusals of civilian workers to expose themselves to the terrifying raids, not a single major vessel sunk on December 7th had been refloated by the end of May 1942. Admiral Nagumo doggedly occupied and controlled the approaches to the Hawaiian Islands in a 360 degree encirclement, refreshing and resupplying his task force with replacement ships, supplies and men from Japan fleet-based assets.

Jap Subs on the Prowl

Daily since early November 1941, Stations *Hypo*, the U.S. Navy Communications Intelligence (COMINT) site in Hawaii and *Cast*, a sister station at Cavite in the Philippines, had been monitoring twice-daily Japanese high frequency (HF) Manual Morse radio broadcasts, which were encoded by *JN-25* codebooks. Direction Finding (DF) fixes consistently located the source of the broadcasts in Tokyo. Although the broadcast's frequencies and callsigns were changed every seven days, the U.S. radio operators were able to recognize the rhythms and keying characteristics of individual Japanese Morse operators, which helped to maintain continuity on the transmitter. While the *JN-25* code had not been broken and the underlying texts could not be read, the *Hypo* and *Cast* eavesdroppers took note of the standard format of the Tokyo broadcasts.

Morning and evening, Tokyo always came on the air with a string of tuning "Vs" and then went right into its message: "DE" (meaning "from") its callsign (such as "KO3A") and then two five-number groups transmitted three times, followed by one more five-number group. Broadcasts always ended with the radio procedure sign requesting acknowledgement, "ZEV." *Hypo* and *Cast* carefully recorded a large number of extremely brief HF *JN-25* messages from individual callsigns (such as "4LUY," "TGRE," and "UO2S") that immediately followed each of the Tokyo broadcasts. These were believed to be outstation responses acknowledging receipt of the broadcasts. The *Hypo* analysts suspected that Tokyo was transmitting compressed messages as codewords.

```
// IN HERE   // VAW

082135ZDEC

MONITORING FREQS 8285 AND 7730 //

VVV   VVV   VVV

VVV   VVV   VVV

DE   KO3A   KO3A   KO3A

20919   64276   20919   64276   20919   64276
65622   ZEV   //1336Z


VVV DE   4LUY   90290   36046   // 1337Z

VVV DE TGRE   33038   29573   //1338Z

VVV DE UO2S   40388   75192   // 1338Z

[31 ADDITIONAL CALLS BETWEEN 1338Z AND
1353z
```

U.S. Navy radio intercept log

By December 4th, between 30 to 40 Morse "acknowledgement" messages consisting of a four-character callsign and two five-number groups were being intercepted on two of four frequencies - two used during daylight and two others at night. The radio frequencies transmitting the acknowledgements were appropriate for use over thousands of miles. On the air for too short a time to permit direction finding bearings, the short messages were suspected by Joe Finnegan and Tom Dyer, *Hypo* radio traffic analysts, as probable acknowledgements to codewords being broadcast from Tokyo.

The long-distance frequencies used suggested the acknowledging senders were somewhere out in the mid-Pacific. Finnegan and Dyer, joined by radioman Ham Wright, briefed Captain Joseph Rocheford, *Hypo's* OIC, on their analysis. The briefing reasoned that acknowledgements back to Tokyo would probably not be sent individually by a large number of vessels traveling in company, therefore the acknowledging stations were most likely scattered. The extremely brief responses were obviously a security measure, intended to protect the senders' identities and locations. The Navy analysts expressed admiration for the disciplined teamwork demonstrated by the enemy radio operators; as a group, they were able to cram three, sometimes four "acknowledgements" into the space of one minute. Listening intently, Rocheford concluded that the acknowledging outstations were probably Jap submarines and the number of responses suggested that as many as 40 subs were deployed and keeping their locations secret, communicating no more than necessary to tell Tokyo they were still OK in response to codeword queries of their operational status.

American anti-submarine defenses were basically ineffective in 1941 and, since December 7th, the U.S. Navy had lost several destroyers and minesweepers to Japanese torpedoes between the West Coast and Hawaiian waters. Japanese sub captains had perfected a reconnaissance technique in which their boats were brought to periscope depth and their propellers stopped. "Hovering" dead in the water with only the stub of the periscope protruding but creating no wake, the subs were virtually impossible to spot with the naked eye or through binoculars and loitered for hours at a time, keeping watch on their assigned sectors for targets. Captain Rocheford had personally briefed Admiral Kimmel of his suspicion that up to 40 enemy subs were out looking for U.S. targets in the Pacific and he repeated the briefing for Admiral Nimitz as soon as he had replaced Admiral Kimmel.

Nimitz fretted about the many Jap subs he suspected were stalking his carriers. He ordered the two Pacific Fleet aircraft carriers,[4] which were miraculously spared by the first Pearl Harbor attack, to sail back to the U.S. West Coast, ostensibly to shore up coastal defenses but as much to save them from destruction. The two carriers, *Enterprise* and *Lexington*, had been away from Pearl Harbor to deliver aircraft to the Marines on Wake and Midway Islands. Both flattops plus their destroyer escorts immediately sailed for the U.S. as a task unit, making an elongated southern arc, zigzagging toward Central America and then north along the coast of *Baja California*. Both carriers still had their Fairchild light *GK-1* scout planes aboard and kept them up in a defensive search mode during all daylight hours. Giving the Panama Canal approaches wide berth, which were correctly suspected of being heavily patrolled by Jap subs, the carriers safely slipped into San Diego. Hawaii, however, was left without any aircraft carriers and only a handful of Army P-40 *Warhawk* fighters to defend Oahu. With the U.S. West Coast under an invasion threat, Hawaii's situation was grim and potentially as expendable as Wake, Guam, and the Philippines had been.

---

[4] *Enterprise* and *Lexington* were in the Pacific, under CINCPAC's control. *Yorktown* had been transferred to the Atlantic Fleet. *Saratoga* was in Bremerton, Washington for repairs.

The West Coast Offshore

Japanese Type-I[5] submarines increasingly attacked the U.S. Pacific shoreline, taking a heavy toll of coastal merchant shipping, and occasional Navy destroyers and auxiliaries, impudently laying mines, and shelling strategically important facilities, such as refineries, port areas, and railroads along the coast.

In May 1942, a Japanese "*Glen*" float plane, launched at night from a Type-I submarine offshore, dropped two bombs and thousands of leaflets announcing an imminent invasion over Newport, Oregon. The raid caused little actual damage but great panic and acute government embarrassment. Two weeks later, there was a repeated float plane attack over Eureka, California. Leaflets with the same invasion warning were dropped but, this second time, a bomb hit a house killing two small children. Rage against Japan swelled but was quickly redirected against the Roosevelt Administration, when it became apparent there were no practical defenses against these nighttime coastal raids.

Japanese Kugisho E14 "Glen" float plane on submarine deck being readied for take-off

---

[5] Long-range submarines.

Axis Forces Press the Soviets

Joseph Stalin

The Soviet Union's Far East ports on the Sea of Japan and Sea of Okhost were effectively blockaded as the Japanese torpedoed any vessel venturing out into open waters. The Soviets lacked effective anti-submarine capabilities and the Soviet Far East Fleet had no means of replacing its losses.

Shrinking Soviet naval assets were confined to port for safety, ready to steam out, if an invasion from the sea appeared imminent. However, a Japanese army group moving north on land from occupied China took up positions along Manchuria's border with the USSR causing panic among the civil population, which began streaming west as refugees

Fearing an imminent cross-border invasion and occupation that threatened to cut the vital Trans-Siberian Railway, Stalin rushed troops, armor, and a token section of ten IL-2 *Sturmovik* tactical fighter-bombers to fortify the border. Soviet troops, in hard-won, firm control of Eastern Finland after invading in 1939, were withdrawn and placed in the lines facing the Germans, who had easily occupied the Baltic States. Little Finland, which had gained world acclaim for its gallant stand against the Russian bear, was only able to celebrate reunified independence for less than a week. Softened-up by *Luftwaffe blitzkrieg* air strikes, Finland's defenses could not withstand the overwhelming German pincer movement originating in occupied Northern Norway and Latvia.

The hasty Soviet redeployments diluted the defense of European Russia against German forces of *Unternehmen Barbarossa* (Operation Barbarossa), which were penetrating deeply since invading on 22 June 1941. Skirmishes and cross-border forays from Manchuria tied-up Soviet forces, which needed a steady stream of reinforcements and resupply. The drain on Soviet army formations facing the Germans on the western front forced their withdrawal into winter quarters, permitting the Germans also to batten down, reinforce and reëquip while awaiting the spring thaw. General Günther von Kluge convinced Hitler to gamble on a continued cessation of fighting during the winter months and a percentage of German ground troops was rotated by rail out to rest areas with heated barracks and mess halls.

None of the ten deployed *Sturmoviks* survived to fire a shot in anger against the Japanese. Always difficult to maintain and especially so in winter's cold and damp, three of the

IL-2 Sturmovik

Sturmoviks were unable to continue the long flight after landing at refueling fields.

One IL-2 was wrecked in an emergency landing after turning back. The remaining six were tracked by Japanese Communications Intelligence units, which reported their in-flight radio chatter and flight plans to a small airfield outside the village of Boreya, near the Manchurian border. All six were caught on the ground and destroyed in a Japanese airstrike on the field the same afternoon they arrived. Having learned a costly lesson about mobile maintenance, further deployment of Soviet tactical aircraft was abandoned and Soviet Army formations on the Manchurian border were continuously harassed by unopposed Japanese fighter-bombers that took a heavy toll on facilities, exposed equipment, and troops in the open.

With the arrival of Spring 1942, coordinated *Wehrmacht* and *Luftwaffe* attacks relentlessly pushed the Red Army back. Regrouping amongst the ruined buildings of Stalingrad, Soviet commanders lured the Germans into a savage contest for the city.

The protracted Battle of Stalingrad began in August 1942 and stretched unabated into winter. The fighting caused terrible losses on both sides and the city was essentially reduced to rubble by artillery and air raids. The poorly-armed *Sturmoviks* were no more effective against German *Panzer* formations than they had been in Manchuria. In defense of the strategic city, the Soviets exhausted all their in-country military supplies and were on verge of abandoning Stalingrad when the extreme cold forced the Germans to pull back as they had the previous year.

2

THE FIGHTING ENDS IN EUROPE

Suppose that lacking U.S. supplies and support, the overmatched British and Soviets were defeated by Germany?

The Alternative History . . .

A *de facto* occupation line was observed by both sides with no further attempted penetration by German ground forces after the spring of 1943. From March to mid-September of 1943, the *Luftwaffe*, enjoying complete air superiority, savagely bombed strategic and military targets, as well as most Soviet cities and towns within range. With trans-Atlantic supplies from the U.S. cut off and the unopposed *Luftwaffe* destruction of Soviet ground transportation systems, there was widespread starvation throughout the western part of the USSR. Stalin agreed to a truce in September 1943 that acknowledged German occupation along the *de facto* front in exchange for a cessation of aerial bombing that would allow rebuilding of road, rail, and canal systems.

Stalin also agreed to maintain a force of one million able-bodied "guest workers" who would labor for food and shelter in *Nazi*-occupied Poland. Stalin jumped at the opportunity to scour the western USSR for Jews, gypsies, criminals, and the mentally ill. Employed in the mines, in road and rail heavy construction, and every hazardous or unpleasant form of work, the Soviet "guests"

Winter 1943:
Extent of German occupation of the
Western USSR in Operation Barbarossa

lived in cramped, unsanitary barracks, were malnourished, and generally brutalized by inhumane working conditions. Their survival rates were appalling but not of concern to either their German masters or to Stalin, who was content to be relieved of responsibility for them and to replenish the supply, with no questions asked.

Britain Stands Precariously Alone

After the collapse of France in 1940, the Royal Navy tried unsuccessfully to persuade fearful small boat owners to cross the English Channel in a rescue attempt under the fire of German artillery and *Stuka* dive bombers. Abandoned by their timid countrymen, 250,000 British troops surrendered on the beach at Dunkirk to avoid further casualties and were ignominiously marched off toward POW camps in *Nazi* Germany. Front-page photos in the London papers deeply shocked the British population and later caused great distress in the U.S. and Canada.

Shortly after the 1940 Dunkirk surrender, *Luftwaffe* bombers began attacking strategic targets in the UK in preparation for a cross-Channel invasion. All of the *Chain Home* air defense radar towers in the south and east of England were quickly toppled and COMINT stations listening to *Luftwaffe* crews were repeatedly bombed, forcing the evacuation of RAF "Y" Service wireless operators and analysts from their listening posts.

Although kept secret from the British public and almost all of the forces, the major disruption of COMINT operations sharply reduced the flow of intercepted German *Enigma*-enciphered messages to Bletchley Park. "ULTRA" cryptanalysis of the *Enigma* ciphers was dealt a serious set-back and work on *Kriegsmarine* U-Boat and *Luftwaffe* bomber communications traffic was suspended for

Chain Home *radar towers*

much of 1940 after an airstrike by the *Luftwaffe* He.111 unit, KG-55, based at Villacoublay, France, damaged the RAF "Y" Service intercept station at Chicksands Priory in Bedfordshire.

Without any advanced warning capabilities, the RAF and Army anti-aircraft gunners were essentially blind until the drone of approaching enemy bomber engines could be heard.

Chicksands Priory

The RAF, which had first demonstrated superb gallantry against large bomber formations escorted by fighters, lost precious pilots and aircraft at an unsustainable rate. Most of Most of Fighter Command's squadrons were dispersed to northern Scotland to stem the attrition of aircraft and crews, holding them in reserve against an expected German invasion across the Channel. Bomber aircraft were also moved to sanctuary bases in Scotland. With RAF Fighter Command basically out of the fight, the *Luftwaffe* enjoyed unopposed air superiority and accepted the smaller risks posed by anti-aircraft guns forced to operate without radar support.

With the RAF effectively neutralized, the *Luftwaffe* followed a disciplined, scripted targeting scheme for the remaining months of 1940 and well into 1941, systematically destroying RAF Bomber Command's major bases, maintenance facilities and fuel stores. Bomber Command was effectively marginalized as it was no longer able to operate from bases in England, which were within striking range of strategic German targets. The British aviation industry was repeatedly attacked from the air. Following a sudden daylight attack on the Vauxhall plant at Luton that killed 55, civilian aircraft technicians balked at working in plants that were subject to sudden bombing raids, slowing aviation production to a trickle.

Royal Navy and commercial shipping facilities from Liverpool around to Edinburgh were relentlessly attacked during this period. *Stuka* dive bombers knocked out key railroad bridges leading to port areas and returned regularly to strafe repair crews. Britain's capacity for importing foodstuffs, oil, and raw materials became a shambles with widespread destruction of port facilities and vessels sunk alongside wharves and in harbor main channels. Although self-sufficient in coal, which was used for generating electricity and powering its railroads, Britain was cut off from customarily reliable sources of petroleum on which ships, aircraft and military vehicles were critically dependent. The British Army began rebuilding and training at camps in Scotland harder for the *Luftwaffe* to reach but the Dunkirk debacle had shattered confidence at all levels and most planners believed that no more than a delaying action was to be expected from the Army, if the Germans invaded. Civilian morale plummeted and Parliament, soberly considering the Army's unreadiness and the supply crisis restraining the Navy and Air Force, began debating how best to make terms with Hitler to avoid invasion and occupation.

American Vulnerability and Confusion

In the Atlantic, German *Kriegsmarine* U-Boats and commerce raiders operated for most of 1942 without effective opposition by the U.S. Navy or Army Air Forces, both of which suffered from inaccurate open-water navigation.[6] German commandos and saboteurs were successfully landed on beaches from Texas to Newfoundland and heavily damaged numerous transportation and industrial assets, occasionally targeting civilian facilities to terrorize citizen morale. Composed of repatriated Germans, who had lived in the U.S., speaking fluent, native English and familiar with American culture, these teams were supplied and sheltered by fanatical American *Bund* organizations, eager to keep the U.S. out of war with a resurgent Germany seen by its admirers as rightfully triumphant. With the exception of a single spectacular apprehension, the U.S. was ineffective at interdicting coastal landings or preventing sabotage. The Congress and the more influential newspapers and magazines, dismayed by Pearl Harbor, the obviously neglectful defense preparedness, and government inability to manage the sabotage threat, hectored the Roosevelt Administration and began to sway public opinion toward a resumption of isolationism.

Montana Congresswoman Jeanette Rankin, who had cast "no" votes against war with Germany in 1917 and again in 1941, publicly agitated for *rapprochement* with Germany and Japan for a cessation of hostilities.[7] She was strongly supported by women's groups, which frequently demonstrated and paraded in big cities, gaining front-page photo coverage and approving, isolationist editorials from sympathetic newspapers.

Jeanette Rankin

---

[6] As late as the 1980s, the author discovered that U.S. government aircrews patrolling the Gulf of Mexico were unable to report the position of a suspicious vessel with sufficient precision for the crew of a second aircraft to visually acquire it without an area search. Furthermore, on "grey" days, when the sea and sky were close to the same color, high altitude (over 10,000 feet) visual contact with a vessel had to be maintained continuously. If the observer looked away momentarily, the vessel would be lost and would have to be reacquired by renewed search.

[7] Representative Rankin's vote against war with Japan in 1941 was the lone "no" vote cast.

The anti-war movement was joined by the major labor unions, which were falling increasingly under the control of Socialists and Communists.

The U.S. Navy's anti-submarine capabilities were inadequate for the threats it faced. Admiral Ernest King, the Chief of Naval Operations, pursued an ineffective policy that favored chasing reported U-Boat sightings over escorting convoys.

In April 1942, a U-Boat wolf pack sank an unprecedented 18 cargo vessels of a convoy bound for Arkhangelsk, plus two U.S. and one Canadian destroyer escorts.

Admiral Ernest J. King

The loss of so many Merchant Seamen from one convoy triggered a labor strike that was supported by longshoremen and teamsters in ports from Delaware Bay to Portland. Brigadier General Dwight Eisenhower was so frustrated by the anti-submarine strategy that he wrote in his private diary that the war effort would be helped, if someone shot Admiral King.

The longshoreman's strike was broken after 22 days by the Army but isolated clashes that cost lives on both sides left uneasy bitterness and difficulty in resuming convoy operations in support of Britain and the Soviet Union. Trans-Atlantic convoys were suspended for a reassessment in May 1942 as Britain and the USSR were forced to tighten rationing of all consumables. The RAF slipped to a thirty-day supply of aviation gasoline, eliminated nearly all pilot training and sharply restricted Channel and North Sea reconnaissance.

On the west coast, headline-grabbing Japanese hit-and-run attacks within U.S. territorial waters fueled an isolationist mindset that grew into a flood of demands to Congressmen that the Asian war was none of the U.S.' business. A small majority in California, Oregon and Washington State opined that a swallowing of pride and an accommodation with Japan that ended the attacks and allowed the resumption of trade was preferable to war and possible invasion by barbarous Japanese troops, whose wanton butchery was shown in graphic movie newsreels.

3

THE 1942 MID-TERM ELECTIONS

Suppose a discouraged, pacifist electorate sent anti-war candidates to Congress?

The Alternative History . . .

Heading into the 1942 Congressional elections, the mood of the nation was simultaneously angry and anxious. In districts across the continent, incumbents were on the defensive, trying to rationalize how the federal government had been so badly fooled and so poorly prepared militarily. Veterans' organizations began calling for investigations and were not mollified by Administration insiders, who privately counseled dropping the issue, lest FDR be forced into revealing intelligence secrets. Senator Robert La Follette, Jr., galvanized the Progressive Party, whose congressional candidates pointedly attacked both Republicans and Democrats as having been equally "asleep at the switch." Progressive candidates, led by La Follette, the Senate's leading isolationist, made it clear that they wouldn't appropriate any funds for military capabilities beyond Homeland Defense.

Women, farmers, and union members, urged on by "America Firsters" such as Charles Lindbergh and Socialist Norman Thomas, elected 217 Progressives, Socialists and allied third-party candidates, capturing a slim House majority and 19 Senate seats.

In the south, a coalition of *Bund* organizations and the KKK put forth eleven successful Democrat candidates for the House and one for the Senate, all of whom ran openly on anti-war, isolationist platforms but secretly concealed fascist views. Scattered small third parties elected three more Congressmen favoring similar policies.

Charles Lindbergh

The new legislative balance in Washington was shifted dramatically to reflect the isolationist national mood but, at the time, it wasn't clear that many of the anti-war isolationists also held mixes of racist, anti-semitic, and segregationist views.

With international trade upset and staggering in the Western Hemisphere, an already-nervous New York Stock Exchange, frightened by the political prospects, declined almost as steeply as it had at the start of the Great Depression in 1929. A growing wave of businesses started closing their doors, causing a sharp rise in the unemployment rate to 11%. The dramatic fall of agricultural prices caused by the loss of European and Asian export markets challenged farmers to pay their bills and mortgages while worrying how seeds and supplies for spring could be purchased. Great numbers went into bankruptcy as lenders called in their loans. The unemployment rate among farm workers soared and idle migrant laborers were marooned in place without incomes or unemployment benefits.

Food, cotton, and tobacco packed for export rotted on docks and in rail cars and the back-up clogged the transportation chain all the way back to small farms, which were forced to abort harvesting. The interruption of beef exports caused overcrowded stockyards, forcing cattle ranchers to keep and feed stock they had planned on shipping to market. No American shipyard laid the keel of a new commercial vessel in all of 1942 and most locked-out their employees and chained their gates. The value of the U.S. dollar declined precipitously.

Around the country in ports on all three coasts, docks and the trucking companies and railroads that served them, were in severe crisis. All three industries laid off major percentages of their employees, retaining only the minimum necessary to handle trade with Canada and Latin America. Almost immediately, the competition for the remaining jobs escalated into racial tensions and demands by white workers, as "real" Americans, for priority over minorities. Employers, in perpetually fragile relationships with their employees' unions, avoided crippling strikes and the expensive damage that unknown saboteurs could cause by protecting the jobs of white workers.

Unemployed Black longshoremen quickly recognized the widespread discrimination and staged noisy protest demonstrations in major cities, joined by unemployed Black truck drivers, railroad workers, and warehousemen. Bloody clashes erupted in many cities, resulting in several Black beating deaths and uncounted injuries. The worst violence occurred in Mobile, Alabama, where a waterfront demonstration was routed by white union members swinging axe handles.

The scattering mob left six dead and fourteen badly injured in the street. A band of white toughs then followed three injured Black demonstrators taking a shortcut and limping through Texas Street Park, held them up at gunpoint, beat them to the ground with their axe handles, and lynched them from tree limbs. From a crowd of nearly 100 onlookers, no one intervened.

Ultimately, over 2500 Mobile curiosity seekers visited the scene before the Coroner's Office took the bodies down. The Mobile Police reported that the identities of the perpetrators were unknown.

Across the country, cautious police refrained from involvement in the brawls and the news photos of the lynched demonstrators hanging in a Mobile park discouraged further protests

The Axis Powers Wage Economic Warfare

Having access now to more oil than all their domestic consumers and military users combined could even use wastefully, the three Axis powers, as an OPEC-like cartel, flooded the international market. The price of crude oil collapsed, forcing a halt to much of the U.S.' pumping capacity and idling most of the workforce in oil fields, refineries, and delivery. The U.S. sank to its lowest point of the Great Depression. The rationing of most commodities, begun in 1942, was tightened as marketplace stocks began to dwindle even as supplies rotted in the distribution chain. The surging unemployment caused acute unrest across the nation that was visible in ubiquitous bread lines and noisy protest gatherings. Incidents of rail yard and warehouse pillaging became a commonplace remedy for feeding hungry families. The desperate mood of a growing majority, spreading inwards from the coasts, cried out for a quick return to some semblance of normalcy and an immediate end to the terrible Axis attacks.

4

1943 - THE ARMISTICE

To keep out of war, suppose the U.S. signed a humiliating armistice with the Axis?

The Alternative History . . .

Immediately after learning the off-year elections results, a somber FDR agonized over the worsening military situation and a domestic economy seemingly beyond repair by even his New Deal programs. Receiving no better useful advice from his Cabinet, Roosevelt directed Secretary of State Cordell Hull to open negotiations with Germany and Japan on a cessation of hostilities. From positions of strength originating in the U.S.' anxiety to stop the deadly attacks, the two Axis powers made heavy-handed demands. Japan applied ages-old Asian *"talk-talk; fight-fight"* pressure by intensifying attacks along the West Coast while the talks went on in Geneva, skillfully leading Americans to press FDR to agree to anything that would make the attacks stop. Japan demanded retention of all U.S. territories she occupied on the agreed date of an armistice. After weighing the probable reclamation costs in casualties, the U.S. agreed to a transfer of the occupied Micronesian and Aleutian Islands. Although the names of the transferred Aleutian Islands were changed on their maps, the Japanese quietly abandoned them as too remote, too cold, and strategically no longer needed.

Japan shrilly excoriated the U.S. as maliciously racist for its post-Pearl Harbor internment of Americans of Japanese descent. Tokyo insisted upon and Washington granted their immediate release and the restoration of Japanese immigrant and *Nisei* [8] homes and businesses. Roosevelt was acutely pained by this Japanese demand, which he knew instinctively would forever haunt the civil rights policy aspect of his presidential legacy. In the autumn of 1941, as strained Japanese-American relations appeared headed toward some form of hostilities, unimpeachable Communications Intelligence, provided by the breaking of Japanese diplomatic codes, revealed ongoing espionage and the readiness of some Japanese-Americans on the West Coast to assist an invasion by their ancestral countrymen. Immediately following the Pearl Harbor attack, when an invasion was greatly feared, Roosevelt approved the internment of the Japanese-Americans as a means of eliminating a credible fifth-column threat. In the face of the new Japanese demands, Roosevelt's natural inclination was to release the internees but to publicly justify the forced relocations by disclosing the underlying intelligence. Rear Admiral Theodore S. Wilkinson, Chief of Naval Intelligence, passionately persuaded the President to keep the code-breaking secret as an essential capability the U.S. would surely need in coming days.

As part of the armistice, the U.S. also guaranteed exports to Japan of strategic commodities that had previously been embargoed with 75% of those cargoes to be carried by Japanese flag vessels. The Japanese, however, had only wanted to cause the U.S. to "lose face," having had no real intention of buying commodities and permitting the U.S. any export opportunities when they were already stealing what they coveted in Asia.

After very difficult, prolonged negotiations, an armistice was finally signed in May 1943 between the U.S., Japan and Germany with Germany representing Italian interests. Chilly relations thawed only slightly as the months passed. The U.S. was anxious for any exports that would ease the prolonged Great Depression.

---

[8] Japanese-Americans born in the U.S.

By the end of 1943, however, German merchant ships were calling at American ports and *Norddeutcsher Lloyd's* passenger liners were bringing German tourists with eagerly-sought *Deutschmarks* to New York.

Cordell Hull subsequently recalled that under these great reverses, Franklin Roosevelt aged visibly and began a long slide into detached depression. Hull believed that the president became increasingly unable to concentrate and passively allowed his assistants to make most of the important decisions and signed documents without really understanding their contents.

Franklin Delano Roosevelt

Frustrated by his painful leg braces and complaining of frequent severe headaches, Roosevelt yearned to retire from the public spotlight to his Hyde Park estate and morosely decided not to run for a fourth term in 1944.

The momentous public announcement that FDR planned to step down sharply rocked the nation and its political parties, large and small. Under severe criticism from all quarters and a near-total collapse of party confidence, the Democrats regrouped under Vice President Henry A. Wallace, who began quietly trying to consolidate party power.

The U.S. granted *de facto* diplomatic recognition to Japanese puppet regimes in China, Manchuria, Korea, Malaysia, Thailand, Burma, Hong Kong, and the Philippines. Additionally, the U.S. agreed to limit the construction of new capital ships, to scrap and not rebuild the sunken remnants of the Pacific Fleet at Pearl Harbor and to restrict all armed naval vessels to an area east of longitude 160 degrees in the Pacific.[9]   In distressing embarrassment, FDR approved language pledging that the U.S. would not intercede in any future relations between Japan and Australia or New Zealand. Additionally, the U.S. conceded not to construct any military aircraft with a range in excess of 2000 miles and a payload of over 8000 pounds.[10] These U.S. guarantees were to be verifiable by on-site Japanese and German inspection teams.

To add emphasis to its cease-fire demands, Japanese aircraft and submarines repeatedly conducted coordinated night time attacks on west coast civilian areas during the negotiations. Although civilian casualties and actual destruction were light, the combination of night-time wailing sirens and U.S. defensive impotence fueled emotional pressures on Washington to settle quickly and permit a return to some semblance of pre-war calm. The settlement with Japan, in the form of a signed armistice, brought the attacks to an end but was a bitter pill for many in the U.S., who experienced national shame for the first time in U.S. history.

Germany demanded that the U.S. free the Panama Canal Zone and transfer canal operations to an international commission, although U.S. merchant ships but not naval vessels were to be allowed its use. The U.S. agreed to restrict its Atlantic Fleet to the Western Atlantic and the Gulf of Mexico. In the agreement, armed U.S. naval combatant vessels were to be restricted from sailing south of the 24th parallel or further east than the Virgin Islands. Cordell Hull, the U.S. Secretary of State was too emotionally overwrought to attend the armistice signings in New York and San Francisco, sending deputies in his place. His biographer later quoted Hull as marking the signings as the lowest point in his fifty years of government service.

Although there was extensive newsreel coverage from Pearl Harbor of dismantled ship parts being loaded on to barges and

---

[9] No further west than the Hawaiian Islands.
[10] Effectively limiting the U.S. to no bombers bigger than a B-17.

towed off as scrap, the Navy kept secret the careful, concealed salvage of 16- and 14-inch battleship guns. After the armistice took effect, these big guns were shipped to Oregon, then covered with Douglas fir logs on rail flatcars, and sent to the Watervliet Arsenal in New York State. Cleaned and refurbished, the guns were shipped in pairs to Army forts to become new Coast Artillery batteries. Fort Miles, on the Delaware Atlantic coast, received the first 16-inch *Iowa*-class guns for its new Battery Smith and kept them pointed out to sea, ready to engage German raiders.

U.S. Army 16-inch Coast Artillery Gun

5

THE AXIS TRIUMPHANT

Suppose victorious Axis powers were given free rein by the former Allies?

The Alternative History . . .

Japan Dominates Asia

Buoyed by their successful humbling of the U.S. and answerable to no external authority, Japanese troops indulged in rapacious, murderous rampages against hundreds of thousands of civilians in Chinese, Malaysian, Philippine, Thai, Burmese, Korean, and French Indo-Chinese[11] cities. Uncounted thousands of girls and young women were spared from slaughter only to be transported for forced prostitution, most not surviving their humiliating ordeals for very long and never accounted for.

Prince Konoye, the Japanese Prime Minister, informed Emperor Hirohito of the Army's and Navy's triumphal successes. The Prince assured the Emperor that, now having assured access to essential commodities and having provided for the security of the Home Islands, Japan planned no further military invasions

---

[11] Occupied by France, the countries of Vietnam, Laos, and Cambodia were known by the pre-war name of French Indo-China.

Emperor Hirohito

Admiral Isoruku Yamamoto

To mark the occasion, the emperor wrote a moving poem in praise of Japanese forces and their *bushido*[12] ethic, which was broadcast on the radio as part of the victory announcement. The emperor elevated Admiral Isoruku Yamamoto[13] to *Danshaku*[14] in the aristocracy and awarded him an imposing oceanfront estate.

Detailed economic and demographic studies by Keio University had persuaded Japanese ruling circles that the United States and its population were too large and the Pacific Ocean too wide to allow an economical occupation. Japan was also reluctant to attempt controlling large, culturally alien populations so invasion of the U.S. mainland was never an actual part of Japanese planning. However, an invasion of the Hawaiian Islands was seriously considered but ultimately disapproved as strategically unnecessary.

---

[12] Traditional code of Japanese warriors, stressing honor, discipline, bravery, and simple living

[13] Architect of the Pearl Harbor attack.

[14] 男爵, the rank of baron in the Kazoku (aristocracy).

The Axis Dominant Across Europe and the Mid-East

In Europe, hostilities were concluded across the Continent on September 30, 1943 and Germany celebrated S-E Day (*Sieg in Europatag* or V-E Day) on October 10, coinciding with the national holiday, *Erntedankfest Sontag* (Thanksgiving Sunday).

The Germans insisted on a free hand in occupied Europe, reserving the right to invade and occupy any state in Europe or Africa whose actions threatened its occupied territories or occupying garrisons. The U.S. granted *de facto* recognition to German annexation of Austria, the Sudetenland, and a wide strip of Poland running all the way to the Baltic Sea. The rest of Poland was occupied by *Nazi* troops. Sweden and Switzerland preserved their neutrality but were both coerced into allowing a small uniformed German "diplomatic" presence. The two neutrals were also bullied into permitting *Gestapo* detachments positioned at border-crossings to screen for and turn back escaping Jews.

Spain and Portugal

General Francisco Franco

Franco's Spain, already allied with Germany since 1937, bloodlessly. deposed the British from Gibraltar and fortified the peninsula with large coastal artillery pieces provided by Germany. Franco interfered in Portuguese affairs, finessing a puppet government that followed Franco's foreign policy and granted Germany naval base concessions in the Azores that projected *Kriegsmarine* control of vast areas of the mid-Atlantic. Franco also granted Hitler naval and air bases in the Canary Islands. All Jews and gypsies, who could be identified, were transported from Spain and Portugal by rail under the most inhumane conditions to death camps in Germany and Poland.

Germany took over Suez Canal operations and closed it to all non-Axis naval vessels.

The *Nazi* Occupation of Europe

Across the European continent, Germany enforced a brutal occupation of captured territory that featured a near-total enslavement of industrial and agricultural labor, the continuous export of commodities to Germany as indefinite "reparations" and "policing" charges. Newspapers, radio, and education were tightly censored. Obscure dialects were forbidden in publications and radio broadcasts, which were limited to carefully screened news, sportscasts, and music. To cow native populations, the occupying Germans were careful not to tamper with traditional local cultures but native book and magazine publishing virtually disappeared in the occupied countries and only German-produced films with subtitles were shown.

When the first TV sets appeared in 1947, they received only *Nazi* propaganda and censored programming, including local football matches, German films, and children's shows that subtly combined cartoons with propaganda.

The Italians occupied and immediately began plundering portions of Africa, the Balkans, Greece, and the islands of Malta and Crete. Hitler approved so highly of his ally Mussolini that he had Architect Albert Speer design a replica of the Vatican's St. Peter's Square for Berlin, with a triumphal statue of *Il Duce* [15] as its centerpiece. As the crowning touch of the *Führer's* master schedule, which planned for victory over all his enemies by 1950, Berlin was to be Hitler's capital of a new World Empire.

---

[15] Benito Mussolini's self-adopted title, "The Captain."

Latin America

The South American dictatorships were already on friendly terms with *Nazi* Germany and it suited Hitler to allow his faraway fascist allies to continue, as before. He was unconcerned with the small numbers of South American Jews, who were already severely suppressed. Both Germany and Japan acquired strategically placed naval bases along the Atlantic and Pacific coasts of South America and both Axis powers were granted generous landing rights for aircraft and airships. Mexico was seen by both Germany and Japan as perfect for collecting intelligence on the U.S. and were invited by *Presidente* Manuel Avila Camacho to station agents and to build HF and VHF[16] radio intercept stations at various mountain points along the border from California to Texas.

The Mid-East

Germany occupied and claimed all British and French territories and interests in the Mid-East and immediately seized control of oilfields, pipelines and oceangoing tanker ports. Under plans brokered with Hitler by the fascist Grand Mufti of Jerusalem, Arab monarchs, warlords, and tribal chiefs cooperated in the roundup and exile of their native Jews, estimated to number in the hundreds of thousands. Neither the Germans nor the Arabs had any need of slave labor in the region so the most cost-effective approach to the Mid-East genocide was for local "enforcers" simply to march the Jews for days toward crowded barbed-wire compounds in the desert. Arab collaborators took the opportunity to add troublesome social misfits and business enemies to the march. Stragglers and resisters were clubbed senseless and left to die, their bodies to be collected later. Deprived of food, water, and shelter from the blazing sun, none in the compounds survived. Bulldozers buried them deeply along with the barbed wire and fenceposts. The endlessly shifting sands completed the natural

---

[16] High Frequency and Very High Frequency.

restoration. By *Ramadan* 1950, no traces of the desert death camps remained.

The Channel Islands and Bermuda

Immediately after the fall of France in 1940, Germany seized, occupied and fortified the Channel Islands, off the north coast of France, which had belonged to Britain since the 13th Century. Much of the islands' populations had evacuated to England before the Germans arrived, leaving behind homes, vehicles, and other personal belongings that the occupiers put to good use. Airfields on the islands of Guernsey and Jersey became home to *Luftwaffe* bombers and fighters and served as jumping-off points for bombing raids on southern England and shipping in the Channel.

The fuel-starved Royal Navy Bermuda Squadron, now cut off from its supply sources in Britain and North America, was frequently harassed by German naval shelling throughout the spring and summer of 1941, destroying hundreds of homes and killing many civilians, who were slow in seeking shelter. Bermuda's two Coast Artillery batteries, consisting of only two 8-inch and two 155mm pieces, were outgunned by German warships, which cautiously stood off outside the range of the Bermuda guns.

Finally, two British destroyers staged a gallant nighttime rear-guard action with the *Kriegsmarine* off Bermuda that permitted the rest of the squadron to sail for Barbados, taking along the island's small British Army and Royal Marines garrisons. RAF maritime patrol aircraft also escaped in low-level nighttime flights to South Carolina, where they were later blown up by the U.S. Army, thereby defusing threatening German demands that the aircraft and their crews be handed-over. The remaining military facilities and stores were torched as the Royal Governor declared Bermuda "open" and the Germans landed unopposed in the ports of Hamilton and St. George. Bermudian men and women wept openly as *swastika* flags were raised at government buildings all over their islands.

Within 30 days, a *Luftwaffe Staffel* [17] of Bf 109 fighters was shipped to Bermuda in crates, reassembled and were in operation flying combat air patrols. In another 30 days, a *Staffel* of Ju 88 bombers was flying ocean reconnaissance patrols. Worrying intelligence on these developments as well as a *Kriegsmarine* surface and submarine presence in the Bermuda ports of Hamilton and St. George quickly reached London and Washington.

Ju 88s

Bf 109

On December 10, 1941, just after the Japanese attack at Pearl Harbor, two Bermuda-based Ju 88s carrying auxiliary fuel tanks, flew at wavetop level to within 30 miles of Morehead City, North Carolina, turned southwest till off Long Beach, South Carolina, and returned to Bermuda. Flying at night and below radar coverage, the Ju 88s' roaring *Jumo* engines were heard and reported by two U.S. Navy vessels and a Coast Guard cutter as "unidentified aircraft." Air Raid sirens wailed in American cities all along the East Coast, most not sounding until long after the *Luftwaffe* bombers had already turned for home. The German probe was a rude wake-up call for the U.S. Government, the defense establishment and panicked, bewildered citizens, most of whom were frozen by their ignorance of where and how to seek shelter from an air raid.

---

[17] Squadron

33

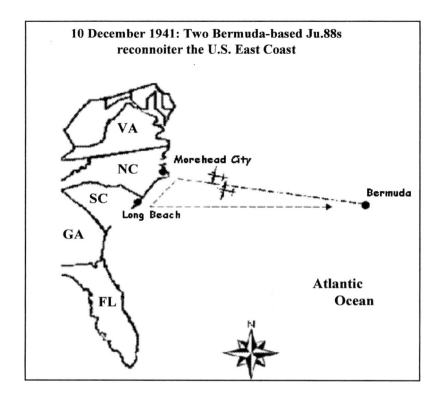

10 December 1941: Two Bermuda-based Ju.88s reconnoiter the U.S. East Coast

VA

NC

Morehead City

Bermuda

SC

Long Beach

GA

FL

Atlantic
Ocean

Navy Department analysis concluded that the aircraft were probably Germans flying from Bermuda and, with the wounds of Pearl Harbor still bleeding after only 72 hours, Washington was deeply shaken by confirmation of its worst fears: the east coast was as vulnerable to air attack as Pearl Harbor had been. Details of the Ju 88 incident were classified "Secret" and the American public was never informed but Navy and coastal defenses were put on highest alert.

A week later, on December 18 and on three dates in January 1942, jumpy U.S. anti-aircraft batteries in Georgia, South Carolina and on ships fired thousands of anti-aircraft (AAA) rounds into the night sky at imagined German raiders. Similar false alarms and AAA firing were experienced along the coast of California and in the Hawaiian Islands.

The deployment of AAA guns, searchlights, sound detectors, and overlapping primitive SCR-268 radars was prioritized for coastal defense from Key West to Bath, Maine. What was not known, at the time, was that the Ju 88 bombers had only a combat range of 1800 miles and could carry either a payload of bombs or auxiliary fuel to fly to targets on the U.S. East Coast and back to Bermuda but not both. The Bf 109 fighters were limited by their very short range and so could not escort bombers to the East Coast.

These major limitations plus the absence of fighter pilots' overwater navigational capabilities were well-understood by the Germans, who had no plans in 1942 to bomb the U.S. from Bermuda. Some in the German high command even expressed anxious misgivings about the Bermuda occupation being an unnecessary "bridge too far" and worried about the island's isolation. Separated from the Azores by just over 2100 miles of open ocean, in an era pre-dating sophisticated air navigational aids, Bermuda superficially gave the appearance of a menacing outpost for naval operations and intelligence collection but, in view of the extended supply line from Western Europe, was never a planned staging point for an invasion of the U.S. This strategic thinking was not deduced by the U.S., however, and the U.S. Navy, Coast Guard and Army Coast Artillery observed high levels of readiness, keeping a wary eye on Bermuda and its occupiers. The U.S. Navy and Army Air Forces grew accustomed to Ju 88 reconnaissance flights off the East Coast, which in time seemed less provocative as the *Luftwaffe* scrupulously observed a 30-mile stand-off line. The German flights, however, continued to be classified "Secret" and withheld from public disclosure.

A German Presence on the North American Doorstep

Despite bitter but toothless British and Canadian protests, the Germans forced a humiliated France to cede the Gulf of St. Lawrence islands of Ste. Pierre and Miquelon. Kept by France after the cessation of Canada to Britain in 1763, the small islands just off the west coast of Newfoundland, had remained French territory. The Germans renamed the islands *Sankt Peter* and *Neues Deutschland* and occupied them as a naval and submarine base. Although surrounded by U.S. and Canadian forces that could have easily overwhelmed the islands' garrisons, Germany declared a "Security Zone" around the islands, enforced by fast E-Boats and Bf 109 fighter planes.

A despairing Winston Churchill, hopefully pressing for the U.S. to fight, warned his trusted ally, Franklin Roosevelt. His decoded telegram, signed "Former Naval Person," urged Roosevelt that:

"... YOU MUST INVOKE AND UPHOLD YOUR MONROE DOCTRINE AND BY FORCE OF ARMS PREVENT THE HUN FROM ESTABLISHING A FOOTHOLD IN THE WESTERN HEMISPHERE STOP UNLESS HERR HITLER CAN BE MADE TO VIEW THE COSTS OF A NAZI PRESENCE ACROSS THE SEA AS TOO HIGH MEXICO AND THE CARIBBEAN ISLANDS WILL BE NEXT STOP THE GERMAN FLEET WILL BE YOUR CLOSE NEIGHBOURS ..."

FDR's aide, Harry Hopkins, reminded him that President Andrew Johnson, citing the Monroe Doctrine, had massed troops just north of the Rio Grande in 1867, to help Napoleon III decide to pull his French troops out of Mexico. Hopkins exhorted the adoption of a posture of military readiness but FDR wasn't so sure the U.S. should act unilaterally. However, stirred by Churchill's note and mulling Hopkins' advice, Roosevelt and his top military and naval aides plus Sumner Welles, an Undersecretary of State, flew to Quebec for a hastily-arranged meeting with Prime Minister McKenzie King, who had also received cabled encouragement from Churchill.

VC-54 "Sacred Cow"

Aboard the Presidential aircraft, *Sacred Cow*, a workable strategy for dealing with the new German naval base was earnestly debated along firm, ideologically-split positions.

The generals and admirals were confident that the Germans could be easily overcome and that Germany would not attempt long-term support of combat operations against the U.S. or Canada. By strongly enforcing the Monroe Doctrine without delay, the U.S. would force both Germany and Japan to consider the logistical costs of any future territorial ambitions they might have in the Western Hemisphere.

The advisors in uniform conceded that there would be a painful price to pay in terms of both military and civilian losses but strongly urged a military solution. Sumner Welles, expressing conciliatory views that would certainly not have been agreed by Cordell Hull, the Secretary of State, saw the minor German military presence off Canada as merely symbolic and not worth the American deaths it would cost to dislodge them. Sitting close to the President on the noisy four-engined VC-54, Roosevelt was able to hear and understand Welles better than those advising military force on the other side of the wooden conference table, resonating with the propeller-engine vibrations.

Whatever it was that swayed his judgment, Roosevelt later slipped into easy agreement with Prime Minister King at their meeting in the *Chateau Frontenac* hotel that the German presence was a *fait accompli* and held to his promise to the American people to keep out of war. The German base would not be attacked.

Chateau Frontenac, Quebec

Advised of the Quebec meeting and correctly guessing its purpose, Joachim von Ribbentrop, Germany's *Reichsaussenminister* [18] served strongly worded notice in personally-signed letters to his Canadian counterpart and to U.S. Secretary of State Hull, warning of harsh punitive reprisals for any aggression.

Year-long weather conditions around the two small islands are predominately foggy and kept the patrolling German E-Boat crews jumpy. In an effort to keep snoopers and potential saboteurs well away, the *Kriegsmarine* harassed Canadian fishing boats and ferries with unannounced live-fire exercises into the surrounding waters and the Bf 109s aggressively buzzed Air Canada commercial flights between Nova Scotia and Newfoundland, underlining von Ribbentrop's threats.

Joachim von Ribbentrop

Cautious Canada suspended the direct air service and rerouted the daily ferry, adding four hours to the crossing but avoiding confrontation.

---

[18] Foreign Minister

The most immediate impact on the U.S., although not realized until long after the damage had been done, was the deployment of a *Sicherheitsdienst* [19] Communications Intelligence (COMINT) unit to the newly-renamed island of *Sankt Peter*. Although the mountain-top base of this COMINT unit bristled with tell-tale High Frequency and Very High Frequency antennas in numbers excessive for support of a small two-way communications station, its radio interception operations were conducted in deepest secrecy. The *Verbindungs-51* unit (*VB-51*) was able routinely to eavesdrop on military, naval, and aircraft communications throughout New England and, occasionally, as far south as Washington.

Depending on atmospheric conditions and the altitudes at which aircraft were flying, *VB-51* could listen to and plot the positions of Army Air Forces planes over the U.S. mid-west and deep south. One of *VB-51*'s early contributions was the report of a U.S. Army transport using callsign "W3HUV" reporting its position over Concord, New Hampshire and then requesting landing clearance at *L'Ancienne Lorette*, an airfield near the City of Quebec. *VB-51* found the callsign in a reference list as belonging to the air transport *Sacred Cow*, used by President Roosevelt. *L'Ancienne Lorette* was identified by the frequency on which *Sacred Cow* called it: 121.7 megacycles. [20] It was the *VB-51* report that tipped von Ribbentrop to the summit meeting.

Selected English language intercepts collected by *VB-51* were *Enigma*-enciphered and sent to Berlin for translation and analysis. Specially-cleared German commanders and vessel captains were provided a daily situation awareness summary that plotted ship positions, described field training exercise themes and participating units, and the itineraries of VIPs, who flew in "Special Air Mission" transports based at Bolling Field in the District of Columbia.

---

[19] Security Service
[20] The modern convention is to express cycles as "hertz" as in 121.7 MHz.

Germany also announced further plans to militarily occupy portions of Greenland, owned by now-conquered Denmark, and Iceland. Naval bases and airstrips were established at *Nuuk* (renamed *"Logistikbasis Edelweis"*) and at *Qaqortoq* (renamed *"Ankerplatz Eisbär"*)[21] on the Greenland coast but were not continuously manned through winter.

In addition to infantry and *Gestapo*, naval and air units were deployed to Iceland for broad ocean reconnaissance and for enforcing offshore "Security Zones" around both islands. With the capability to surveil the major shipping lanes between Europe and North America, the *Kriegsmarine* was now master of the North Atlantic. U.S., Canadian or British naval and commercial shipping sailed at its pleasure and *Kriegsmarine* destroyers frequently stopped and harassed cargo and fishing vessels, "impounding" valuables with impunity and arresting "wanted" persons, who disappeared permanently.

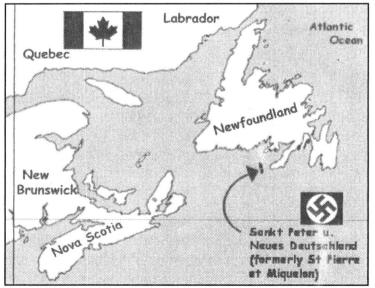

---

21 Supply Base "Edelweis" and "Polar Bear" Anchorage

6

POST-ARMISTICE AMERICA SWALLOWS HER PRIDE AND REPRIORITIZES

Having avoided war, suppose an isolated pacifist America tried to make the best of a tough domestic situation?

The Alternative History . . .

A humiliated American Nation sought comfort by assuring itself it had been spared the horrors of war they had seen in movie newsreel coverage from Asia and Eastern Europe. Prayers of thanksgiving were offered across the continent and some American philosophers redefined "patriotism" to include exercising restraint as a better alternative to bloody conflict.. Taking stock, the leading administration economists concluded that the U.S. was self-sufficient in food, oil, coal, wood, electrical power, and most minerals but would need to make painful adjustments for the loss of exports.

The economists noted that the country's transportation infrastructure was operable and recommended very strongly that domestic transportation capability be temporarily nationalized. None of the economists ventured an encouraging prediction of economic recovery and there was consensus that the Depression would continue until natural influences launched a new phase of the business cycle. Their recommendation to President Roosevelt was that the price of avoiding war was high but, despite the military and diplomatic reverses, the nation could survive. The

U.S. should make the best of it and now move on. Making the "best" of high unemployment, business stagnation and acute hunger and health care needs was especially difficult for Americans near the bottom of the economic ladder. Their mood was the despondent, restive anger of a neglected lower class.

The West Point Conference

In mid-January, at West Point, a humbled joint conference of senior War, Navy and State Department staffs gloomily assessed the military situation, trying to peer into a future dominated by ruthless enemies at the doorsteps to the east and west. After a full morning of vitriolic finger-pointing and ungentlemanly venting of great frustrations that bordered on fisticuffs, conferees grudgingly began seriously working toward an inevitable conclusion that, either the U.S. must secretly work around the armistice terms, waiting patiently for an offensive opportunity to fight, or to adjust to the harsh armistice terms and move on.

The few remaining hawks from what once had been the U.S.' most dependable champions stood little chance against overwhelming voices of negativity, who predicted severe retribution for discovered breaches of the armistice, including the possibility of invasion, occupation, and repatriation of formerly Mexican territories. It was nearly unanimously believed by the senior Army and Navy planners that Bermuda and the small islands off Newfoundland could be overwhelmed and held but the accommodationists, without disputing that the islands could be taken, were emphatic in disagreement that such adventurism had lasting strategic value. They counseled, successfully, that the Germans had clearly demonstrated a readiness to mete out highly disproportionate reprisals and that the islands were not worth the blood of the American civilians, who would have to pay the ultimate price.

One faction of those favoring accommodation, led by senior Foreign Service members of the State Department, piously rationalized that national honor and integrity demanded adherence to truce terms agreed in good faith. The accommodation faction cited pacifist newspaper columns and editorials as evidence that the preferred notion of a non-competitive, non-confrontational U.S. was gaining sway with national opinion. Counter-responses by a few hawks were dismissively shouted down as the "too little, too late" ideas of disgraced military leaders, whose planning and preparation failures had paved the way for national humiliation.

The very detailed balance sheet produced after a week of heavy-hearted deliberations was highlighted by a dramatic shift away from long-range offensive capabilities to a vision of hardened Homeland Defense. Abandoned long-range bomber plans were to be replaced by pursuit fighters, torpedo planes, troop transport aircraft and overwater reconnaissance capabilities. Major naval combatants and troopships, now disallowed by the armistice terms, were bypassed in favor of submarines, destroyers and fast motor torpedo boats. Coast Artillery for the defense of harbor entrances and critical assets on shore was prioritized and all three coastlines would bristle with big guns and overlapping radar coverage.

To maximize mobility when responding to attacks anywhere in the continental U.S., a network of defense highways and railroads would be constructed and the 82nd and 101st Airborne Divisions would be built-up and provided troop transports to airlift them to any U.S. hot spots. The curricula at the Military and Naval Academies were overhauled to reflect a Homeland Defense doctrine. Finally, Communications Intelligence was prioritized with concentration on both radio and commercial cable message traffic and code-breaking.

Although the West Point meetings produced a loose consensus, the issue of how an ambitious new defense program would be paid for by a nation still in the grip of the Great Depression surfaced. German, Japan, and Italy were bursting at the seams with the raw material fruits of their conquests and the U.S.' ability to match their defense spending seemed an impossibility.

Within days of their return to Washington, many doubters were writing memos and speaking at staff meetings about the sober need to control costs, stretch-out some programs and to combine or eliminate others. Ideas for financing defense spending through the sale of War Bonds were dropped as impractical during a depression characterized by high levels of unemployment. The prevailing attitudes of the 1930s, which had been unrealistic about threat assessment and which had neglected defense preparedness, remained prominently represented at the highest political levels and served to quiet the protests of younger, action-oriented visionaries. American isolationists were content while the silenced military hawks were extremely anxious to be in a defense-only posture.

Dawn of the Nuclear Age - Race for the A-Bomb

The West Point conferees were not included in and knew nothing of a low-key but Top Secret meeting in an unpretentious classroom in historic Nassau Hall on the campus of Princeton University. Henry Stimson, the Secretary of War, and a small handful of his most senior R&D staff traveled there under cover in non-descript cars to meet with Albert Einstein, Leo Szilard, and other leading nuclear physicists from the University of Chicago.

The scientists convinced Secretary Stimson that Germany would soon successfully develop an atomic bomb, and with German help, Japan would too, but that so also could the U.S. Stimson returned by car to Washington that evening and immediately began a discussion with the despondent President into the wee hours that led ultimately to the Manhattan Project.

Henry Stimson   **Albert Einstein**

Stimson's diary suggests that FDR was unable to stay fully awake at their meeting and probably didn't grasp the significance of what he authorized to begin. Although no workable visions were available to define possible enemy nuclear targets and how the U.S. might deliver a nuclear weapon, it was clear to the military hawks that an atomic capability would be an essential deterrent to foreign invasion from the sea and German nuclear blackmail.

In April 1940, the Germans had invaded and occupied Denmark. Just before the Danish surrender, the world's leading researcher on atomic energy, Niels Bohr, a Dane, was almost successfully exfiltrated to Britain by the RAF to keep him out of German hands. However, the pilot of the *Anson* aircraft sent to fly Bohr out decided not to risk landing in the dark.

Pilot Officer Jones' log later noted that he had made three low-level approaches and could see the signal lights displayed by the Danish underground but not the trees at either end of the clearing. German troops, alerted by the sound of a low-flying twin-engined aircraft, swooped in and seized Bohr, who was handed over to the *Gestapo* and secretly put on a train heading south to Germany.

Neils Bohr

Coerced by the *Gestapo* to reveal the location of his atomic energy research papers, which were collected and brought to Germany, Bohr was held *incommunicado* and relentlessly debriefed until *Nazi* physicists believed they had effected an exhaustive knowledge transfer.

By mid-1942, the Germans were working on a heavy water reactor, were moving uranium from Czech mines to Germany, and were well on the way to developing an atomic bomb. Bohr disappeared from history without a trace.

The Manhattan Project

At a secret base in the remote New Mexico desert, the Manhattan Project got underway to produce "the gadget" but was quickly penetrated by German, Japanese, and U.S. *Nazi* espionage agents. Hitler personally vetoed recommendations to finesse U.S. abandonment of the program, opting instead for expected valuable developments that could be secretly acquired for the benefit of the German effort. Hitler also believed that U.S. success could be denied through selective sabotage. Some Manhattan Project employees with the highest security clearances brought with them doubts about their personal roles in providing the U.S. an atomic terror weapon and voiced them in what they believed were private conversations among colleagues. They were easily discovered by the German espionage agents among them and a key few were shortly transferring data or performing mathematical sabotage, working quietly for failure in pursuit of a "greater good."

Cheated of better news by research sabotage in the form of deliberately looking in the wrong places, Major General Leslie Groves provided a discouraging progress report to President

General Leslie Groves

Roosevelt in early 1943 that noted his inability to realistically forecast the accomplishment of key program milestones.

In early 1943, German scientists were predicting the assembly of a prototype nuclear explosive device by September 1945 and a smugly-confident Hitler saw no further needs from the U.S. Manhattan Project. When his spies in Washington and Alamogordo, New Mexico reported Roosevelt's secret decision to slash spending on the quest for an atomic bomb, Hitler danced a few happy steps in his office. The General Staff's Strategic Target Planning Bureau reported to Hitler that all the contingency targets for atomic weapons were in North America or deep in the Soviet Union; none were in Europe or Africa. The General Staff recommended, accordingly, that the development of a heavy-lift, long-range bomber capability had extreme difficulties and should be bypassed in favor of rocket-delivered atomic warheads launched from towed ocean platforms, close to North American targets but still in international waters. Hitler approved and directed Albert Speer, his munitions chief, to acquire weapons-grade uranium in sufficient quantity for 25 ten-kiloton V2[22] warheads by October 1945 and for a further 25 by January 1946. The news of Roosevelt's atomic cut-back decision was supplemented by War Department direction to defund design research on the XB-29 bomber program, pleasing Hitler further.

German Missiles and the Fall of the British Empire

Germany briefly rested and recovered from the costly invasion of the USSR and the Battle of Stalingrad. While his attention had been on the Eastern Front, Hitler had deëmphasized his designs on

---

[22] Hitler's "V" weapons were Vengeance Weapons (*Vergeltungswaffen*) such as the V1 and V2.

Britain, satisfied that the naval blockade and continuing airstrikes against transportation targets kept Britain in a neutralized, non-threatening state. With the *Barbarossa* mission now accomplished, Hitler shifted his thinking back to Britain and turned over his personal sketches and schedule to senior army planner, General Franz Ritter von Halder, for a cross-Channel invasion jumping-off from Normandy and Le Havre in June 1944. Hitler's rough estimate included a D-Day invasion force of 250,000 troops and six *Panzer* divisions landing in three main areas followed by a further 200,000 troops over five days. The *Führer's* penciled arrows on a map specified *Fallschirmjager* [23] air drops and disembarking troops in the British deep water ports of Plymouth, Bristol, and Southampton on the 6th of June. The idea of landings on British beaches not linked by roads suitable for military trucks and tanks had always been seen as logistically impractical and was never seriously considered.

At a preliminary meeting with naval planners, von Halder was briefed on serious problems about crossing the Channel. At the time, Germany had neither invasion nor sealift experience that included crossing a sizeable body of water to enemy shores. Senior *Kriegsmarine* admirals advised that troop transport capacity for putting a landing force of 250,000 plus all their equipment ashore was grossly inadequate and could not be available for at least nine months, possibly a year. The admirals also had no satisfactory approaches to berthing deep draft vessels in British ports having sunken ships at their bomb-damaged docks. Von Halder's only good news came from Herman Göring, who gave glib personal assurances that whatever airlift was needed would be available to ferry the *Fallschirmjager* battalions from airfields in France to their drop zones. Von Halder noted that Göring had not consulted any documents for his remarks but did not challenge him.

Hitler totally rejected von Halder's concerns, humiliated him in front of the staff, loudly insulting his loyalty and competence, and

---

[23] Paratroops

fired him on the spot. The job was given next to *Generaloberst*[24] Nickolaus von Falkenhorst, who had led the successful invasions of Denmark and Norway in 1940. The *Kriegsmarine* repeated its earlier dismal assessment for von Falkenhorst, adding an additional worrying intelligence conclusion.

Skillful British deception devised by the Special Operations Executive at Milton Earnest Hall in Bedford and the MI-5 "XX" Committee[25] fooled the *Abwehr* [26] into believing the British Army could set harbors and landing beaches on fire. Keeping his nerve, Von Falkenhorst realized he had better offer a *"win-win"* proposition, if he wanted to save his job and miraculously convinced Hitler that invasion and occupation of the British Isles was not necessary for accomplishing the *Reich's* long-term goals. Britain could be brought to her knees and led to come to terms acceptable to Germany without the expense of an invasion and investment in sealift that probably would have no further usefulness.

According to von Falkenhorst's plan, *Unternehmen Seelöwe II* [27] would vault Hitler to the position of the first head of state to conquer another without invading. Keen on flexing his technology muscles and impressing his Japanese allies, Hitler warmed immediately to von Falkenhorst's idea of raining V1 and V2 missiles on Britain. He made an emotional public speech complete with wild eyes and grasping arm gestures that threatened devastating damage, if Britain did not immediately capitulate. Winston Churchill's response, in a radio address from the House of Commons, took the form of exhorting British civilian preparedness to fight with farm implements, if necessary.

---

[24] Colonel-General, the equivalent of a U.S. 3-star general.
[25] The "XX" Committee operated the "Double Cross" system, which is claimed to have "turned" every German spy in Britain, who wasn't executed, into a double agent feeding misleading intelligence to the *Abwehr*.
[26] German Military Intelligence
[27] Operation Sealion II

V-2 Rocket

Churchill called for "Victory at all costs, victory in spite of all terror, victory however long and hard the road may be; for without victory there is no survival."[28] Hitler promptly directed the rocket launches to begin.

In *Seelöwe II*, fully 9521 V1 "Buzz Bombs" and then 1150 V2 rockets, each with one-ton high explosive warheads, were launched against British target areas. 'Till the start of the missile war, Britons had only experienced air-dropped 500-pound bombs, which were demoralizing but did not shake the ground as severely as the new, heavier warheads.

Hitler crowed about his rocket weapons to Baron Oshima Hiroshi, the Japanese Ambassador in Berlin. Oshima dutifully communicated important news to Tokyo via HF radio messages in a diplomatic code that was being read by American cryptologists, who also read Tokyo's instruction that Oshima offer to buy some of the V2s. Hitler agreed and 12 dismantled V2s were taken by submarine to Japan. Although willing to share the rockets, Hitler kept his emerging nuclear capabilities secret from the Japanese, who were known by the *Abwehr* to be working on their own program. Japan reassembled eleven of the V2s and modified six of their warheads to carry deadly chemical weapons transferred from Army Unit 731, based in Harbin, Manchuria. The remaining dismantled rocket went to a Mitsubishi plant in Osaka, where reverse-engineering was immediately started. The resulting Japanese rocket design was designated "I-GO-4."

Although the German V1s and V2s were unreliable by modern standards, with many failing to complete their planned trajectories,

---

[28] Text of Churchill's actual remarks to the House of Commons on May 13, 1940

and were too inaccurate consistently to hit targeted towns, the British people soon became highly agitated. Slow-flying Buzz Bombs could be heard and seen approaching and many were shot down by anti-aircraft fire and the RAF. However, the certain knowledge that, when a V1's tell-tale pulse jet engine quit, it would fall somewhere nearby, was overwhelming.

The anxiety took a heavy toll on the populace but was quickly bypassed by paralyzing panic as the supersonic V2s, traveling 3500 miles per hour began falling silently and suddenly from their 50-mile high apogees. With a combat range of only 200 miles, the London area and Southern England absorbed the full blow. Gradually, Churchill's pep-talks became less convincing and British courage eroded in the face of the 1150 successful V2 blasts that killed over 2700 and injured 6500 without warning during the second half of 1944. Edward R. Murrow, broadcasting to the U.S. from London, sobered Americans with his admonition that, if the Germans weren't stopped, they would be attacking the U.S. next.

The MI-5[29] intelligence report on Germany's nearly-operational V3 rocket, with a 350-mile range, dealt Churchill a numbing blow. He was tortured by the futility of wasting what was left of RAF aircrews on well-defended German launch sites scattered across France, Belgium, and the Netherlands and felt Britain nakedly defenseless. Except by capitulation, Britain had become utterly powerless to stop the murderous rain of V2s. And with their longer range, the new V3s could be launched at Southern England from even further beyond reach on the Continent or could start falling on the industrial cities of the Midlands.

Confronting the inevitable but unable to bring himself personally to participate in a surrender, a stooped, somber Churchill requested the King to ask Deputy Prime Minister Clement Atlee to form a new government.

---

[29] British Intelligence service

Winston Churchill

Churchill went home to Chartwell a broken man forcing thoughts of suicide from his brain. He spent his remaining days writing his memoirs and painting landscapes, expecting his imprisonment by the *Gestapo* in the near term.

To the immense relief of the English people, who had desperately prayed for deliverance from the missile terror, Atlee asked the Swedish Ambassador to relay a note to Berlin proposing an immediate truce. Atlee then directed the First Sea Lord[30] to order the surface fleet scuttled in deep water and the Minister for Air to order the RAF to destroy its combat aircraft. A small number of Brits with selected critical specialties, such as cryptanalysis, radar, and nuclear physics were evacuated by submarines from Holy Loch in Scotland to Halifax, Nova Scotia. Most of these eventually traveled on to the U.S. The Royal Family insisted on staying in Buckingham Palace. With pomp and celebration, the Germans released and repatriated the quarter-million British troops captured at Dunkirk and kept in POW camps since 1940.

As *Generaloberst* von Falkenhorst had promised, Britain had been conquered without invasion.[31] Hitler's terms for the UK were economically and politically harsh but Foreign Secretary Anthony Eden managed to convince the Germans that Britain would cooperate without being occupied. Although no German troop formations were to be stationed in Britain, Germany forced Eden to agree to teams of plain-clothes inspectors attached to the German Embassy in London, who could travel at will to verify Britain's observance of the truce terms. Although never agreed as

---

[30] Equivalent to the U.S. Secretary of the Navy

[31] Actually, the 1943 Italian surrender of the Mediterranean island of Pantellaria after sustained U.S. aerial bombardment marks the first time in history that militarily-defended territory was surrendered without having been invaded or besieged.

within their portfolios, the German inspectors included undercover *Gestapo* and *SS*, who clandestinely caused Britain's Jews substantial anxiety.

At the stroke of a pen, the British Empire dissolved. Canada, Australia, New Zealand, India, and the Union of South Africa declared their independence but retained symbolic, politically insignificant commonwealth ties. In exchange for concessions and guarantees that would be blatantly revoked later, India granted Japan naval bases at Madras and Calcutta and agreed to permit Japan to "consult" in the formulation of Indian foreign policy.

British colonies in Africa and Asia were ceded to the Axis powers. In Britain, the prices of tea and sugar quadrupled overnight. In a 48-hour period, the Royal Navy slipped from first in the world to insignificance. Throughout Britain, the mood was universally somber. The sudden V2 explosions had stopped and Britons would go on living but stiff upper lips were in very short supply. Grown men on buses and in the Underground avoided eye contact as a device to forestall weeping and sobbing.

Germany's well-kept secret that several V2s were successfully launched from platforms towed by U-Boats in the blandly-named *Unterhehmen Prüfstand-XII* [32] kept Americans and Canadians. ignorant of the coming nuclear threat to North America.

---

[32] Simply "Test Bed XII"

7

A NEW DIRECTION FOR AMERICA

Suppose FDR retired after three terms and a new political agenda emerged in Washington?

The Alternative History . . .

1944 - Roosevelt Steps Down

Franklin Roosevelt's decision to retire after his third presidential term threw the election of 1944 into a mad scramble. Both the incumbent Democrats and opposition Republicans bore the brunt of vitriolic blame for the disastrous military and diplomatic embarrassments. Vice President Henry Wallace found no room in which to distance himself from FDR's failed economic, foreign and defense policies. Wallace was kept consistently off-message and on the defensive by standard bearers of the new challengers, the American Citizens Party (ACP).

The ACP was a loose amalgamation of formerly small third parties, which had gained strength in the 1942 off-year elections. Norman Thomas, the socialist, who had been continuously anti-war since 1917 and an outspoken "America Firster," easily won the ACP's nomination. He frequently cited, as an example of his level-headed social policy experience, his strong opposition to the Roosevelt-Wallace Administration's relocation of West Coast Japanese-Americans to concentration camps. Charles Lindbergh became Thomas' unlikely ally by focusing on their defense and isolationist policy agreements and was selected by Thomas as his Vice Presidential running mate. To underscore the ticket's anti-war platform, Thomas tapped Jeanette Rankin early-on as his Secretary of War and the lady pacifist campaigned vigorously, winning very high favorability marks from women. Senator Robert La Follette Jr., whose Progressive Party had done well in 1942, also joined forces with Thomas. La Follette subordinated his own presidential ambitions to become Secretary of Agriculture and to have an influential voice in other cabinet appointments; La Follette specifically insisted on naming union-leader John L. Lewis as Secretary of Labor.

Thomas and La Follette had a private gentlemen's agreement that Thomas would serve only one term, stepping down for La Folette's own 1948 candidacy and the next vacancy on the U.S. Supreme Court. As part of his southern strategy, Thomas brought Governor Eugene Talmadge of Georgia into the campaign and appeared with him across the South. Talmadge was an early financial backer of Thomas' campaign and gave Thomas the assurances he wanted to hear about his personal politics. In a commitment Thomas would come to regret, Talmadge, an outspoken white supremacist and advocate of print censorship, was introduced as the next Attorney General and the man who would appoint the next head of the FBI.

Norman Thomas   *Robert La Follette Jr.*   *Eugene Talmadge*

With the backing of German and Japanese money, so cleverly laundered that the main candidates didn't know the original sources, the ACP ran a model campaign. Thomas and La Folette pledged responsible stewardship of the resources and affairs of a nation basically on its own and reaching peaceful accommodation with the Axis powers through appeasement. The ACP handily won the White House, both houses of Congress, and many state governorships. Naive ACP candidates accepted lavish campaign funds from clandestine American fascists in exchange for promises they were soon asked to fulfill.

The post-Pearl Harbor shame and hostilities-ending armistice yielded an acrimonious atmosphere in which none of FDR's outgoing principal officials nor the senior Civil Service leadership retained enough reputation or charisma to earn a prestigious position in a Norman Thomas administration, which was inaugurated on March 20th, 1945. Secretary of State Cordell Hull retired from public life and J. Edgar Hoover left the FBI. Harry S. Truman was not reelected to the Senate and retired to Independence, Missouri, where he tried and failed again in the haberdashery business.

Thomas, a committed Conscientious Objector, Lindbergh and La Follette brought to Washington a pacifist-isolationist ideology characterized by the rejection of any international alliance that obligated the U.S. or used the military as an instrument of national power. Thomas had no practical defense or foreign relations experience but knew enough of both subjects and their players to dislike them thoroughly as incompatible with the accomplishment of important social goals. Senator Gerald P. Nye, the North Dakota isolationist, became Secretary of State. Thomas ignored defense and foreign policy, delegating White House contact with Nye and the State Department over to the Vice President.

The influence to be wielded by the War and Navy Departments was deliberately downgraded and the administration turned away from most of the successful industrialists, financiers and the generals and the admirals, instead bringing into the federal government "known-quantity" union organizers, state and local legislators and police officials, plus mid-level military and naval officers with good leadership reputations but no disproven policy involvements. Confident of the electoral mandate they believed they had been given, Thomas, La Follette and their principal domestic advisors set to work on raising the minimum wage, controlling rents and prices, fostering near-universal collective bargaining, subsidizing farming and farm prices.

As Thomas had promised, Jeanette Rankin, the arch-pacifist, was named Secretary of War, pledging to restrict the Army's capability for getting the Nation into trouble by reducing its funding to basic subsistence levels. Rankin had the support of a majority of American women for her vow that, while she was the Secretary of War, no American boys would kill or be killed in combat. As an exception to the cold shoulder given to industrialists, Henry Ford was asked to become Secretary of the Navy and agreed for only two years to oversee the conversion of the Navy's mission to coastal defense. Ford had a public reputation as an anti-Semite and his anti-union philosophy clashed with President Thomas' views. However, Vice President Lindbergh, Ford's long-time confidante, convinced the president of his indispensable manufacturing savvy and industrial leadership.

Low on Thomas' list of priorities, the War and Navy Departments were also delegated to Lindbergh. Lindbergh was naturally inclined toward military defensive capabilities but thought it futile to attempt catching up to and matching the Axis powers militarily and was swayed by the force of Jeanette Rankin's personality. Military uniforms disappeared from White House security details and ceremonies; service bands performed for Washington social occasions in civilian clothes.

Even before the Inauguration Day celebrations had quieted-down, the American unholy alliance of organized crime, the KKK, assorted "militias," and the German-American *Bund* shifted into high gear, making plans and collecting IOUs. Ruthless thugs, who belonged in jail, were instead appointed to federal and state agency offices, judgeships, key legislative committees, and senior law enforcement positions by unsuspecting administration officials new to the Washington and state capital scenes.

Simultaneously a Klansman and member of the *Bund*, George Strong was one of those, who should have been in prison but became a paid consultant to the Federal District Attorneys of all three Alabama districts and was named a member of a newly-formed Regional Law Enforcement Coordinating Council for Florida, Georgia, Alabama and Mississippi under the U.S. Department of Justice. In this latter role, George recommended the funneling of federal grant monies to police forces in those states and represented them to the FBI. Law enforcement became the "old boys' club" for several of George's Klan and *Bund* friends and many more like them.

It was the opportunity to channel federal grants that made George a rich man. George also profited handsomely by facilitating the smuggling of drugs by Organized Crime through the all the Gulf ports from Pascagoula, Mississippi to Tampa, Florida. He became a generous host, who distributed largesse in exchange for loyalty but was feared as a well-connected boss who could order business-crippling labor strikes and enemies killed through his KKK and *Bund* contacts. For Blacks in the U.S., it was not a happy time to be alive.

Franklin Roosevelt retired broken-hearted to his home at Hyde Park, morosely living-out the rest of his days as a wheel chair-bound recluse, shorn of power and influence. At the urging of his wife, Eleanor, he had just begun writing his memoirs when he died of a massive cerebral hemorrhage on April 12, 1945.

Germany the Nuclear Superpower

Albert Speer traveled to Berchtesgaden in August 1945 and advised Hitler that an atomic device was ready for testing. Looking out at the snowcapped alps from the sunny terrace of his

Adlersnest [33] retreat, Hitler enthusiastically approved Speer's plan for an underground test in an abandoned salt mine (Codenamed "*Teufelshöle*")[34] outside Lüneburg in northern Germany. "Everything is ready," Speer gushed. "We have assured that no radioactive material will vent into the atmosphere and we are ready with a communiqué about an underground earthquake, if questions about a seismic event are asked."

Germany's ten-kiloton device (Codenamed "*Kleiner Junge*")[35] was successfully detonated deep in the old salt mine on September 4th. There was no venting and a brief shockwave, measuring 3.2 on the Richter Scale, was measured in nearby Lüneburg.

The few citizens who asked about it accepted the earthquake explanation from *Professordoktor* Klaus von Kädich, head of the Geology Department at Lüneburg University. There was only perfunctory newspaper coverage of the "earthquake" and none outside Germany.

Albert Speer and Hitler

Germany's Spectacular Mid-Ocean Demonstrations

Back in the Berlin *Kanzlerei*[36] on September 9th, the *Nazis* decided to publicize their triumph after a lengthy discussion of secrecy versus disclosure. Wishing to capitalize on his new power, Hitler not only ordered a *communiqué* but directed an above-ground demonstration to which his allies and some

---

[33] Eagle's Nest
[34] Devil's Cave
[35] Little Boy
[36] Chancellery

remaining enemies would be invited. Although he wanted an immediate demonstration, an impatient *Führer* reluctantly agreed to a date that would permit the necessary preparations and was convinced by Himmler of the significance of November 11, erasing forever the stigma of the humiliating Great War armistice in 1918. Hitler also saw an opportunity to intimidate the new American President, Norman Thomas, who had been in office since March. Vice President Charles Lindbergh was asked by Thomas to attend the demonstrations.

Werner Heisenberg, Germany's leading nuclear scientist, also argued against any atomic explosions that might scatter radioactive fallout on Germany or on German occupation troops on the continent, urging instead, a point at sea 400 miles west of the Azores. VP Lindbergh was flown out to the mid-ocean site in a Navy *Catalina* flying boat and was given a royal reception on board the battleship *Tirpitz*. The two-part demonstration programme for Saturday, November 11, 1945, named *Ausstellung Thorsblitzen*,[37] opened with the launches of two V3 rockets from platforms that dramatically and unexpectedly surfaced behind the U-Boats that were towing them.

The disbelieving, wide-eyed observers watched transfixed through binoculars as deck cranes lifted the V3s out of the submarines, erected them on the platforms, transferred fuel from the submarine, and connected the cables. A narrator explained the sequence of events over public address loudspeakers in four languages. Twenty-five minutes after the platforms had surfaced, the rockets roared straight up and then arced to the south, finally disappearing from sight.

For Part Two of the exhibition, the observers' vessels were repositioned a safe upwind distance from the captured French tanker, *Ville de Saint Mâlo*. Germany's second atomic device

---

[37] Exhibition Thor's Lightning

(Codenamed *"Fettmann"*)[38] had been put aboard, hidden from view by a wooden shed on a steel tower.

The narrator explained that the weapon aboard the tanker could be carried by the rockets demonstrated earlier and counted-down, in German, from *"zehn."*[39] In mid-ocean, observers from 26 countries, including Japan, Italy, the U.S., Britain, Canada, and the USSR saw through tinted goggles, the bright flash that eclipsed the overhead sun. They felt the powerful shockwave that set off permanent fearful trembling, and watched the mushroom cloud that signaled the dawn of a new age, far worse than the humiliating conventional defeats some of their countries had recently suffered.

In the U.S., the White House and most of the Congress could not come to grips with the significance of the German weapons demonstrations. Those who had not seen the missile launches and the mushroom cloud had difficulty understanding the eye-witness descriptions, trying unsuccessfully to relate the word-pictures to newsreel images of large explosions, perhaps somewhat larger. President-elect Norman Thomas, disdainful of all things military, refused to permit the German weapons developments to intrude into his priorities and deferred to the VP.

Lindbergh assured the Nation: unless provoked, the Germans would have no cause to hit the U.S. with atomic weapons and

---

[38] Fat Man
[39] Ten

there would be no danger, if good economic relations could be established. Having anticipated the German atomic demonstration, Lindbergh had resolved to work for the termination of all U.S. work on an atomic bomb as quickly as possible to forestall German thoughts of preëmption. He had obtained concurrence from Thomas, who only vaguely understood Lindbergh's explanation but was eager to transfer newly-available defense funds to his favored social programs.

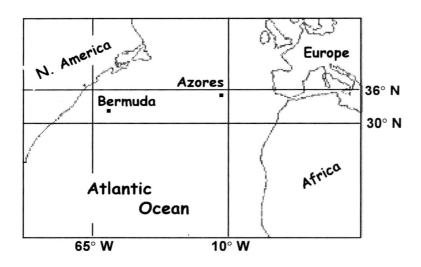

8

THE SECRET CANADA VISIT

Suppose a Nazi-led conspiracy plotted to foment and exploit civil rights strife in the U.S.?

The Alternative History . . .

In fog so thick, the men on board were unable to see the dock they had just stepped from, the black-hulled trawler marked "NS-88" and homeported in Halifax, eased out of *Wagnerhafen* (formerly Miquelon Harbor, renamed) at 11:15 pm and headed due west at a cautions ten knots. For their departure, the harbor, dock, and trawler lights were all completely blacked-out to keep NS-88's very brief visit secret. Captain Terry Ryan confidently studied his compass heading and tachometer shaft revolutions as the trawler chugged ahead in the dark. Checking their watches, the captain and Rob O'Rourke, the First Mate, nodded in agreement when they had been underway for exactly twenty-six minutes and twenty seconds and ready to change course. Ryan spun the helm till the compass read 045 degrees and throttled the engine to "ahead two-thirds" while O'Rourke switched on the trawler's lights, which illuminated the enveloping fog and defined it as a mass of swirling droplets of moisture. About every minute, Ryan sounded a long blast on the trawler's foghorn, causing his passengers to jump until they learned, after the fourth blast, to watch him reach for and pull the horn cord.

"We will be at Pass Island in forty-three minutes, *Herr Obergruppenführer*," Ryan informed his principal passenger. "That's in foggy Newfoundland."

Reinhard Heydrich pulled the fisherman's duffle coat closer around his throat against the cold damp, responded, "*Danke*" and huddled with his two traveling companions, speaking German in low voices.

In thirty minutes, the VHF radio speaker crackled the message, "Holly this is Lady Chesley. Come in Holly." Ryan gave two horn toots and turned to face Heydrich. "That is Marlowe, right on time." In five minutes, Ryan slowed to a careful crawl, magically passing a buoy with a red light and bell, close aboard to port, producing triumphal, knowing chuckles from the captain and mate, both of whom gave smiling nods to their passengers. In minutes, a second buoy slipped through their view and a dull light appeared dead ahead, low down on the surface. Ryan steered straight for the light, which grew brighter as they approached.

O'Rourke trained the trawler's searchlight on the light they were approaching and Ryan reversed then idled the engine. The faint outline of a wooden pier became visible and a coil of rope suddenly came out of the night, landing noisily on the deck forward of the pilot house, again startling the passengers. O'Rourke pulled on the rope until the trawler nudged against the pier, looped it around a cleat, and then killed all the lights. Marlowe, standing on the pier with a boat hook, pulled the stern snug against the timbers. The German passengers disembarked without delay and, from the pier, Heydrich said softly to Ryan, "*Danke, danke Herr Kapitän. Auf wiedersehen.*" O'Rourke put the Germans' three small seabags on the pier and cast off as Marlowe pushed the vessel away from the pier. Ryan slowly reversed away from Pass Island immediately and in seconds, the blacked-out trawler was swallowed by the fog and could only be heard gently bubbling away.

Marlowe led the Germans to a large blue Buick that he had left idling with the heater on. All four men were grateful to get out of the penetrating fog and into the car's warmth. Marlowe turned on the headlights, put the car in gear and headed slowly across the bridge for the small town of Grole, arriving shortly at Juliana's Inn, a small fishing lodge.

Inside, the hotel owners had long gone to bed and the only member of the staff who greeted the new arrivals was Juliana's Black Labrador Retriever, Shadow, with whom Heydrich bonded immediately.

The *Obergruppenführer's* private room and a double room for his aides were ready with the keys laid out on the counter. Marlowe bid the visitors "good night" and left. The Germans were all in bed by 1:30 am. Heydrich came down for breakfast at 7:30 dressed for waterman's work at sea and joined his similarly-attired aides, *SS-Obersturmführer* Wilhelm Führbeck and *SS-Untersturmführer* Johann Baerwalt, who were already drinking coffee with the three Americans they had come to meet.

All traveling on forged identity documents, KKK National Grand Dragon Sam Green, Grand Kleagle Robinson Byrd, and *Bundesführer* Fritz Kuhn had arrived the day before, driven by aides who were in the inn but not joining the others for breakfast. After introductions that were accompanied by broad smiles and firm handshakes, Juliana wheeled in a hearty Canadian breakfast of eggs, bacon, potatoes, biscuits, and big pot of coffee and then left the dining room, closing the door behind her. Heydrich smiled at her but remained silent. Shadow sat close-by, watching the *Obergruppenführer* eat and eventually shared half of Heydrich's bacon and a buttered biscuit.

During the following business discussion, which plotted the details of the planned suppression of America's minorities, Heydrich fondly petted the dog and scratched behind his ears. When Shadow brought his tennis ball and placed it in Heydrich's lap, he repeatedly sent the Lab scampering across the room to the silent annoyance of Sam Green, who felt the German wasn't concentrating.

To Green's relief, Heydrich finally got down to business. As he began speaking, *Untersturmführer* Baerwalt set up a wind-up phonograph player near the door to the kitchen and started a record of the first movement of Beethoven's Fifth Symphony at a moderately-loud volume.

"*Danke mein junge*," Heydrich said to Baerwalt, explaining to the others that "Beethoven will guard our privacy." He then began by suggesting that, so long as inferiors were allowed to corrupt the North American populations, the Master Races would never be able to rest easily and realize the lofty world ideals the *Führer* had defined.

Heydrich continued, explaining that his colleague in Berlin, referring to Adolph Eichman but not naming him, saw the North American problem in simple terms: prosperity and international harmony were dependent on Aryan purity free of the distracting conflicts that invariably arise in racially-polluted populations. "If America would ship its money-hoarding Jews to Europe, Germany would take over from there. Her Negroes were indolent, mentally-deficient sub-humans best shipped back to Africa and put ashore or even dropped over the side in mid-ocean. Heydrich added with a smirk, "But there are too few boats so we must find other ideas."

America's Chinese would always take needed jobs from the superior races by accepting low wages; the Chinese would do well as agricultural workers in Mexico and could easily be transported there. Finally, that part of the native Indian population that had not been successfully assimilated should be forcibly confined separately on reservations in the west." Future immigration to the U.S. and Canada would be carefully planned by cooperative governments and strictly limited to provide living space for selected Aryans. Every eight minutes, Baerwalt restarted the Beethoven phonograph record, keeping the "sound fence" active and making Sam Green visibly squirm, especially when Heydrich prevented Baerwalt from cutting-off Beethoven's coda by merely raising his index finger from the table and moving it left and right.

Synchronizing his remarks to the opening notes of the restarted Beethoven symphony, Heydrich next laid out a set of tactical objectives the Americans agreed they could accomplish and the meeting went on to consider the development of a schedule and how communications would be handled. The discussions lasted through a working lunch at which Heydrich, who never ate fowl, fed all of his turkey to Shadow, sheepishly asking the others not to inform Juliana on him. The group took a half-hour break after lunch, which Heydrich spent outside, playing ball with the Black Lab.

Their afternoon session reviewed various contingencies and how information would be fed to the world press for maximum effect. Heydrich's financial assistant, *Obersturmführer* Führbeck, informed the Americans that operating funds for their use would be in the customary bank accounts in ten days. By 4:00 pm, the sun was low on the horizon and the conferees were all watching the time. The Germans were to be picked up by the trawler at 6:15 pm to travel back to *Wagnerhafen* in secret darkness. The Americans had a long drive ahead of them to their first stop-over. All agreed they were ready to adjourn. No one had taken any notes at the meeting about which no historical record had been created.

Untersturmführer Baerwalt packed-up the phonograph and produced a bottle of aged Canadian rye whiskey that had been given to the *Obergruppenführer* as a welcoming gift by the Commandant of *Wagnerhafen*. Heydrich toasted his new associates with, *"Prost"* but found the whiskey too sour for his own taste. He set his glass down, still mostly full while the Americans and his aides downed theirs. The small group circulated making their "goodbyes." While shaking hands with Sam Green, Heydrich asked to be remembered to George Strong, being careful not to use George's former name. Green brightened at hearing Heydrich's commendation of one of the *Bund's* most reliable leaders. In their car, driving away, Green complained to his Klan companion, Byrd, that the Beethoven music was burned into his brain and he would never be able to turn it off inside his head.

Stepping outside into the early evening darkness, Heydrich grudgingly welcomed a repeat of the previous night's fog as a provider of stealth. As the Germans were getting into Marlowe's Buick, Shadow approached Heydrich, his tail wagging vigorously. Unabashedly, the genocidal murderer bent forward, held Shadow gently by his long ears, and kissed him on the top of his head. *"Gut* boy!" he told the Lab in his accented English. Later, Juliana found the open bottle of rye whiskey and added it to her bar stock, never knowing the identity of the guest who left it behind.

9

Endlösung, THE FINAL SOLUTION ACHIEVED

Suppose an unchecked Hitler had completed the Holocaust?

The Alternative History . . .

A nuclear-armed Adolf Hitler was adored by Aryan Germans. He was virtually deified after conquering Europe and, with their Japanese ally, bringing the English-speaking nations to heel. Convinced by unrelenting propaganda that they were a morally superior master race delivered personally by Hitler to a position of deserved dominance from confiscatory post-World War I reparations restrictions and disrespect, the *Deutschevolk* basked in Europe's highest standard of living. With all segments of the economy rigidly controlled, average Germans lived large from the open stealing of raw materials from occupied territories and the enslavement of conquered peoples. *Volkswagens,* now accessible to most German workers, scooted everywhere via modern *Autobahnen* and the abundance of luxury foodstuffs, inexpensive electric and gasoline, and bargain-priced vacations at the prime resorts of occupied Europe were enjoyed by a contented population. In Germany, the good life was a much appreciated gift from Hitler and the nation's invincible armed forces.

All of the fighting from 1939 to 1943 had taken place outside Germany; not a single enemy boot or bomb had disturbed German soil. From fairytale medieval towns and richly productive farmland to the muscular robustness of her heavy industry, Germany's cleanliness, attractiveness, and disciplined efficiency sparkled. Her occupied neighbors, however, presented a much bleaker picture. In addition to the bestial brutality visited on invaded populations, the overrunning *blitzkrieg* attacks had been maliciously and unnecessarily destructive to infrastructure and dwellings. The *Nazis* felt no obligation to rebuild any more of the war damage than was minimally necessary to produce and transport the spoils back to Germany. The victims were stripped of their surviving cultural artifacts that made places nice to live in. Occupied populations were deliberately impoverished as a device to keep them docile and, with the exception of collaborators, who facilitated oppressive occupation and took their share of the *Nazi* loot, captive populations were overworked, malnourished, ill-clothed, and in declining health.

Having bought into repetitive anti-Semitic propaganda, reinforced by *Nazi*-controlled media and art, the prevailing attitude among Germans was that the post-World War I economic difficulties and social unrest had been launched in 1917 by the Jews in collusion with Soviet Bolsheviks. Banishment of the Jews from lands where they didn't belong and denial of their sharing in Germany's hard-won luxuries was quietly accepted as just retribution. The mass deportations via rail yards in population centers large and small had been noisy spectacles and the *Nazis* didn't try to conceal them. It was public knowledge that Jews in large numbers were being sent into deserved punitive exile. While most Germans approved, the few who were repulsed learned quickly to keep silent. Everyone had heard stories of dissenters either being lumped-in with the herded Jews or mysteriously disappearing. No moralizing emerged from the press, the church, the universities, or anything resembling a political opposition in Germany.

The luckier Jews got out of Europe before 1939 and the start of the deportations, reaching sanctuary where they related harrowing experiences of harassment, property confiscation, and physical abuse. Even without embellishment, their descriptions of the

Kristallnacht [40] depredations were horrific and thought, at the time, to be the low point of German anti-Semitism. As the *Nazi* persecution and genocide increased in proficiency, the borders were closed and emigration became almost impossible. *Grenzpolizei* [41] shot first and questioned later, if suspects too close to the border appeared to be planning to cross. By June of 1940, France had fallen and anxious Jews scrambled their way to Marseilles and the hope of an American visa, good for fleeing Europe. Anxious to avoid confrontation with France's Vichy Government, the Roosevelt Administration ordered the Consulate in Marseilles to deny the Jews visas.

This unpleasant task fell to Hiram Bingham, the U.S. Vice Consul, who strongly disagreed with the policy but turned the pleading Jewish refugees away. Under the terms of the Franco-German armistice, Vichy France delivered those Jews for transportation to the death camps. The *Nazis* enforced strict suppression of foreign news correspondents. International postal and telephone connections were strictly censored and, as greater numbers of Jews were relocated to the camps, the outbound flow of news was reduced to a trickle. Germany released no information on its genocidal crimes.

Those outside Germany, who had loved ones or close business associates on the inside were gripped by concern and frantic at the loss of contact. Appeals to host governments and to German embassies were fruitless. In particular, the U.S. Government publicly feigned ignorance, however, from 1939 through the end of 1944, was receiving chilling intelligence that hinted at an organized mass slaughter in progress.

From clumsy early beginnings in 1939, the *Nazis* classified as *Streng Geheim* [42] the Jewish, gypsy, and other *Untermenschen* [43]

---

[40] Literally "Crystal Night," in reference to the great quantities of broken glass in the streets of German towns. During the night of November 9, 1938, rampaging *Nazi* rioters smashed the shop windows of many Jewish-owned businesses.
[41] Border Police
[42] Top Secret

genocide, known as the *"Unternehmen Euthanasieprogramme T-4."*[44] Great care was taken to keep the program's details, death camp locations (designated "14-f1-3 units"), and murder statistics from disclosure. All paper documents were stamped *Streng Geheim,* registered, and, when no longer needed, destroyed by witnessed burning. Teletype messages were enciphered by four-rotor *Enigma* [45] encryptors and telephone speakers were circumspect, carefully talking around the sensitive aspects of conversation in home-made codes.

***Four-rotor* Enigma cipher machine**

With so much of the European continent and surrounding waters occupied by the Germans, getting close enough to intercept radio communications was extremely difficult, effectively drying-up most reliable Communications Intelligence (COMINT). After 1940, U.S. COMINT was reduced to only a few clandestine listening posts in Switzerland, Sweden and Britain. Operating a very small number of High Frequency and Very High Frequency radios, these undercover facilities with scant, overworked staff, were focused on the highest intelligence priorities.

Desperate for strategic warning of any further hostile Axis activities, those few available interception resources emphasized German military, nuclear research and diplomatic radio traffic over whatever communications the Germans used to support the shipment of human freight to the death camps.

---

[43] Subhumans
[44] T-4 Operation Euthanasia Program
[45] An enciphering device. The 4-rotor version produced Germany's most secure ciphers of the war.

In the absence of reliable COMINT, U.S. intelligence on the genocide relied almost exclusively on the reports of occasional travelers, who had been in occupied Europe, and even these people were pumped more for strategic intelligence than news of the Jewish plight. Still, enough connectable dots were in the hands of the State Department and the American Jewish community to penetrate the veil of secrecy Germany had pulled over the holocaust.

10

PROVOCATIVE CRUISE OF THE IRON FLEET

Suppose a taunting German fleet appeared off the U.S. coast?

The Alternative History . . .

The decoded incoming cablegram marked 'FLASH" from the Royal Canadian Navy base at St. John's, Newfoundland started young sailors in whites flat-out running the halls in U.S. Navy Headquarters in Washington. In the 1940s days before copiers, office automation and local area networks, teletype machines were loaded with 5-ply papers separated by carbon paper. The yellow original and the top three carbon copies of the Canadian message, all rubber-stamped "SECRET" in red ink, were rushed by the runners to the offices of the Chief of Naval Operations and three of his senior deputies. The Communications Center immediately started printing additional copies from the punched-paper tape that had been created when the message was decoded.

In the CNO's office, Commander John Crowley, the CNO's aide, scanned the message and took it right in to Admiral Ernest King. King read the brief text twice and instructed Crowley to ask the Battle Staff to assemble in the Command Center in ten minutes. King then wrote the names of others on the message, including the President's naval aide, who should see the message and handed the yellow paper to a WAVE yeoman before heading to the Command Center himself. By the time Admiral King reached the

Command Center, a copy of the Canadian message had been read and the Senior Watch Officer had the giant wall map of the world tagged with the last-known position of the *Kriegsmarine's* fearsome *Atlantische Eisenflotte*.[46]

Amid lavish ceremonial fanfare accented by brass bands, flowers and bunting, dignitaries in formal dress, bellowing ships' horns, and smartly-dressed crews at attention on all the decks, the Iron Atlantic Fleet, champions of German sea power, had made a striking departure from Kiel harbor on April 9, 1945, captured by the world's photojournalists and newsreel photographers.

500 *Luftwaffe* bombers in *staffel* formations overflew the departing ships at an altitude of 100 meters,[47] creating a vibrating roar on the ground that affected the balance of many standing onlookers.

The *Führer* himself attended the ceremony, watching from the luxury yacht *Sachsenhausen* and had to cover his ears as the bombers thundered low overhead. The power-projecting tour was the *Führer's* own idea, inspired by Teddy Roosevelt's having sent the U.S. "Great White Fleet" off on a world tour in 1907.

Bismarck

The tour's principal audience was recently-inaugurated President Norman Thomas.

After their departure from Kiel, the naval giants *Bismarck* and *Tirpitz*, accompanied by heavy cruisers *Scharnhorst*, *Graf Spee*, *Deutschland*, *Gniesenau*, and *Prinz Eugen*, plus fifteen destroyers and fleet support vessels had next put in at occupied Copenhagen

---

[46] Atlantic Iron Fleet
[47] Approximately 300 feet

and: Stavanger, Norway; Bruges, Belgium; Rotterdam; and Le Havre. Prime Minister Clement Atlee apologized to an adamantly opposed King George VI and then advised a nonplussed Commons that the Cabinet had approved a 48-hour "good will" visit by the German ships to Plymouth. Black crepe, usually reserved for mourning displays, hung from the windows of many English homes to signal that the German presence was a bitter pill to swallow. However, the people of Plymouth, traditionally a Royal Navy town, and the German crews ashore on leave behaved politely and German money was gratefully accepted by pub landlords, shopkeepers, tattoo artists, and opportunistic "good time" girls.

At the conclusion of the visit on April 22nd, Admiral Günther Lütjens, in Bismarck, ordered each ship in the formation to fire a one-shot salvo from each of its main guns in salute as the fleet got underway from Plymouth. Although the guns were all pointed out to sea, the powerful concussions broke windows, set pigeons flying, and made young children cry.

Before the smoke had cleared, over 200 Luftwaffe bombers based in Northern France and the Channel Islands roared over the harbor and the departing ships at very low altitude. Adult Britons cringed in memory of the recent wartime bombings and ruefully looked around at the ruins that still littered some Plymouth streets, muttering anti-*Nazi* oaths to themselves.

Admiral Günther Lütjens

Lütjens next headed for bunkering and provisions at St. Nazaire on France's Atlantic Coast and then steamed to the Azores, putting in at the port of *Angrodo do Héroismo* on the island of Terceira. Three days later, on April 30th, the sunrise revealed the Germans suddenly gone and U.S. naval intelligence had suspicions but no hard sightings or radio intercepts that revealed where the fleet had headed or if it were still intact. After a further two days without any intelligence suggesting that the Germans had sailed back to Europe, there were many American high-placed hunches that Lütjens was either heading for the *Kriegsmarine* base at *Sankt Peter* or the Caribbean and South America.

The German bases in Greenland, *"Ankerplatz Eisbär"* and *"Logistikbasis Edelweis"* were still locked-in by winter ice and assessed as improbable ports-of-call. The Secretary of the Navy directed that no information be released that would alarm the general public or reveal that the U.S. was only guessing at where the Germans might be heading.

Early on May 4th, the fleet was spotted by a *Sunderland* flying boat of the Canadian Maritime Patrol, heading for the island of *Sankt Peter*. The tiny port offered insufficient anchorage for the whole fleet so only Bismarck and the destroyer Z17 *Von Roeder* were berthed while the rest of the ships bobbed offshore.

Short Mark III Sunderland

At dawn on May 8th, a Canadian fishing crew out of Sydney, Nova Scotia stared in disbelief as the fog-colored German seagoing giants materialized out of the drizzle, heading southwest towards New England. The fishermen, trembling in fearful anticipation of being blown out of the water, still dutifully contacted the Canadian Coast Guard, which made a report by radiotelephone to the Navy in St. John's that formed the basis of the coded cable that was flashed to Washington:

```
GERMAN FLEET SIGHTED
081030Z⁴⁸ NORTH OF SABLE
ISLAND NS HEADING
SOUTHWEST.
```

Within the hour, dozens of additional sighting reports came in, originating from freighters, ferries and aircraft. For the remaining daylight hours, sighting reports totaled in the hundreds, although the accuracy of numbers and types of ships varied widely, with some reports erroneously claiming to have sighted German aircraft carriers. CBC Toronto was first on the air with broadcast bulletins, quickly echoed by U.S. networks and the threatening German fleet was the subject of huge headlines in all U.S. newspapers. The American public was agitated and stirred to great anxiety by hyped predictions offered by the leading radio news commentators. The U.S. Navy's Atlantic Fleet went on maximum alert and positioned all available combatant ships along the East Coast right on the edge of the three-mile territorial limit but with strict orders to stay within home waters and avoid offering even the slightest provocation.

When the lead destroyer, of the German formation, the Z16 *Friedrich Eckoldt*, blinked her position as 125 kilometers off Nantucket Island, Lütjens ordered the whole fleet to Battle Stations, in keeping with his sailing orders. At breakfast aboard *Bismarck* before going ashore in Kiel, Grand Admiral Eric Rader had wished Lütjens a happy voyage, lamented that he could not participate in so historic a German accomplishment, and putting on his uniform cap, soberly reviewed the fleet's sailing order, documenting his specific rules of engagement with the Americans:

---

⁴⁸ 6:30am Atlantic Time on the 8th

- The fleet was to very conservatively observe the U.S.' claimed 4.8 kilometer[50] territorial limit by coming no closer than 25 kilometers[51] to any U.S. land.

- No fleet vessel was permitted any courtesy visits in U.S. ports, even if invited, and Lütjens was to handle any emergencies and maintenance difficulties within his own resources.

- The fleet's accompanying screen was to position destroyers between the fleet's main combatants and any U.S. Navy or Coast Guard vessel that approached, permitting no American approaches closer than 4 kilometers.[52]

- The fleet was to maintain scout plane reconnaissance during all daylight hours. Scout planes were to avoid closer contact than 4 kilometers with any U.S. aircraft and ships.

- Crews of all ships were to remain at Battle Stations when the fleet was within 100 kilometers[53] of any U.S. territory. While at Battle Stations, the fleet was to be blacked-out and to observe ship-to-ship radio silence, communicating only by flag hoists or signaling lamps. During ship-to-ship radio silence, only *Bismarck* was permitted to report the fleet's position daily at midnight and noon via *Enigma*-encrypted High Frequency radio to the communications station, *VB-51*, on *Sankt Peter* for relay to Berlin.

---

[49] Sailing Order
[50] 4.8 kilometers = 3 miles
[51] 25 kilometers = almost 16 miles
[52] 4 kilometers = 2.5 miles
[53] 100 kilometers = 80 miles

- The fleet would be provided tactical Communications Intelligence support by the *B-Dienst* [54] detachment embarked in *Scharnhorst*. Upon the detected flight of any American aircraft, all radars other than air surveillance sets were to shut down.

- If need be, Lütjens was authorized to resort to arms if American warships should try to prevent the fleet from exercising their right of way in international waters. "Keep Away" warnings by flag hoists or signaling lamps should be given first, followed by warning shots across the bow, before any firing for effect. Fleet vessels were always authorized to return fire, if fired upon.

- Expected hostile American action was to be reported with the codeword, "*Weizenmehl*." In the event of actual hostilities, radio silence was to be broken and reports radioed to *Sankt Peter* and Berlin in plaintext.

The Iron Fleet Off the U.S. Coast

At 1512 hours Eastern Standard Time, Destroyer Z16 reported her arrival at *Punkt Gustav*,[55] on latitude 40°-30', 25 kilometers off New York City, and the fleet changed course, steering 225 degrees and slowed to ten knots, maintaining a 25-mile offshore track. The turn was reported by the crew of the U.S. Navy blimp, K-11, out of Lakehurst Naval Air Station, New Jersey. K-11, flown by Lieutenant (jg) Frank Lunney, was a long-endurance reconnaissance platform, and was inching ever closer to the German fleet to photograph individual ships in as much detail as possible.

---

[54] *Beobachtungsdienst,* German Navy Communications Intelligence Service
[55] Point "G" in the German phonetic alphabet.

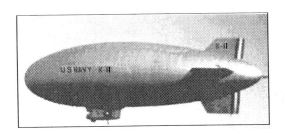

When Lütjens felt K-11 was crowding too closely, he ordered Bismarck and Tirpitz each to launch an *Arado* Ar 196 aircraft from their on-board catapults. The two *Arados* intercepted the blimp and *Leutnant* Erich Baumgartner, flying the lead plane, fired warning shots from his twin 20mm machine guns.

Lt. Lunney watched the tracer rounds zipping closely by and immediately turned toward shore, disappointing Baumgartner, who was hoping to be able to shoot the blimp down. Lakehurst Operations ordered Lunney to approach no closer than ten miles but to climb to 6000 feet and continue pacing the Germans.

Later the same day, the aircraft carrier USS Ranger (CV-4) launched a section of twelve *Hellcat* fighters while just off Virginia Beach. Under orders to approach no closer than five miles from the German ships, the *Hellcats* were picked up first by destroyer Z16's radar and reported by blinker lamps throughout the fleet.

Bismarck and Tirpitz each launched their two *Arado* Ar 196s, which intercepted and flew parallel to the blue fighters but staying well outside their own prohibited 16-mile buffer. Baumgartner was aloft again but soberly watched the twelve Hellcats, feeling no strong desire to engage them in his low-performance float plane.

Newspapers in Germany and Japan later published front-page photos of the small *Arado* seaplanes apparently blocking the American fighters from approaching the fleet and accompanying captions poked fun at the U.S.' feeble response. A week later, photo reprints, complete with the *Nazi* captions appeared in

American newspapers, embarrassing the Thomas Administration and the Navy in particular.

Arado Ar 196

The First Army Headquarters Command Post at Fort Jay, New York, was monitoring intelligence on the German fleet's movements and plotting successively reported positions on a large Plexiglas map. With no troop transports sighted, the Army's intelligence assessment was that the probability of invasion was low and, while First Army's infantry and armored divisions were placed on RED Alert, they were all kept in garrison. Army Air Forces bomber units were loaded for anti-ship missions and all their crews were recalled to bases.

Based on blimp K-11's reports, the Germans were estimated to be 16 miles off-shore, well within the 22-mile range of the battleships' 15-inchers and the cruisers' 11-inchers. The fleet's combined main armament brought to bear sixteen 15-inch and thirty-six 11-inch guns that could easily reach U.S. targets on shore.

Leaves and passes for all Coast Artillerymen were cancelled and batteries along the Atlantic seaboard were placed at Readiness Condition I but ordered not to open fire without direct authorization to do so from 2nd Coast Artillery District at Fort Totten, New York. However, once the Germans had sailed below the 40th parallel, the readiness of the cannoneers in New York and New England was lowered but no leaves or passes were allowed.

Colonel Henry K. Roscoe, commanding the 21st Coast Artillery Regiment at Fort Miles, Delaware had his gun batteries manned and ready with powder and armor-piercing projectiles loaded for maximum range. All of his regiment's SCR-296 radars were scanning the ocean approaches to Delaware Bay all the way south to the Maryland line.

Searchlight batteries at water's edge kept their generators running as they themselves tried to escape the cold on-shore winds and blowing sand under their parka hoods. Artillery fire controllers were in-place up in their towers, just behind the beach, searching the horizon for German ships with binoculars and azimuth telescopes.

Coast Artillery Searchlight Battery at Fort Miles

Cummings' Finest Hour

Staff Sergeant Frank Cummings was too jumpy to eat the meal that had been brought out by the chow truck to Battery Herring, overlooking the Delaware beach from a scrub-covered dune. His coffee had gone stone cold and the wind had blown his ham sandwich off the toolbox he was using for a table. The sandwich had separated, landing mayonnaise-side down in the dirt but Cummings ignored it.

For the fifth time in the last hour, he walked the short distance from his six-inch gun platform to the battery bunker's observation slit to ask if anything was being reported from the towers or radars. With more than a hint of annoyance in his voice, Corporal Arthur Fitzhugh replied, through the slit, that he would check once again. Using the hand-cranked field phone, Fitzhugh called Tower #6 on the beach just north of Rehoboth Beach.

An equally annoyed corporal, scanning the ocean with an azimuth telescope from his tower perch, 60 feet above, curtly replied, "Still nothing. But we *will* report if we do see *anything*, Mac." With the field phone handset still to his ear, Fitzhugh gave Cummings his answer by merely shaking his head "no" and raised his binoculars to his eyes, ending the conversation.

Cummings walked the few steps back to his gun and, one more time, counted the six-inch armor-piercing projectiles and powder bags that had been brought out by his gun crew's Ammunition Squad. It didn't occur to him that the totals were unchanged from the last several counts he had taken.

Next, he moved alongside Private Martin Trimper, the gun pointer seated behind the gun's heavy steel shield. "You OK Marty?" Cummings asked him, as much a check on himself as on Trimper. "Yeah Sarge. But we been sittin' here for three hours. How much longer we hafta stay here?" From his seat on the other side of the gun, Private Bobby Cropper, the range setter, chimed in before Cummings could answer, "Yeah. How much longer?" Cummings shot back, "Till we're relieved dammit; till we're relieved. If the *Krauts* come within range, we gotta be ready to fire." He noted the tension in his own voice as he dried his sweaty palms on his green fatigue pants, well aware of his elevated pulse and agitated tone.

Cummings' gun platform was in the open air on a dune above the beach, just outside the massive Battery Herring concrete bunker. A briny mist reduced the visibility out to sea to three miles. The sky, the ocean and the mist were all uniformly grey. Cummings squinted out to sea but not a speck of the horizon was visible. The back of the sergeant's neck tingled when he considered the possibility of a German spotter watching him through a grey submarine periscope and directing a battleship broadside right at him. His mouth was so dry that he couldn't swallow as he again replayed in his mind his expectations for an artillery duel with the German fleet.

He wrestled with the reality that the Battery Commander, safe inside the bunker, would excitedly urge his six-inch gun crew to keep firing 105-pound projectiles as quickly as they could reload and re-point the gun, regardless of any incoming rounds exploding nearby. He knew with certainty he would need to fight the instinctive self-preservation impulse to run for cover while he summoned courage to stay with his gun and fight the Germans. Unless he stood right next to the young privates on his crew and calmly led them step-by-step, his gun would be out of action and the green kids might even bolt.

He wasn't sure how brave he was going to be himself and, in his imagination, he couldn't picture himself any further through the scenario. Never, in his ten years of laid back weekend drills in the Delaware National Guard, did the A&P produce manager from Georgetown think he would ever be placed in this dangerous position.

Cummings longed to be at home with his wife and daughter and wondered if they knew where he was right then. He had a strong urge to run back to the phone booth outside the Administration Building to call his wife and little girl, in case it was his last chance to speak with them.

The townspeople of nearby Lewes and Rehoboth Beach, Delaware, who were following the German fleet's progress on the radio news, correctly surmised that the absence of soldiers on pass in the two towns meant that they were probably at battle stations, ready to exchange fire with the powerful German fleet and the word spread like wildfire.

Fearing a furious artillery duel that would spill over into the two towns, many loaded their families and what treasured possessions they could grab into cars and farm trucks and fled west, away from the ocean.

At 1036 hours Eastern Standard Time, Colonel Henry K. Roscoe, Fort Miles Commander, read an intelligence bulletin that placed the German fleet 17 miles due east of Atlantic City, New Jersey and headed straight in his direction. Unable to sit still, the colonel donned his helmet and walked briskly out of his office, instinctively feeling for the .45 hanging on his thigh. Roscoe hopped into his jeep and drove over to the Battery Smith concrete casemate that housed the fort's two 16-inch guns with the regiment's longest range that had been salvaged from the Battleship *West Virginia*, sunk at Pearl Harbor.

Colonel Henry K. Roscoe

Satisfied that the two gun crews were ready and eager to fight, he headed over to the battery's underground plotting room. The Battery Commander, Major Donald Everitt, assured Roscoe that they were as prepared as they could be: the projectile and powder details were fully manned and ready, he was in telephone contact with the battery's azimuth and range readers in the beach towers and everything was in order.

"If you gave me a fire mission, I could hit 'em easy 17 miles out but remember, Colonel, we can't *see* 'em till they're within 14 miles of the beach."[56]

---

[56] Fort Miles' fire mission plotting rooms depended on azimuth and range solutions based on visual observations from the towers. The tallest Fort Miles tower afforded only a 14-mile view to the horizon. Knowing that beforehand, the *Kriegsmarine* planners restricted the fleet's approach to no closer than 16 miles.

Troubled by Everitt's warning, Roscoe got back in his jeep and made the rounds of the other gun batteries within the fort. Roscoe was fully aware of the fire control towers' 14-mile line-of-sight capability but had never before that moment thought of it as a liability. Without a triangulated fix on the enemy ships from the towers, they could almost certainly not be hit by his slow-firing 16- and 12-inch batteries.

Fort Miles, Delaware: A Coast Artillery Fire Control Tower

For the first time, Roscoe wondered why the towers had not been built taller, affording a view to a more distant horizon. He also remembered that, in an exercise earlier that year, airborne artillery spotting from blimps and observation planes was found to be totally ineffective because the observers could only guess at their *own* positions, forcing useless estimates of moving target locations.

Roscoe's thoughts next shifted to how badly Fort Miles was outgunned. His two heaviest batteries, 16-inch Battery Smith and 12-inch Battery 519, which had previously only fired single test shots, could theoretically sustain an unverified rate of fire of only one round per minute from their total of four guns.

Intelligence on the German ships worried Roscoe; 52 big guns capable of firing broadsides twice per minute at his stationary emplacements would turn his beachfront installation into an exploding scene from hell for gun crews in the open air. The colonel's earlier strong sense of a personal call to historic stand-and-fight duty ebbed to an unspoken prayer that the *Huns* would just keep on going.

Wilhelm Metzger the Navigator

From the starboard rail of Destroyer Z16 *Friedrich Eckhold,* *Kapitänleutnant* [57] Wilhelm Metzger strained for a glimpse of the Delaware coast through his binoculars. As lead navigator for the fleet underway, Metzger was meticulously plotting the destroyer's position minute-by-minute and had ordered the duty signalman to flash a report by lamp that Z16 had just crossed into the field of fire of Fort Miles' biggest weapons, the twin 16-inch guns of Battery Smith. The signal had been acknowledged by the Battlecruiser *Scharnhorst,* two kilometers astern off Z16's port side.

The young navigator glowed inside with the satisfying thought that his message would be relayed throughout the whole fleet underway and that he was being relied upon by all his comrades from the admiral on down.

Metzger reëntered the bridge, walking the few steps back to the chart table and bent again to study the intelligence map of the New Jersey, Delaware and Maryland shore. Stamped "*Geheim,*" [58] the map displayed a 25-mile arc centered on Cape Henlopen, extending offshore to represent the "*40 Kilometer Effectiverbereich – 406mm Küstenartillerienbatterie* (2)." [59]

Looking at Z16's position just inside the big guns' range, the navigator's earlier confidence suddenly fluttered with the realization that now, American 4000 kilogram [60] high explosive projectiles could reach his ship and blow it to bits. Conscious of a flushed warmth growing from head-to-toe, Metzger looked astern for a moment, and - reassured that mighty *Scharnhorst* was still in position – went back to the starboard rail and resumed his

---

[57] Navy Lieutenant
[58] Secret
[59] 40 kilometer (approximately 25 miles) Effective Range – 406 milimeter (16-inch) Coast Artillery battery, two each
[60] Approximately one ton

binocular search for land, all the while mindful that from 27 kilometers out,[61] the earth's curvature made the view impossible.

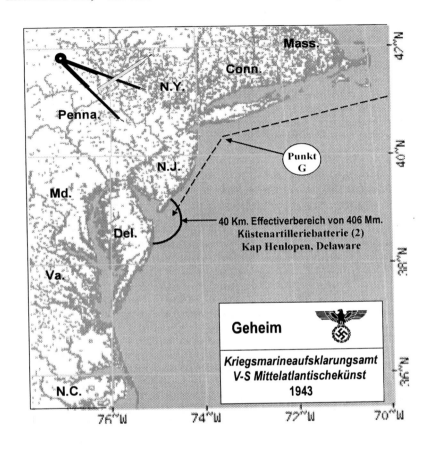

Silently, he reviewed the drill and the math: "If they open fire, I will see the muzzle flashes against the clouds immediately. We will then have only 45 seconds to change course to seaward before the projectiles hit the water.[62] *Kapitän* Vogelmann will immediately order the change of course on my word and he will break radio silence to alert the rest of the fleet. We shan't hear

---

[61] Approximately 17 miles
[62] In actuality, a 16-inch projectile, fired with a muzzle velocity ofapproximately 2600 feet per second, would be in the air over 40 seconds before impacting at its target area.

their guns till almost two minutes after they have fired[63] but I may see muzzle flashes again nearly a minute after their first salvo."

The rolling sea challenged Metzger's keeping the heavy binoculars trained on where he believed Fort Miles to be and he thought his heart had stopped when momentary glare flooded his vision. Metzger's throat constricted as he discounted what he believed must have been an illusion and not the expected muzzle flash. Stunned by the momentous decision facing him, he tried unsuccessfully to count off the expected 40 seconds to impact in panicked contemplation that he had failed in his duty.

What seemed an eternity passed without any nearby splashing projectiles, reflected muzzle flashes, or distant rumbles. Paralyzed in time and space, his elbows braced firmly against the rail, Metzger was afraid to shift the aim of his binoculars and stared at a magnified grey horizon until he heard *Kleinlicheroffizier* [64] Eschers cry-out that Z16 was crossing out of Fort Miles' 16-inch gun range. If Navigator Metzger could keep to course, the fleet would not be visible from shore and no American guns could reach them for the rest of the cruise.

Jolted back to the present, Metzger shouted, "Make position report to *Scharnhorst*" and moved to sit next to the chart table, his back turned to the rest of the bridge crew. He discovered his fingers trembling and sweat breaking out above his upper lip, grateful that no one could see him.

Shortly, when his breathing had evened and the trembling stopped, the young navigator went back to work, reassured by the normalcy of the ship's progress and the businesslike calmness of the sailors around him.

---

[63] Metzger would have estimated the speed of sound to calculate the time the rumble of the shots would take to cross the 17 miles from shore.

[64] Petty Officer

The Crisis Eases

To almost universal relief ashore, the Germans did keep going. Later, a blimp from the Naval Air Station at Weeksville, North Carolina reported the Germans 50 miles south of the Delaware-Maryland line and heading south at an estimated speed of twelve knots. 2nd Coast Artillery District lowered Fort Miles' readiness level to Condition II three hours later. In another two hours, Destroyer Z-16 signaled its arrival at *Punkt Siegfried* [65] and Admiral Lütjens ordered a fleet change of course to 090 degrees, heading due east and away from the U.S. coast.

Reinhard Hardegen

Tensions relaxed on both sides and Lütjens authorized the cruiser *Prinz Eugen* to stop long enough to *rendezvous* with submarine U-123 for the transfer of a sailor needing an emergency appendectomy. *Korvettenkäpitan* Reinhard Hardegen, the U-Boat's skipper, permitted his broadly-smiling crew to come up into the fresh air and collect produce and movies and to banter with their genuinely affectionate comrades on the cruiser.

Later, over cold beers in the billeting area, many of the younger 21st Coast Artillery cannoneers bemoaned their missed opportunity to see "action" and reassured each other that they would have sunk every *Kraut* ship they sighted. Pleased with the troops' high morale, Colonel Roscoe decided not to burst their bubble but he began composing two documents.

The first was a recommendation for a unit citation, acknowledging its courageous preparedness for combat. The second was an "After Action Report" to 2nd Coast Artillery District that expressed worried concerns about the limited horizon visible to Fort Miles'

---

[65] Point "S" in the German phonetic alphabet.

fire control towers and the low rate of sustained fire the fort could expect to maintain against an offshore enemy.

Inside the now-quiet Battery Herring bunker, a trembling Staff Sergeant Frank Cummings closed the door of the parts storeroom behind him and, with racking sobs, shed the first salty tears of his adulthood. In a few minutes, his swollen tensions released, the composed sergeant went in search of his gun crew to share a celebratory drink. He never described his concealed fear, his demonstrated courage, or his momentary emotional breakdown to anyone but, for the rest of his life, he was silently proud of having stayed at his post doing his duty in the face of enormous odds. He knew it was a defining moment of his life.

Most Americans sighed in reprieve but closed-door sessions in Washington and military headquarters were grim. The U.S. had dodged a bullet but the Germans' close pass revealed an unready capability to assert itself defensively. Already bitterly but invisibly divided, the national security players in the Thomas Administration and both houses of Congress succumbed to dovish versus hawkish finger-pointing recriminations that led to a search for a comprehensive solution that would please everybody. Political considerations displaced and diminished the security issues. No constructive courses of action could be agreed and the crisis ultimately subsided.

 Back in Kiel harbor, *Kapitänleutnant* Wilhelm Metzger stood proudly as Admiral Lütjens hung the Iron Cross around his neck, congratulating his distinguished navigating accomplishment. Forever proud of his role in guiding the historic cruise and a frequent attendee at shipmate reunions but sobered by the reality of having confronted gripping fear, Metzger took his private, unrevealed memory to his grave after a comfortable retirement.

11

THE *OUTFIELDER* AFFAIR

Suppose some American patriots planned to resist German domination of the Western Hemisphere?

The Alternative History . . .

Curtis LeMay

Feeling himself in virtual exile at Great Falls Army Air Base, Montana, Colonel Curtis LeMay's frustration level had brought him to the point where either some productive relief or a nervous breakdown must occur. He had been devastated by his country's earlier acceptance of humiliating armistice terms and its docile response to the German missile and atomic weapon demonstrations in November. LeMay's moods swung between deep depression and white-hot anger. He wasn't getting much sleep and was frequently nauseous. It was a painful, low blow when his old friend, Boeing Director of Flight and Research, Eddie Allen, told LeMay that the War Department had defunded all further work on the XB-29 project. Feeling the cancellation the "last straw" and no longer wishing to carry on, LeMay submitted a letter of resignation that was personally torn to pieces by his mentor, General Ira Eaker, who didn't ask but instead ordered him to soldier-on. "Your country can't afford to lose you, the Air Forces can't afford to lose you, and don't ever think for a minute you are alone in your agony."

The only available outlets for LeMay's rage were an increase in work tempo, the punching bag at the Base Gym, and his consumption of cigars, which had trebled. As a B-17 group commander in the Army Air Forces (AAF), LeMay began training his flight and ground crews non-stop in bombing simulated naval vessel targets and had brought the 401st Bombardment Group (Heavy) to a keen edge of readiness and proficiency.

Colonel Curtis E. LeMay

The men in his command, however, were confused and continually questioned each other about why the 401st was working so hard while they knew of no other groups doing anything more than just going through the basic motions.

LeMay couldn't have explained it satisfactorily and, on his part, incessantly peppered his superiors and contemporaries with complaints about what he saw as the U.S.' shameful unwillingness to stay strong. He heard lots of unhelpful consolation and commiseration.

The aviator's anxiety level peaked when he read General Hap Arnold's summary after Arnold, in turn, had heard General George C. Marshall's personal observations of the November German rocket and atomic demonstrations in the mid-Atlantic. To LeMay, the Chief of Staff was in awe of the displays of power and capability, which seemed to a subdued Marshall unmatchable by the U.S. Marshall had been deeply impressed by the V3 rocket demonstration and was troubled by the German narrator's cheery forecast of a longer-ranged rocket, the V-4, by year's end. Marshall was already aware of long-range German plans for a two-stage rocket capable of throwing a 20 megaton warhead one thousand miles.

LeMay couldn't accept Marshall's implicit defeatism as official Army policy or an attitude he could himself adopt. Driven to "do something" before the situation became irretrievable, he began sketching out a plan to neutralize German capabilities to threaten the U.S. from its Bermuda and Gulf of St. Lawrence island outposts before the offensive rocket capability could be brought to bear. After days and nights poring over maps and revising his calculations, he wrote out a terse message, sent by teletype to San Antonio. The message advised his friend and confidant Jimmy Doolittle, that he would be at Randolph Field on Thursday, 20 December and would come to his office at 1400 hours.[66]

On a map held up by thumbtacks, LeMay began to explain to Lieutenant Colonel Doolittle what would eventually become Operation *Outfielder*. Almost as soon as he grasped where LeMay was headed, Doolittle was on his feet, excitedly tracing imaginary lines on the map with his pipe stem and offering additional ideas. From the imagination of the two aviators, an executable attack plan began to take shape and even addressed the key issues of further planning, training, logistics and the preparation and fitting-out of staging bases.

Lt. Col. Jimmy Doolittle

At the most elementary level, the mission of *Outfielder* was the destruction of German naval and submarine facilities and *Nazi* capability to launch rockets from platforms towed by U-Boats staging from Bermuda and the former French islands in the Gulf

---

[66] 2pm.

of St. Lawrence. A heavy bombardment group of 48 B-17s would launch from the base at Presque Isle, Maine, codenamed *Push Cart*, to strike German targets on the Gulf islands, codenamed *Fenway Park*. A medium bombardment group of 48 B-25s from Langley Field, near Norfolk, codenamed *Golf Bag*, would fly at wave top altitude to hit Bermuda targets, codenamed *Polo Grounds*. The planners agreed that the two raids needed to be synchronized to keep one or the other target area from going on alert and taking defensive measures. Additionally, they were of one mind on the need for daylight bombing, which would eliminate a security risk, if the Canadian or Bermudian undergrounds were needed to mark targets at night.

Fighter cover would be provided by the Royal Canadian Air Force out of bases in New Brunswick and Quebec and by U.S. Navy fighters launched from an aircraft carrier selected by the Navy and codenamed *Wood Screw,* between North Carolina and Bermuda. Once the *Luftwaffe* fighters had been neutralized, the B-17s and B-25s would shuttle back-and-forth between their staging bases and the target areas until Bomb Damage Assessment concluded that the mission had been fully accomplished. The air campaign would be followed immediately by Canadian troops landing on and capturing the islands off Newfoundland and U.S. Marines taking Bermuda. In the general concept, if either invasion was unsuccessful, at least the island bases wouldn't be able to support offensive rocket launches.

At just before 8pm, Doolittle realized that the Officers' Club kitchen was about to close and they rushed out to Doolittle's car. As they were driving, Doolittle animatedly exclaimed, "This could work!" and next asked LeMay, "But how are we going to sell this to the top brass, let alone the White House?"

"For now, this has to be Top Secret, Le May replied. "First I need to bring Hap[67] on board and persuade him to get MacArthur to

---

[67] General Henry "Hap" Arnold, Chief of the Army Air Forces.

convince Marshall[68] to support us. In the meantime, let's put our intel guys to work on target selection and ops to planning the routes. Also, we can start training on our own authority. Let's just keep a cover on it. I'm not going to fully read any of my staff in on the details yet"

General Henry "Hap" Arnold

General Henry "Hap" Arnold had known LeMay for years and was proud of LeMay's many pioneering achievements that publicly boosted Army aviation. Three days after he called the general's secretary, Miss Starke, to ask for an appointment, LeMay was in General Arnold's office, explaining the *Outfielder* concept.

LeMay asked Arnold, who had been listening intently without interrupting, to sell the Army leadership on the idea, beginning with General Douglas MacArthur. Arnold had not stopped repeatedly pinching his chin with thumb and forefinger since LeMay started and was thoughtfully silent, while LeMay waited for a reaction.

"Yes. We absolutely must be able to do this," Arnold finally agreed. "I want you and Jimmy to work out the details and begin crew training. I'll start preparing to brief MacArthur. His planner, Dwight Eisenhower, a one-star I often see at budget meetings, is level-headed and discrete. Doug trusts Ike. And I'll get Glenn Barcus[69] down here from New York to get things rolling at Presque Isle and Langley. Staging out of those two will need a

---

[68] General George C. Marshall, U.S. Army Chief of Staff.
[69] Glenn O. Barcus, later Lieutenant General, on the staff of First Air Force at Mitchel Field, NY in 1943.

great deal of preparation and will be difficult to hide. To protect the plan, we may have to go through the same motions at several other bases. I'll pull together additional staff support on this end. Getting White House's budget approval will be a tough nut to crack. And in any case, to pull this off, we'll have to get the whole Army and Navy put on alert and be ready to move forward to solidify, especially in the mid-Atlantic." Arnold stood and took LeMay's hand, looking him right in the eyes. "Remember: training only for now. Keep me advised every step of the way. Don't exceed your authority or get out in front of me by doing anything dumb. We will need firm approvals from the White House and the few friends we have in Congress; you leave those to me. You've conceived a brilliant idea and I'm mighty proud of you! But, if this gets out . . ."

LeMay left Arnold's office feeling a new man. He and Doolittle immersed themselves in the *Outfielder* planning, grateful for being away from Washington and the East Coast, where many of their contemporaries were directly affected by civil unrest and the heated politics over curtailing civil liberties. The two airmen were relieved when the controversial National Emergency Powers Act was finally signed and riots eased off but never permitted themselves to lose their planning concentration.

Outfielder Moves Forward

With most of official Washington riveted to recent domestic social unrest and German fleet movements, the senior staff offices were only able to muster a reduced level of scrutiny of what appeared to be routine army budget line items. Arnold skillfully walked the *Outfielder* proposal through its required approvals, collecting the necessary signatures, by assuring reviewers that "We should proceed as if we are going to get White House approval with the understanding that we must go as far as we can within the legal limits of our authority."[70] At his personal direction, two new AAF Groups were established in April 1946 with aircraft and support equipment transferred from other units.

The 6950th Aerial Support Group, consisting of three squadrons of B-17Cs commanded by Colonel Curtis LeMay, was based near Phoenix at Luke Field. The *Fenway Park* targets on the German-held islands in the Gulf of St. Lawrence were assigned to the 6950th. The 2167th Reconnaissance Group was formed at Goodfellow Field, near San Angelo, Texas, with three squadrons of B-25B bombers under the command of Lieutenant Colonel Jimmy Doolittle. The 2167th's *Polo Grounds* targets were to be in Bermuda. LeMay exercised interim operational control of Operation *Outfielder* and reported directly to "Hap" Arnold's Deputy for Plans, Major General John Morrison, Jr.

B-17 Cs

B-25 Hs

For Operations Security, Arnold arranged for improvements similar to those being made at Presque Isle and Langley Fields to also appear to have been started at Lowry Field near Denver, at Hamilton Field near San Francisco, and at Spokane Air Base. Construction and the movement of people, equipment and supplies at all five bases were quickly detected by both Japanese and German intelligence but not considered of sufficient significance to rate more than brief mention in routine summary reports. The stand-up of the two new groups, oddly named "reconnaissance" and "support," however, raised the eyebrows of senior German

---

[70] A very close paraphrase of the 1946 position taken by General Dwight Eisenhower concerning the creation of an independent USAF.

officers. *Luftwaffe* Headquarters in Berlin requested the Japanese to open case files and emphasize collecting Communications Intelligence on the new Goodfellow and Luke Field tenants.

Japanese COMINT Scrutinizes *Outfielder*

Hideki Watanabe was the chief of U.S. air intercept operations at Station *Ni-88*, high on the north slope of *Cierro Prieta* mountain, just south of the Mexico-Arizona border. At an elevation of over three thousand feet, *Ni-88* was well-positioned to listen-in on U.S. aircraft HF radio transmissions and, occasionally, those in the VHF band. U.S. bomber crews included radio operators, who typically kept in contact with their home bases via Manual Morse signaling and relieved the boredom of long practice missions with extended contact sessions that were easy prey for Japanese COMINT.

Watanabe, raised in California, was fluent in English, and permanently bitter about his post Pearl Harbor internment by the Roosevelt Administration at a camp in Wyoming. His parents had lost their farm near Los Angeles and he longed for a chance at revenge. He already knew that B-17s had recently arrived to stay at Luke Field in April and that additional B-25s had taken up residence at Goodfellow Field, a known B-25 training base. With Tokyo's new emphasis, Watanabe raised the collection priorities of the Luke and Goodfellow Base Operations and had his operators start logging aircraft callsigns and event times. Watanabe also arranged for an increase in intercepts of the Luke and Goodfellow towers from clandestine sites on the top floor of the Hotel San Carlos in downtown Phoenix and in what appeared to be a Chinese laundry on Woodruff Street in San Angelo. *Ni-88* and two sister intercept stations in Mexico also began taking Direction Finding (DF) lines of bearing on the airborne bombers' airborne position reports and requests for landing instructions.

In only four days of signals collection, many of the B-17s and B-25s had been equated to their respective squadron callsigns.

Within ten days, *Ni-88* was able to forward an Air Order of Battle (AOB) summary for both U.S. groups that included estimated aircraft totals. The estimate was based on numerical callsign suffixes, such as "Oboe-4," "Baker-12," or "Zebra-16," with no suffix number higher than "16." All of Doolittle's B-25s could be separated from the older Goodfellow training squadron based on callsigns alone.

With the callsigns known, the air-to-air and air-to-ground radio communications of aircraft from both groups, enabled their assigned unit frequencies to be identified. On the first of each month, when all the squadrons routinely changed to new callsigns (such as "Hammer-4," "Crown-12" or "Pepsi-16"), their continued use of the previous month's frequency proved the callsign changes to have been a waste of time as *Ni-88* was able to continue following the flight activity.

When B-25 "Crown-8" lost an engine and made an emergency landing at Kelly Field near San Antonio, *Ni-88* was able to report it and also to report the aircraft's return to Goodfellow, four days later.

April 1946		
AOB for 2167th Reconnaissance Group, Goodfellow Field, San Angelo, Texas	**Aircraft**	**Callsigns**
Group Staff	1 C-47	Rocky-1
21st Reconnaissance Sq	18 B-25B	Cobra-1 to 18
24th Reconnaissance Sq	18 B-25B	Arrow-1 to 18
25th Reconnaissance Sq	18 B-25B	Flash-1 to 18

April 1946		
AOB for 6950th Aerial Support Group Luke Field, Phoenix, Arizona	**Aircraft**	**Callsigns**
Group Staff	1 C-47	Jello-1
221st Support Sq	18 B-17C	Kodak-1 to 18
252nd Support Sq	18 B-17C	Slam-1 to 18
271st Support Sq	18 B-17C	Pike-1 to 18

Late one afternoon, one of Watanabe's most studious linguist/analysts, Itoyama Hagihara, created a hand-drawn map based on bomber position reports and DF "fixes," where lines of bearing crossed. Using the map to illustrate, Hagihara briefed Watanabe that all the B-17s and B-25's seemed to be flying repetitive routes. For the past week, small formations of B-17s flew a pattern from Luke to a point approximately 65 kilometers south of Lubbock, Texas, turned due north till right over Lubbock, and then returned directly to Luke, a one-way return flight of about 880 kilometers.[71]

The "reconnaissance" B-25s flew in sections of four to six aircraft from Goodfellow to a point 40 kilometers northeast of Mayfield, Missouri turned to a southwest heading till over Mayfield and then returned to their base, a one-way trip back of approximately 1170 kilometers.[72] Hagihara suspected the B-25s descended to altitudes too low for their transmissions to be heard during the short 40 kilometer leg to Mayfield but he wanted to study that further.

---

[71] Approximately 550 miles.
[72] Approximately 730 miles.

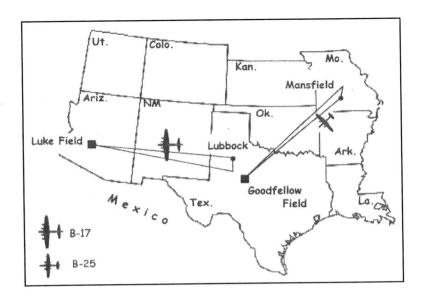

Operation Outfielder bomber training profiles – Spring 1946

On several occasions, as many as 33 B-17s and 41 B-25s were detected aloft at the same time, flying their same established routes. By noting the times that individual aircraft reported their positions over Lubbock ("Checkpoint Easy") or Mayfield ("Checkpoint Item"), Hagihara believed the formations were. strung out in "trail" so that the later arrivals overflew positions previously visited by the planes ahead of them.

Watanabe, looking at the clock and anxious to head down the mountain to the *cantina* in town, to see the *señorita* barmaid he was romancing, wasn't concentrating and attached no special significance to the repeated flight patterns. He included Hagihara's data the next morning in a daily summary as "purpose unidentified" in a teletype message sent it to Tokyo at "Routine" precedence

Franz Bergmann

Ni-88's routine summary report reached Tokyo, and was decoded three days later. A copy was placed in the "in-box" on the desk of *Hauptman* [73] Franz Bergmann, a *Luftwaffe* Communications Intelligence exchange officer stationed at Air Force Headquarters, Naruto Air Base, near Tokyo. Bergmann was fluent in Japanese and had adapted easily to the local culture, enjoying the cuisine, the formal rituals of restaurants and teahouses, and especially the attentiveness of *geishas*. Franz had learned to savor green tea but thought the Japanese were insane for their habit of very frequent bathing. The German officer never caught on that, by frequently suggesting he join them at a bath house, his Japanese co-workers were giving him subtle hints about his personal hygiene.

The summary report of the patterns repeatedly flown by the American bombers intrigued Bergmann. Spending hours in the intelligence agency's library, he paged through American atlases, gas station roadmaps, telephone yellow pages plus all the files he could locate on Missouri and the north Texas area. Nothing he read helped the young intelligence officer understand why repetitious bomber missions would be flown over those areas. He sent a query to Berlin for any available intelligence on what was on the ground in the Lubbock and Mayfield areas that might have a connection with bomber training, specifically asking about any mobile radars or parked communications trucks. He also asked the Japanese Air Force intelligence section to which he was attached to create overlay maps for the B-17 and B-25 sorties, annotated with numbers of aircraft, times of reaching their waypoints, and the distances between waypoints. When he received the maps, he began making measurements with a set of navigational dividers, looking for commonalities but saw nothing of interest.

Finally, he measured the total distances covered between the home bases and Lubbock and Mayfield and began experimenting with a

---

[73] Captain.

piece of string scaled to 880 kilometers on a large wall chart of the U.S. studded with colored map tacks representing various military installations and marked *KIMITSU* [74] in Japanese. Bergmann began tracing 880 kilometer arcs around Luke Field but found nothing of apparent significance in either the US or Mexico and had no better luck with same length-of-string technique applied to Goodfellow Field.

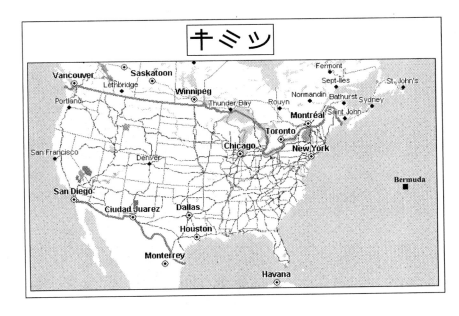

Believing he was on to an answer but feeling puzzled, his train of thought was broken by a Japanese Air Force enlisted man, who advised that a staff meeting would start in ten minutes. Bergmann drained his cup of green tea and went to the conference room. At the staff meeting, the German was asked to prepare an administrative report and, back at his desk, put his pieces of string aside.

Although he often looked at the large wall map and wondered about the significance of the pattern flights, Bergmann was

[74] Top Secret

basically preoccupied with other more pressing tasks. Early one morning, while tasting his first sips of hot green tea, he became aware that *Gunsho*[75] Takeshi Yasuhiro was standing stiffly at attention in front of his desk and Bergmann looked-up. The diminutive sergeant was excited and bursting to begin his customary rapid-fire discourse but he politely maintained his composure, bowed, and waited to be invited to speak.

The Japanese Air Force analyst handed Bergmann an Air Situation Summary Report for May 1946, folded open to Page 27, that had been distributed from Bergmann's own *Luftwaffe Funkaufklärungsdienst*[76] headquarters in Berlin. Had the sharp-eyed Japanese analyst not spotted the paragraph buried inside the report, the item about Presque Isle Air Base might have been ·missed. The summary, in German, reported that on May 3rd, callsign Kodak-1, a probable B-17, had requested landing instructions at Presque Isle thirty-five minutes before callsign Spray-6, a C-47, also requested landing instructions there. The summary also mentioned an unidentified association between Presque Isle and unidentified Project "Push Cart."

Yasuhiro had done thorough research and discovered the Spray-6 callsign was being used by the 89th Transport Squadron at Bolling Field, across the Anacostia River from Washington, D.C. That squadron ferried high-ranking military staff on field visits and Spray-6 was a confirmed C-47 *Dakota* transport. As for the B-17, Yasuhiro was certain that it was using a Luke Field callsign and that the "-1" suffix indicated that either the Commander of the 221st Aerial Support Squadron, Lieutenant Colonel Stone, or Group Commander Colonel LeMay was on board.

In Bergmann's mind, the puzzle-piece snapped into place with a bell-ringing "*ding*." He grabbed his pieces of string and, dragging Yasuhiro with him by the arm, strode briskly to the large wall map. He knew beforehand what he would find; the 880 kilometer

---

[75] Sergeant
[76] German Air Force Radio Signals Intelligence Service

106

string fit nicely between Presque Isle, Maine and the German island bases at *Sankt Peter* and *Neues Deutschland* and muttered to himself *"Wie dumm ich bin!"*[77] Next he placed one end of the 1170 kilometer string on Bermuda and stretched it back to the U.S. east coast. Langley Field! The Americans were rehearsing air raids from Presque Isle and Langley against the German island bases!

Forgetting himself and the strict behavior code observed by his Japanese military hosts, a loudly laughing Bergmann enfolded the smaller Japanese sergeant in a hug and waltzed him around in front of the map. Overwhelmed by the German's rancid body odor, Yasuhiro gagged while a half-dozen nearby curious desk-workers concluded that the conventional wisdom classifying Germans as beneath *bushido* standards was correct.

Göring Warns; Hitler Threatens

 On Monday morning, June 10, 1946, the newly-promoted German Ambassador, Hans Thomsen, formerly the *Chargé d'Affaires* in Washington, personally handed an envelope containing a cablegram to Vice President Charles Lindbergh in the Old Executive Office Building, next to the White House. Lindbergh opened the envelope marked with the seal of the Third Reich and stamped "Most Urgent," pulling out a decoded cablegram addressed to him by *Reichsmarschall* Herman Göring. Under the letterhead with eagle and swastika, the text read:

---

[77] How dumm I am!

8 JUNI 1946

MEIN ALTER FLIEGENDER BRUDER: [78]

DISTURBING NEWS HAS REACHED US ABOUT
APPARENT PLANS BY THE AMERICAN ARMY AIR
FORCES TO TRY TO BOMB GERMAN
INSTALLATIONS IN BERMUDA AND THE FORMER
FRENCH ISLANDS NEAR NEWFOUNDLAND. I HAVE
BEEN TRYING TO EXPLAIN TO MY FELLOW
MINISTERS THAT ALL AIR FORCES MUST
CONSTANTLY PRACTICE TACTICAL SOLUTIONS TO
THEORETICAL PROBLEMS AND THAT THE RECENT
TRAINING BY YOUR B-17 AND B-25 GROUPS IN
ARIZONA AND TEXAS SHOULD NOT NECESSARILY
BE INTERPRETED AS DIRECT THREATS TO GERMAN
FORCES. I MUST INFORM YOU, HOWEVER, THAT
SEVERAL MEMBERS OF THE CABINET ARE OF A
VERY CAUTIOUS VIEW AND WILL REQUIRE
ASSURANCES FROM THE HIGHEST LEVELS OF THE
AMERICAN SIDE THAT NO HOSTILE INTENTIONS
FORM A PART OF THIS UNSETTLING BOMBER
TRAINING. EVEN NOW, THE FÜHRER'S CLOSEST
COUNSELORS ARE PREPARING A REPORT THAT
PROPOSES AN OPTION FOR PREËMPTIVE ROCKET
STRIKES ON THE FORWARD BASES IN VIRGINIA
AND MAINE FROM WHICH AIR ATTACKS ON THE
GERMAN INSTALLATIONS COULD BE STAGED
UNLESS GUARANTEES ARE PROVIDED THAT NO
HOSTILITIES WILL BE UNDERTAKEN.

I HAVE EVERY CONFIDENCE THAT THIS SITUATION
HAS BEEN UNFORTUNATELY MISINTERPRETED BY
REICH OFFICIALS WITHOUT PRACTICAL MILITARY
AVIATION EXPERIENCE AND THAT A MINOR
MODIFICATION OF AMERICAN BOMBER TRAINING
REGIMES ELIMINATING THE APPEARANCE OF
UNFRIENDLY MOTIVES WOULD BRING QUIET

---

[78] My old flying brother

CLOSURE TO THE CURRENT STATE OF UNEASINESS.
I AM CERTAIN WE TWO OLD BIRDS HAVE ONLY THE
BEST OF INTENTIONS FOR OUR TWO GREAT
PEOPLES AND THAT YOU WILL ACT QUICKLY TO
HELP RESOLVE THIS ISSUE. I CANNOT IMAGINE
THAT MEN OF HONORABLE AIMS COULD TEMPT
THE TERRIBLE RESULTS OF ROCKET WARFARE
THAT MUST NOT BE ALLOWED TO MATERIALIZE.

MEIN LIEBER ALTER FREUND, [79] YOU MUST COME
SOON TO GERMANY TO TRY THE CONTROLS OF
OUR NEW ME.262 JET FIGHTER AND TO VISIT ME AT
KARINHALL, WHERE WE MUST TAKE SOME TIME
FOR A PHEASANT HUNT.

Following two additional lines of pleasantries, the cablegram was signed simply, "Göring."

Fuming inside, Lindbergh read Göring's first paragraph twice while trying with difficulty to remain unruffled in Thomsen's presence. He folded the cablegram, laid it on his desk, and with a wan smile, told the ambassador, "Thank you."

Thomsen asked if there would be any reply to which Lindbergh replied, "Not just now." Thomsen straightened to attention, clicked his heels, and wished Lindbergh, "Good morning Mr. Vice President" and turned for the door. Lindbergh couldn't wait to get on the phone with Secretary of War Jeanette Rankin. The Vice President was usually deferential to Rankin's senior stature but his tone of voice communicated his extreme unhappiness with the Army Air Forces in calling a "highest priority" conference in his office in one hour.

Spurred by the Vice President's snappish tone, Rankin asked Generals Marshall and Arnold to join her in the Old Executive Office Building at ten o'clock to discuss a serious aviation

---

[79] My dear old friend,

problem with the VP. The secretary apologized for not being able to better explain the subject of the meeting. At a small round conference table, a flushed, livid Lindbergh looked past Rankin and directly confronted the two generals with the substance of Göring's note and challenged them for an explanation. General Arnold told the truth about being prepared with an operations plan, in case the Army Air Forces were called upon in an emergency. General Marshall backed up Arnold, assuring Lindbergh that it was training only and that no schedule even existed in its most preliminary form. Somewhat relieved, the Vice President excused his three visitors but immediately called his naval aide into his office.

Late that afternoon, Lieutenant Commander Neil O'Conner was back at the Vice President's desk with an informal briefing that described the B-17 and B-25 groups at Luke and Goodfellow Air Force Bases, the number of hours that were flown in the past thirty days, the costs of "support" facilities at Presque Isle and Langley as well as the deceptive construction already begun at the other "cover" bases. O'Conner named LeMay, Doolittle and Barcus and put them in a box labeled "Project Outfielder." On direct orders from Chief of Naval Operations King, O'Conner made no mention of Vice Admiral Wilson Brown, who had been quietly working on providing fighter cover for *Outfielder* over Bermuda, using the carriers *Lexington* and *Hornet*.

Generals Marshall and Arnold stuck to their "planning-training" story and managed to keep their jobs. Arnold successfully protected Glen Barcus, who was not disciplined. The 6950th and 2167th groups were disbanded. Before the end of June, their aircraft and support equipment plus all air and ground personnel were scattered throughout the Air Force, leaving no traces behind them. LeMay and Doolittle[80] were transferred to harmless

---

[80] Actually, LeMay went on to become Chief of Staff of the Air Force. Doolittle, as a Major General, commanded Northwest Africa Strategic Air Forces in 1943 and managed *Operation Corkscrew*, the bombing of Pantelleria that forced an enemy surrender without being first invaded. (See Footnote #30).

Washington desk jobs, where they could be watched. Both officers left the service that autumn and established a successful cargo airline that was eventually bought-out by *Lufthansa Airfreight*.

Having fatally squashed *Outfielder* in the U.S., Lindbergh got word to Canadian Prime Minister McKenzie King. King received and accepted assurances given by Wing Commander David Pownall and Squadron Leader James Muir, commanding officers of Number 423 and Number 425 Fighter Squadrons, that they would never entertain so insubordinate an act as supporting an American attack on the German islands. The *Outfielder* matter was closed without so much as a written entry in the history of Canada or the RCAF officers' diaries.

Hitler Reacts to *Outfielder*

Fully six weeks after the episode had faded, the *Oberkommando der Wehrmacht* [81] tried to gently brief Hitler on *Outfielder* in upbeat terms, trying to avert another of the *Führer's* infamous tirades. Preferring that Germany not risk having to logistically support cross-ocean operations, the OKW strove to confine international relations with Western Hemisphere countries - most especially with the United States - to bullying diplomacy. Knowing full-well, however, that any conspiracy to conceal information such as the *Outfielder* discovery invited an indictment and prompt execution for treason to set an example for others, General Alfred Jodl himself tried unsuccessfully to slip the *Outfielder* item into the crowded agenda being quickly stepped-through. Hitler's ears went up, however, and stopped Jodl, asking for details and then more details and was soon on his feet, roaming the room while he repeatedly smacked the back of his right hand into his left palm and ranting about the Americans spitting in his eye. The OKW generals cowered silently in their chairs, avoiding eye contact with Hitler or each other. "Those sneaky American

---

[81] Armed Forces General Staff

cheats give me no rest. They are constantly put up to no good by their scheming Jews and must be watched like mischievous children. . . if it's not one thing, it's another."

The *Führer's* first opportunity to surface the incident publicly came at a state dinner for Haj Amin al-Husseini, the Grand Mufti of Jerusalem on July 6th. The Mufti had raised and led a division of moslem *Nazi* troops and was accorded the status of an SS general by Hitler. At a microphone-studded podium, Hitler *ad libbed* extemporaneous remarks into his prepared welcome that warned of terrible, punishing reprisals for any nation that dared disturb international peace with aggressive acts against German forces operating anywhere. Emphasizing his points with horizontal pointing-finger slashes above the microphones and rolling his eyes demonically, he carried on long enough to make the Grand Mufti wonder what all that had to do with him. Newspaper readers and newsreel viewers outside Germany, however, were frightened by the thinly-veiled threats to rain atomic rockets on their cities, if they offended Hitler.

The Grand Mufti visits Hitler in Berlin

12

PRETEXT FOR THE U.S. *Kristallnacht*

Suppose American factions could have been manipulated into acts that provoked the Germans?

The Alternative History . . .

Obergruppenführer Reinhard Heydrich had taken great pride in his personal accomplishments for Germany in finally cleansing Europe of its troublesome Jews. He treasured the gleaming "German Order" badge, pinned to his tunic, awarded by the Fuhrer's own hand and he often touched it lovingly when he was alone. The outraged invective being poured on Germany by American commentators and Jews, offended him personally and he felt the criticisms unfairly tarnished his historic achievements. Heydrich believed that, except for her own meddling Jews, the American people would have recognized how much the world was now better-off and would have sought *rapprochement* with Germany, acknowledging the leadership of a deservedly-dominant *Reich*. But with the sub-human Jews still polluting Western Hemisphere populations, there would never be uncomplicated peace and beneficial forward progress.

Hitler had learned a lasting, painful lesson from the difficult and costly *Barbarossa* invasion of the Soviet Union. The ineffective 1939 performance of the Red Army's invasion of Finland had led Hitler mistakenly to expect the Soviets to crumble before his brutal *Blitzkrieg*. He now believed, in his evolved thinking, that armed invasion was not the only road to success at his disposal. In an after-dinner hypothetical, philosophical discussion with Baron Oshima, the Japanese Ambassador to Berlin, the two found agreement that everything about a theoretical invasion and occupation of the U.S. by Japan on the West Coast and by Germany on the East argued against the idea.

Both saw the estimates of a million invasion troops on each coast with their equipment plus reserves of another million followed by a steady stream of replacements and resupply as a cross-ocean logistical impossibility. The American land mass was also too vast and too heavily populated to be efficiently occupied and, since both Germany and Japan had positioned themselves as masters of their own spheres of influence, there really were no North America invasion imperatives. Hitler and the baron agreed that, so long as American influence was suppressed and they refrained from interfering in German and Japanese affairs, further military conquests were simply unnecessary. Privately, however, *Obergruppenführer* Heydrich was not so easily convinced. Heydrich sensed, in the emotional Jewish reaction to fears about a suspected Holocaust, the seeds of long-term anti-German agitation that would be a troubling thorn-in-the-side to be dealt with.

As was his daily custom, Ambassador Oshima sent Tokyo a summary report of the previous day's activities and included an abbreviated mention of his after-dinner discussion with Hitler, citing only the subject as "Strategic problems of invading both coasts of the U.S." The HF radio transmission of the summary from the embassy roof in Berlin to Tokyo was intercepted by a Naval Security Group detachment embarked in the cruiser, *USS Baltimore*, and was decrypted and translated. Oshima's "strategic problems" item was distributed to the highest officials in Washington cleared for COMINT, causing great alarm.

Cruiser USS Baltimore

At a hastily-called meeting at the White House, President Thomas' senior national security advisors debated whether the Oshima telegram was an intelligence indicator of Axis invasion plans. Secretary of War Jeanette Rankin was adamant about appeasing the Axis powers, giving them no pretext to invade. Vice President Lindbergh sought consensus for assuring Germany through expanded diplomatic contacts that the U.S. was faithfully adhering to the terms of the armistice, agreed in May 1943, and planned to continue doing so. Secretary of State Nye strongly supported Lindbergh's idea. Secretary of the Navy Henry Ford and the top Army and Navy brass were in agreement with the diplomatic approach but thought it also prudent to exercise plans for a two-coast defense. The pacifists in the room, led by Rankin's shrill denigration, sharply criticized those views as unnecessarily provocative and exercises were not further discussed. A paper review of plans was to be permitted but without any public releases.

Der Führer Stews

Heydrich and his under-cover SS aides had taken a major risk on his own responsibility in going to Newfoundland and fomenting the *Unternehmen Lorelei* [82] provocations in the U.S. Although General Jodl and the senior staff smelled a rat and thought some German involvement must have been likely, Heydrich and his SS co-conspirators allowed Hitler to buy into the apparent authenticity of spontaneous Jewish-Negro protests against the U.S. Government and German interests. Heydrich's most hoped-for scenario blossomed in Hitler's arm-waving, pacing protestations about the dishonorable, untrustworthy Americans, who were not capable of keeping their Jews and other *Untermenschen* in line. *Der Führer* wondered aloud how he had possibly succumbed to feelings of mercy for those unworthy backstabbers and wished he had crushed America as he had Poland and England. He had, however, already forgotten his after-dinner philosophizing with Baron Oshima that had so alarmed Washington.

Hitler stewed about what he saw as American ingratitude for his magnanimous forbearance and worked his grumbling diatribes into every conversation and discussion. No one with personal contact failed to understand the depth of Hitler's annoyance and itch for punishing retribution. In the midst of *der Führer's*

Hitler welcomes Mussolini

distraction by the revealed *Outfielder* affair, Benito Mussolini arrived on the inaugural flight of *Italiano Aereo's* new *Savoia-Marchetti S.M.79C* daily service from Rome to Berlin.

Greeting his Italian ally on the arrivals tarmac of *Flugplatz Tempelhof,* [83] Hitler impatiently cut off *Il Duce's* smiling invitation to look inside his converted bomber, spiffed-up as a luxury transport, and launched into his own anguished lament about having let the Americans off too easily. During welcoming

---

[82] Operation Lorelei
[83] Tempelhof Airport

remarks at the podium, a scowling Hitler, speaking to Mussolini but glaring directly into the newsreel cameras, admonished his Italian friend and the rest of mankind that the important work of remaking the world was apparently unfinished. Mussolini, ever the toady, agreed with and egged Hitler on instead to trying to calm him down.

Referring to " . . . sinister, conniving forces across the seas bent on upsetting the peace that had been won at so great a cost," *der Führer* plainly warned that treachery would be " . . . repaid with a rain of rockets that would be heard across the oceans in Europe and Japan. We will send any who dare to challenge us back to the Stone Age and make their land fit only for spiders and roaches." Listening intently as a translator whispered in his ear, Mussolini folded his arms across his chest, thrust his chin upward in studied concentration, and nodded his unquestioning agreement.

Benito Mussolini

13

GEORGE STRONG

Suppose Americans of divided loyalties could have been recruited for support of Nazi strategy within the U.S.?

The Alternative History . . .

George Strong was one of the very few Americans that Germany invited to attend the 1945, post-war resumption of the Olympic Games in Nürnberg at *Nazi* expense. The games were actually a mere symbolic skeleton of the former world-wide celebration of athletic competition, and were scheduled to cover only four days. Seen more as a *Nazi "Sieg Heil"* celebration than a rekindling of the cherished Olympic spirit, the conquered European countries fielded only teams sponsored by their conquering occupiers; the new U.S. administration was faced with overwhelming "growing pains" and never even seriously considered fielding a contingent. Strong apologized to his wife, explaining that the month-long trip he had "won" was only for one person. Maryellen Strong, a browbeaten, sometimes battered wife and frequent victim of marital rape, was grateful for George's "business trips" and smiled on the inside at the prospect of his being gone for a whole month. Running her tongue over the tooth George's hard slap had chipped, she made sure he heard her, "OK." Two days later, George left to board the rusting former Dutch steamer renamed *Nordstern* in Port Arthur, Texas, bound for Bremerhaven with a cargo of cotton.

To the Alabama dockhand, Port Arthur's water smelled distinctively different from Mobile's and was a part of George's exciting new experience. Having never been to sea himself after so many years working on the docks, George took pleasurable satisfaction from standing at the port rail, watching the scurrying stevedores, the lines being cast off, and the Texas coast finally receding. When the coast became just a thin grey line on the gently rising and falling horizon, George inhaled deeply the clean, tangy saltiness of open salt water and turned to go inside when he noticed a crewman in the stern take down the Stars and Stripes, flown as the customary international courtesy, and replace it with a German naval ensign complete with an Iron Cross. On a pleasurable high induced by the salt air, George felt a comfortable sense of belonging and softly whispered, "*Ja*," to himself.

On board, he met three other Americans: Harry Bauermann, David Robertson, and Eddie Mueller, also going expenses-paid to the Olympics. George could have picked each of them out of a crowd; he and they all looked "Nordic." The four passengers were assigned cabins appropriate for ships' officers and took their meals in the captain's wardroom. Each of the four was a prominent member of the German-American *Bund* from different parts of the country. Their guide for the nine-day cruise was SS *Oberstleutnant*[84] Dieter Lösen, traveling under cover as a merchant mariner. Lösen began the political indoctrination of the Americans on the first evening at a dinner more splendid than any the four guests ever had. Lösen's supply of "liberated" French

---

[84] Lieutenant Colonel

wines and cognac seemed inexhaustible and the travelers were made to feel very special and welcome among friends.

During their "ice-breaker" discussion, the four Americans discovered numerous common characteristics. Three were of German ancestry, all were fanatical members of the *Bund*, all had a pathological hatred of one or more minorities, all had committed serious felonies such as causing grievous bodily harm, grand larceny, or arson. Although none admitted so to the others, two of the four had participated in murders and a third had attempted a murder. All four owned guns and had used them in the commission of a crime. All four were brawlers unafraid to fight and had experience in fighting dirty, seeking more to injure an opponent than to defend himself. By bedtime, George was ever more firmly convinced of the validity of his long-held view that international Jewry, together with the Bolsheviks, had selfishly contrived the global Great Depression that forced Germany to reassert the rights of a sovereign state and that he had chosen the winning side.

Strong had been born Gerd Strohminger in 1893 to Ludwig Strohminger, a naturalized German father, employed as a stevedore on the docks of Jersey City, New Jersey. With his wife dead soon after his new son's birth, Ludwig raised young Gerd alone, disciplined to stand up and fight for himself and to feel pride in his Teutonic heritage. Ludwig spoke both English and German to his son, who grew up bilingual. Always troublesome in class and a quick-tempered bully, intolerant of even the smallest unintended slight, Gerd enjoyed fighting and would provoke after-school fights with Black boys on the basketball court to drive them off, even when he didn't want to play himself. Gerd finally dropped out of school at 15 after being suspended for administering an unprovoked stairwell beating that put a Black classmate in the hospital.

His father got him a job on the Sussex Street docks and Gerd found the freedom from classroom discipline and homework to his liking. With his father's watchful eyes on him, Gerd settled into a regimen of hard work, hard playing, and hard drinking and his adolescent years passed uneventfully. Soon a member of the union's local, a tall blond muscular Gerd was spotted, at age 23, as trustworthy material for handling "special jobs" assigned by union bosses. He took readily to helping with cargo thefts, was a reliable but unobtrusive courier for delivering large sums of cash, and enjoyed the fights that often broke out during labor unrest. With a ready hatred of Jews, Blacks and Irish immigrants, all seen as threats to his job security, Gerd took easily to rushing a crowd of demonstrators, swinging a stick. He was one of the police's "usual suspects" and frequently brought in for questioning but never formally charged.

In 1916 with Europe at war, the U.S., although officially neutral, shipped great quantities of foodstuffs and war materiel to Germany's enemies through ports like Jersey City. Gerd, his father, and other German sympathizers did what they could to delay shipments and damage cargoes destined for Britain, France and Imperial Russia.

Black Tom dockyard after the 1916 explosion

In the wee hours of July 30, 1916, German saboteurs, smuggled secretly into the U.S., spectacularly detonated over a thousand tons of explosives awaiting loading from Jersey City's *Black Tom* dockyard, bound for Russia. Gerd and his father had helped the saboteurs gain access through the *Black Tom* perimeter fence, for which they were both paid ten dollars.

121

It was the most money of his own Gerd had ever held. Father and son rejoiced in the huge explosion and fire, rationalizing the deaths of seven American acquaintances and damage to nearby buildings as acceptable losses of war.

The authorities considered those with the most to gain from the explosion to be most likely responsible. The investigation's preliminary findings, however, could not fix the blame conclusively on Germany, giving rise to newspaper charges of an official "cover-up." Noisy demonstrations, instigated by Russian attachés stationed in Washington, thronged outside the still-smoldering dockyard. Unable to resist a good punch-up and dismissing Ludwig's fatherly advice, Gerd joined some of his workmates at the scene of a noisy, banner-waving protest that accused Germany of an act of war against the neutral U.S. Emboldened by the two large mouthfuls of *schnapps* he had downed from a friend's flask, Gerd waded into the midst of the mob carrying a length of lead pipe.

Before he was disarmed and pinned by a howling crowd, Gerd had cracked two heads, sending one to the hospital and the other to the morgue. Gerd's mates reached their comrade and freed him from the fist-swinging demonstrators just as two policemen blowing whistles showed up. Using high school football skills, some of Gerd's friends blocked the cops while the others spirited him away, however not before Gerd was spotted and recognized.

Seeing his son's bloody nose and mouth and hearing the details from one of the boys, who brought him home, Ludwig Strohminger decided it wasn't safe for Gerd to be at home and the friend took him off to be safely hidden. Within the hour, the police were outside the Strohminger's apartment tenement and Gerd's father was being asked when he last saw his son and if he knew where he might be found.

Prying nothing useful from Ludwig, the police left empty-handed but showed up first thing in the morning at the Sussex Street dockyard, where Gerd worked. His gang boss tried to cover for him but the police interpreted Gerd's absence as evidence that he was a fugitive from justice. Arrest warrants were sworn and posters put up announcing that Gerd was wanted for murder and assorted federal racketeering crimes. His name and an artist's sketch of his face were in the Northern New Jersey and New York City papers that evening and accompanying articles named Gerd as a German sympathizer and *agent provocateur*.

The 1916 *Black Tom* sabotage had not occurred in a vacuum. Strong anti-German feelings had been stirred the year before by a series of German submarine attacks that killed American passengers on four allied ships, most notoriously, the liner *Lusitania*, with over 100 American losses. A 1915 German air attack on the *MV Cushing* had also resulted in American deaths. American outrage continued to simmer but was held in check by President Woodrow Wilson's resolve to avoid the more sobering alternative: war in Europe.

Over the next few days, Gerd Strohminger was convicted in the press of murdering a peaceful protester and of complicity in the seven deaths from the explosion. The German embassy quietly arranged for Gerd to be slipped aboard a boxcar headed south and he was cared for by a succession of sympathetic railroad workers, who fed him and got him to Alabama. In Mobile, pro-German friends were waiting to supply the new George Strong with a forged birth certificate, references going back several years, room and board, and a job interview at Mobile's Palmetto Street Pier.

Although the federal income tax had been enacted in 1913, official records on individuals were much less encompassing than they became with the advent of computers and the integration of federal, state and local data. There was no Social Security Administration keeping national records, no nationwide drivers license or criminal databases and no FBI. George Strohminger started life afresh with a new name, an affected southern drawl but old habits and was forced to isolate himself from his father and old friends, lest the mail, which could be watched, reveal where he was. He scrupulously refrained from speaking German and consequently lost most of his vocabulary over time.

Try as he could, President Wilson lost his hold on American pacifist opinion after revelation of the 1917 notorious *Zimmerman Telegram,* which Americans quickly saw as treachery intended to split up the Union and undermine *Manifest Destiny.* For many older Americans, the Civil War was a still-healing, still-painful sore and the attempted German-Mexican intrigue was too sinister to overlook.

Woodrow Wilson

The tide had turned and soon American Doughboys were on their way to France. Pro-German sentiments became instantly unfashionable and were quickly hidden. George Strong watched as many of his new associates changed sides or seemed to lose interest in isolationism and politics altogether. As would many later American liberals in the 1960s and early in the 21st Century, George hoped the Allies and America would lose against Germany, although his fear of facing murder charges in New Jersey made him hold his counsel and avoid calling attention to himself.

The 1919 Treaty of Versailles and post-war Allied policies punished Germany severely, annoying a small number of secretly-outcast Americans, who quietly retained their pro-German views. Typically uneducated, dead-end job-holders living basically dull lives, the closet outcasts inevitably drifted together for mutual commiseration. Their political discourse well-lubricated with alcohol, this disgruntled minority coalesced around perceived slights and offenses visited on their stratum of society by the government and wealthy elites. Particularly vexing to them were upwardly mobile Blacks seen simultaneously as threats to white employment and suspected of lusting for mesmerized white women. In the eyes of the outcasts, Blacks were much in needed of repression and discipline by the morally superior, white segment of society. The KKK came out of dormancy, offering an attractive vehicle for asserting the manhood of aggrieved white men.

Behind masks and white sheets that cloaked their identities from outsiders, Klansmen terrorized mainly rural Black populations with horrible lynchings and arson. Local law enforcement frequently turned a blind eye and at times was fully complicit in the terror. "Lynch Law" was an unwritten code in many parts of the South and some politicians won elective office by giving it tacit approval. At age 34, George Strong, the childhood bully, racist, and labor head-basher, was a natural for the KKK, just waiting to be asked.

Urged on by what they saw as the manly exploits of upstate enforcers and their counterparts just across the Mississippi line, an after-work bull session in *The Ship* saloon near the Mobile waterfront, first addressed the government's impotence, after more than two years, in ending the Great Depression, the unfairness of income taxes, and, finally, moves by job-seeking "Negroes" to take over their livelihoods on the docks.

Unable to influence the first two problem areas, the right way to handle the "Negro" issue quickly attracted a consensus. Amidst loud exclamations and shouted agreements, a plain-clothes member of the Mobile County Police Department, a late afternoon regular at *The Ship*, quietly gathered a small handful of drinkers, George Strong among them, to a corner. Officer Buford Kermit had kept his eye on George and some of George's cronies for years.

Unaware of his New Jersey origins and name change, Kermit nevertheless knew George to be a foul-mouthed scrapper with an anti-social personality. Although basically ignorant of Civil War history, George threw in easily with die-hard Southern rebels as an anti-government, hateful white supremacist. He rarely spoke a sentence without a four-letter word or racial slur and the presence of women was no deterrent. He couldn't have explained satisfactorily why his old Ford sported a Confederate flag but George intended it as a subtle warning that he was not to be messed with and that it was best to keep out of his way. Rarely without a cold *Jax* beer to drive with, he took pleasure from tossing the empties out to smash in the streets of Black neighborhoods where the kids often ran barefoot.

An obnoxious, aggressive driver who kept a heavy wrench ready as a club under the driver's seat, George's reputation for forcing drivers, who offended or delayed him, to stop or for following them to their destinations to verbally and sometimes physically assault them, was well known in the Mobile area. Taller than most, George commonly invaded the personal space of people, he judged to be in need of intimidation, and characteristically leaned forward over them, forcing them to look up, while he alternately shouted insults and blew cigarette smoke in their faces. A spring-loaded bully, George was quick to take any victim's defensive movement as aggression and immediately shifted into his high-gear slugging and kicking, refusing to disengage until he had seriously hurt his victim. He gloried in having an opponent's blood on his clothes.

Buford Kermit invited the small group of drinkers from *The Ship* to accompany him to a meeting near Dawes, a small town just west of Mobile. They departed the bar singly and crossed the street to where Kermit's small truck was parked. Twenty-five minutes later, they were bouncing down a dirt farm road, well off the highway, finally parking outside an old wooden barn. Kermit got out, was greeted by two shadowy figures, who obviously knew him, and then came back to let his passengers out of the truck.

George was thrilled to be led inside the torch-lit, flag-bedecked building, standing within a coven of sheeted Klansman, listening enrapt to a soft-voiced speaker preaching a volatile, inciteful message from a hay wagon.

When he had finished speaking, he leaned down to be advised that there were new fellows to be introduced. George was surprised that he and the others brought by Officer Kermit were merely referred to as "good old boys from the big city." No names were used and George came away that night without having been properly introduced to a soul. Buford Kermit volunteered in the truck heading back to Mobile that, for now, it was better not to know names; that way their were no identities they needed to protect, if anyone asked.

On three occasions within that year, George was an enthusiastic participant in two hangings of Black men and the torching of a Black family's home. Seeming always reliable to do as bid, he was drawn into the coven's inner circle, where his opinions and suggestions were listened to.

Officer Kermit privately slipped George an old .32 caliber revolver with which he fired the first shot into a hanging Black lynching victim, who was shot a further 28 times by whooping hooded Klansmen.

By 1936, 39 year-old George had risen to high rank within the Klan and was nationally known within the organization but only by his codename, "Dutch from Mobile." He was admired as a "follow me" leader, who didn't merely order others to do what he wouldn't and was a notoriously vicious fighter, who never missed an opportunity to cause severe injury. Additionally, George was socially very well connected. He was proud of the Mobile County deputy sheriff's badge pinned in his wallet and never hesitated to exaggerate its mostly ceremonial meaning when pulling over or detaining Blacks he could rough-up, youths he could "confiscate" from, and women he could molest.

George had long lost count of his own role in lynchings, arsons, beatings and cross-burnings. He had also progressed to the point where his income was being supplemented by "no questions asked" cash payments and he had traveled across the South on expense-paid Klan business, most often as a messenger delivering memorized messages to coven gatherings. Among those who took his phone calls were Governor Talmadge of Georgia, other state government politicians, senior police officials, and a syndicated newspaper columnist. Although he felt safe from the 1916 New Jersey murder charge, he never tried to contact his father and was unaware of his death for over two years.

George's smoldering pride in his German heritage was fanned by movie newsreels of Hitler's brownshirts parading in German cities. He identified with the reëmergence of the German military, the glorification of Aryan youth, and the firm hand being taken in the form of book burnings and repression of the Jews. The assigned Jewish guilt for engineering the Great Depression and their punishment by a resurgent Germany resonated with George, who was committed to the obviousness of Jewish complicity in America's depression and her seeming inability to recover. At a Klan meeting in early 1937, he was pleased to discover that some of his sheeted brethren were also members of the German-American *Bund*. Formed in 1935 on Hitler's personal order, George found himself in enthusiastic agreement with the *Bund's* pro-German positions focused principally on anti-communism, racism, anti-Semitism, and the glorification of German heritage. Already known and trusted by his Klan associates, George was taken into inner circles and given special *Bund* assignments. With income from the Klan, the *Bund*, and cargo thefts on the docks, George reduced his back-breaking longshoreman's work and was "semi-retired," having more time available for out-of-town Klan and *Bund* business.

Dressed in the *Bund's* German-style black uniform and *swastika* armband, George swaggered in downtown Montgomery's Washington's Birthday parade in 1938 and imagined himself subduing disapproving onlookers with his penetrating glare and disdainful sneer. At dinner in the *Berlinergarten* restaurant on Montgomery's University Drive, George sat at the head table with visiting *Bund* dignitaries and was flattered by Fritz Kuhn, the *Bundesführer* himself, who seemed familiar with George's capabilities and reliability. George was deeply impressed by Kuhn's forceful quotation of Washington's admonition to avoid foreign entanglements and later passionately repeated it himself in his own anti-war arguments.

Germany's remilitarization and territorial annexations of 1938 had seriously strained U.S.-German relations and American Jews, outraged by overt *Nazi* anti-Semitism, loudly pressured the Roosevelt administration to intercede.

The nation became starkly polarized. At one end was a pro-German faction composed of "America Firsters,"[85] the KKK, German-American *Bund*, and a large portion of the population holding isolationist, anti-war sentiments. Alarmed by any American posturing that risked armed confrontation, it enjoyed significant newspaper editorial support and the affiliation of prominent government officials.

George and a small group of toughs he personally mentored became proficient at following anti-*Bund* protesters and newspaper columnists home and administering savage, bloody beatings. He was personally involved in torching two hostile

---

[85] Charles Lindberg, the celebrity aviator, was aligned with the America First movement but not the KKK or German-American *Bund*.

newspaper offices and, over time, in the theft and destruction of thousands of bundled newspaper copies headed for newsstands. In a year, his heart bursting with pride, George advanced to be on stage with *Bundesführer* Kuhn on February 20, 1939, at Madison Square Garden, beaming out at over 20,000 cheering *Bund* adherents. First to his feet at numerous Kuhn pronouncements and denunciations, George led frequent interruptions of the speaker with commanding *"Sieg Heil"* and *Nazi* salutes

It was Germany's unprovoked *Blitzkrieg* victories, starting in Poland in 1940 and continuing into Western Europe and Scandinavia, that forced many in the U.S. pro-German anti-war camp to change sides. As he had experienced in 1917, George again watched many he thought were ideologically committed lose interest and drop out of pro-German activities. Many Americans began to worry seriously about the *Nazi* threat and, in 1940, the Congress passed a half-hearted, symbolic military draft law that specifically limited conscription to one year but forbade overseas deployments. German U-Boats started torpedoing U.S. and Allied ships just off the Atlantic Coast, however, just as many voices preached appeasement as those which argued for defense readiness. Many Americans believed, in good faith, that military preparedness would only bring the nation closer to war and steeled their opposition. When the German U-Boat U-552 torpedoed and sank the U.S. Navy destroyer, *Reuben James* in October 1941,[86] the Roosevelt Administration responded with measured restraint, continuing to profess American neutrality.

Even as German forces were tightening their grip on Europe and extending attacks into the Soviet Union and Britain, the U.S. commitment to national defense lacked committed resolve. The Japanese attack on Pearl Harbor was welcomed by Winston Churchill, Joseph Stalin, and George Strong. Although there was initially a patriotic reaction against the Japanese sneak attack and the unexpected German declaration of war, it was soon deflated in

---

[86] The USS Reuben James (DD245) was escorting a convoy in the North Atlantic when torpedoed on October 31, 1941.

the face of powerful Axis thrusts the Roosevelt administration was unready and unwilling to counter, preferring instead a humiliating armistice that sharply curtailed exports and was economically crippling. Standing alone, America had refused to fight.

George had been employed at the Palmetto Street Pier and a member of the Longshoremen's' Union since coming to Mobile as a fugitive from justice in 1916. He regarded his job as "a right" and had unshakeable plans to retire one day with dual pensions from the pier company and the union. The outlet for George's deep-seated racism had always been the jealous protection of his and other whites' livelihoods from Blacks and other minorities and he was ever quick to physical anger by any perceived transgression.

He had held himself in check since the Jersey City dock riot 26 years earlier, worried about the old murder charge, but a group of blacks demonstrating, just outside the *Ship Saloon,* to be able to take away his own job, was a personal affront and more than he could tolerate. Confident in his sheltered status as a Klansman and member of the *Bund,* and rationalizing his aggressive feelings towards the demonstrators as called for by the state of world affairs, George bought his drinking buddies another round, assured them they had an obligation to protect white rights and led them out of the bar yelling and swinging axe handles, into the crowd of Blacks.

14

AT THE OLYMPIC GAMES

Suppose the Nazis trained susceptible Americans for subversion and incitement?

The Alternative History . . .

The *Nordstern* made the Atlantic crossing in eight days. In the relaxed atmosphere of card playing, gourmet dining, boozing, and story-telling, George Strong and his American shipmates discussed, dissected, and absorbed *Oberstleutnant* Lösen's analysis of world economics, politics, and social theory. By the time they had debarked in Bremerhaven, each of the four could have delivered a polished, "party line" indictment of world Jewry for fomenting and continuing the Great Depression. Each could have explained authoritatively how "inferior" races, including Africans, the Chinese, aboriginals such as Native Americans, and mixed-breeds having a percentage of "inferior" blood were a drag on progressive societies and economies. Each could make a case blaming these *Untermenschen* [87] for America's moral decline leading to economic hardship, military unpreparedness, and national humiliation. After the ocean crossing, in a first-class compartment of the *Deutsches Reichsbahn* [88] rolling south toward Nürnberg, the American *Nazis* luxuriated in further pampered

---

[87] Subhumans
[88] German Reich Railroad

133

comfort, looking forward to the spectacle of the Olympic Games and meeting the *Reich's* important dignitaries.

Nürnberg Castle

George and his companions were lodged in the sumptuous ancient Nürnberg Castle and were treated as VIPs. The Americans experienced a whirlwind schedule of banqueting at three daily meals, chauffeured rides to Olympic preliminary ceremonies and then track, swimming, and gymnastic events followed by nightly cocktail receptions.

They were attentively served by a *concierge*, who kept their rooms stocked with expensive cognac and had a different *Fraulein* sent to George's room every night. George had an unbelievably grand time, never learning that he and some of the girls were secretly photographed in case he ever needed to be pressured or controlled.

George was fully caught up in the heady experience of jackbooted guards snapping to attention when his group came and went through the huge castle portal, riding in Mercedes staff cars with fender-mounted flags, and the adoring gaze of pretty *Frauleins*, who smiled from the sidewalks. It didn't occur to George that the American party was buffered from any contact with common people or any members of the press, who had come to Nürnberg in large numbers.

The Americans were introduced to numerous *Nazi* VIPs and posed for photographs with Herman Göring. George was thrilled to have shaken hands with Göring and several German generals, raising his glass to toasts he couldn't fully understand, and to have given a *Nazi* salute to Hitler himself as the *Führer* made a grand entrance. Hitler looked directly at George in his American *Bund* uniform and whispered a question to an aide, then smiled and nodded to the four Americans. George's only disappointment was not speaking more German than the smattering he remembered from boyhood and thus missing conversations he wished he could have started.

Just after dinner on the third day of the Games, a German soldier asked George to follow and led him to a small study, where he found a blond German officer resplendent in silver braid, jeweled military orders, and campaign ribbons. George's first reaction was that this officer looked so much like him, right down to his own receding hairline, he could have been a brother. But George was next stunned and momentarily fearful when the officer put out his hand and said, *"Guten abend, Herr Strohminger."* [89] Switching to accented English, the officer introduced himself as *SS Obergruppenführer* [90] Reinhard Heydrich and gave George a *Nazi* salute, which George returned with a *"Heil Hitler"* in a shaky voice that had lost its drawl and betrayed his apprehension. His former name and the long-ago murder charge flashed through his mind.

"Not to worry, *Georg,*" a chuckling Heydrich consoled, acknowledging the name change but saying it in German. "You are *mit* friends here. You were highly recommended to us. by your *alter Kamerad* Heinz Spanknoebel."[91] It took ten minutes of small talk and several sips from the snifter of dark *Jägermeister* after-dinner liqueur Heydrich had handed him before George was again nearly at ease.

SS Obergruppenführer
Reinhard Heydrich

---

[89] "Good evening, Mr. Strohminger."
[90] SS Top Group Leader, equivalent to a U.S. 3-star general.
[91] Your old friend, Heinz Spanknoebel. In 1933, Spanknoebel actually founded the Friends of the New Germany, a forerunner of the German-American *Bund.* Spanknoebel fled the U.S. as he was about to be arrested for being an unregistered foreign agent.

Heydrich explained that George's *Gestapo* dossier covered his whole life and his family history revealed them to be third cousins. Nevertheless, George sensed that Heydrich meant him to understand that, with knowledge of his background, they had a tight hold on him. However, George, in common with almost all people outside the German government knew absolutely nothing of Heydrich, especially his brush with death on May 17, 1942.

On that date, agents of the Czech government, exiled to London, had skillfully laid an assassination plot in Prague to kill Heydrich, the military governor of the occupied Moravia and Bohemia provinces of Czechoslovakia. Lying in wait for his passing open car, the agents lost their nerve at the last moment and fled instead of shooting and throwing the anti-tank grenade they carried. Spotted running by Heydrich's security escort and seized while still carrying a grenade and guns, the agents revealed the plot and named their co-conspirators under brutal *Gestapo* torture. The whole circle of agents was rounded-up and slowly hanged with piano wire in Heydrich's presence. As a further warning, Heydrich ordered the murder of all the male inhabitants of Lidice and the total destruction of the little mining village.

Only four months earlier, Heydrich had been the chairman of the January 1942 *Wannsee* planning conference, which placed the *Endlösung* [92] program on an industrialized footing and enabled the efficient murder of Jews and other undesirables from Europe in great numbers. Following the failed assassination plot, Hitler personally transferred Heydrich to the *Euthanasieprogramm* to assist in the management of gassing and cremation operations. *SS Obersturmbannführer* Adolf Eichmann was his office neighbor, just across the hall.

A January 1945 status report for the year just ended and jointly signed by Heydrich and Eichmann, hand-delivered and briefed by Heydrich, informed Hitler that the *Endlösung* total was over 11 million undesirables eliminated and that Europe was now

---

[92] Final Solution, the Holocaust

judenrein.[93]   No further Jews, Gypsies, Bolsheviks, Blacks, or mentally ill persons could be found in the occupied territories. The report declared the *Endlösung* mission had been accomplished and recommended that the more technologically-obsolescent *Vernichtungslagern* [94] be decommissioned. As Heydrich and Eichmann recommended, those newer camps that were retained continued gassing and cremating criminals, suspected political rivals, terrorists and the "uncooperative."   Foreign "guest workers," exhausted or made sick from harsh labor regimens, were sent off on recuperative "holidays" to the death camps.

The Heydrich-Eichmann report that *Nazi*-occupied Europe had been ethnically cleansed had two attached appendices. The first nominated over six thousand German military and civilian personnel for medals and contained an additional roster of those foreigners - mainly Vichy French - who had cooperated by identifying and turning-in their countrymen for exile and death, to be appropriately decorated.

Hitler, ecstatic at having accomplished so important a personal goal, signed-off on the medal recommendations and also awarded both Heydrich and Eichmann the German Order, Germany's highest decoration.

Adolph Eichmann

The report's second appendix outlined a concept for continuing the liquidation of Jews outside Germany from where they were largely concentrated, beginning in the U.S. Hitler asked his staff to review that concept but the inner circle, including Herman Göring and Albert Speer, ridiculed the idea because of the great logistical difficulties involved. However, they began to listen attentively, when Heydrich suggested that the Americans might be

---

[93] "Cleansed of Jews"
[94] Death camps

induced to take care of their own Jews and perhaps their *Negers* [95] as well.

After the Olympics

Within 24 hours of the games' ending, Nürnberg and the sports venues emptied-out. All the dignitaries and their retinues departed, leaving the castle mostly vacant and quiet. Immediately, SS and *Gestapo* instructors began teaching the four Americans undercover tradecraft they would need as secret agents of the *Reich* in the United States. With encouragement to begin preparing immediately for the coming new world order, the Americans were to be important players in launching the social revolution that would permit the U.S. to become Germany's cooperative partner. Their training sessions covered dead drop and silent signaling techniques, how to communicate by flashlight Morse Code with submarines and aircraft, setting up safehouses, and methods of concealment and security. Each of the four was privately given instructions to memorize for leaving secret notices at designated points to be recognized by others in a large network of agents and how to exchange recognition signals. They were photographed and fingerprinted so that fellow agents could recognize and authenticate them.

Other lessons included how to spread propaganda, assembling and inciting crowds, plus other techniques that George and his classmates found stimulating. Each was told, that once back home, to draw up secret lists of businesses owned by Jews, Negroes, Indians, and any Bolshevik sympathizers they could identify, complete with owners' names and their business and home addresses. The lists were not to be labeled, must not have any compiler's identification, and were to be securely stored. Jewish ownership or partnership in banks, newspapers, radio stations, and jewelry stores were to be considered a priority.

---

[95] Literally, "blacks"

There was instruction in how to watch for "alert" and "execute" messages in the classified ads of local newspapers, in George's case the Mobile *Register*. George committed to memory that messages for his personal attention would be in "Wanted to Buy" ads including the codewords "Used Radiators." George sat for two hours memorizing pages of other codewords and how to discover their underlying meanings. He had to hand back the pages and George, his upper lip sweaty from the anxiety he hadn't experienced since his hated school days, had his code reading ability tested. To his relief, he passed the tests easily. "You must tell no one, absolutely no one, about the newspaper procedure," his instructor emphasized. "Read them in private. Do not keep the newspapers, do not mark them or cut out any parts of them." Don't call attention to the significance of the newspapers by burning or tearing them into small pieces. Simple disposal of a discarded newspaper in a waste bin is the preferred security procedure."

In private sessions with a finance instructor, the trainees were told to memorize a bank account number they would be able to draw upon for expenses but were sternly admonished about ethical spending and never keeping any personal written records that could link them with the account. There was encouragement to establish discrete working relationships with clandestine militia groups and people with talents for making and transporting explosives. Grave warnings were given about limiting trust and keeping true identities secret through the use of codenames and codewords.

A man with a dueling scar on his cheek and dressed in civilian clothes, who identified himself only as Karl, spoke to them on the last day of training and assured them that they would soon learn of great accomplishments by the *Vaterland* and that they would each be counted upon to play a heroic role in the continuing struggle for Aryan world supremacy. Having successfully completed their training, they had been accepted into the *Soldierly Order of Nordic Men* and were designated *Ehrend-SS Offizieren.*[96]

Karl's *achtung!* and *zieg heil!* brought them to their feet and a *Nazi* salute. Karl led the Americans in taking the SS oath:

> *"I swear to you, Adolf Hitler, as Führer und Reichskanzler, loyalty and bravery. I vow to you, and to those you have named to command me, obedience unto death, so help me God."*

With hearty congratulatory claps on the back, Karl presented each of the Americans a souvenir dagger without any incriminating symbols and led them off to the dining room.

George had thoroughly enjoyed the classroom sessions as he never did while a schoolboy. With mixed emotions, he packed for the return trip to Alabama, reluctant to be leaving Germany. A train took them to the port city of Kiel, where their escort saw them safely on board the *Münchner Jugend*, a break-bulk freighter carrying a cargo of industrial chemicals. On board, their host was *Korvettenkäpitan* [97] Hans Girnus, a *Kriegsmarine* officer traveling undercover as the ship's navigator. Once underway and clear of the North Sea coast, Girnus told the Americans that they would be calling at Havana to unload the drums of chemicals and would be loading molasses, cigars, and rum. "We will have three days in Havana and will then head for New Orleans. You will meet very important people in Havana, who will be counting on your loyalty in coming days."

Girnus led lengthy political tactics "what-if" and role-playing sessions with the Americans on each of the seven days of the Atlantic crossing. At breakfast on the day of their arrival in Havana, he warned them that Havana should be considered unfriendly territory for anyone arriving on a ship of the *Reich*, and

---

[96] Heinrich Himmler referred to the SS as the "Soldierly Order of Nordic Men. *Ehrend-SS Offizieren* = Honorary SS Officers
[97] Equivalent to Lieutenant Commander in the U.S. Navy

lectured them about security. "Havana is full of American agents, who use Cuban girls to collect information from unsuspecting sailors. We may also test your security awareness and loyalty so be alert and be sure to reach home safely," he said with a serious expression on his face. "You have all sworn an oath of obedience to orders. This is an order to watch out for each other and avoid dangerous contacts."

An Unholy Alliance

At Havana's Bahia Hotel, George had a bellhop take his bags to his room and, with Eddie and David, headed for the bar. He noted numerous very fit-looking young men, who seemed to be scrutinizing everyone in the bar and several very attractive women, some American-looking and some George took for Cuban. An pretty blonde woman made eye contact with and smiled at George, whose immediate reaction was aroused interest but David placed a hand on George's arm, cautioning him to leave it alone in case the blonde was a plant. A chastened George refocused on his rum drink.

At dinner, in a ballroom blue with cigar smoke, the four Americans learned that the hotel was completely occupied by Americans. The whole entourage, including personal assistants and bodyguards comprised nearly 250, many of whom apparently knew each other and exchanged warm, back-slapping hugs. George was delighted to spot two Klansmen from Arkansas and a *Bund* member he had met years earlier in New York.

Cuban President Fulgencio Batista, in military dress uniform, entered the ballroom, stopping to shake hands with three expensively tailored Americans.

Fulgencio Batista

From the podium, he very briefly greeted his assembled guests in halting, heavily-accented English. After warmly expressing his *¡Bienvenidos amigos americanos,!* the president left the room escorted by his army security detail, waving in acknowledgement as several applauding Americans shouted out *¡Viva Cuba!* and *¡Viva El Presidente!* George noted that, unlike Hitler's appearance in Nürnberg Castle, which was covered by a small crowd of news photographers, no one photographed Batista.

A Master of Ceremonies, wearing a black pin-striped suit, a black shirt, and a white tie, opened the meeting with welcoming remarks sprinkled with Italian phrases that elicited approving responses from some in the audience. George and his three traveling companions were in the middle of the off-shore convention of an unholy alliance hosted by Batista, the Cuban President.

The MC, using effusive terms of affection in a combination of English and Italian that George couldn't understand, introduced Meyer Lansky, Frank Costello and Vito Genovese. George and his *Bund* cohorts vaguely recognized the Mafia bosses as principals of American organized crime, who enjoyed warm relations with the Cuban Government and a friendly base for their North American operations. Lansky, however, was unhappy to be in league with the KKK and the *Bund* but was persuaded by his Mafia associates that it was "only business" and that "those guys" would be watched and kept at arms' length. Also introduced were The Klan's National Grand Dragon, Dr. Sam Green of Georgia, Grand Kleagles Dewey Wolfe and Robinson Byrd, plus several Klavern leaders from across the South. The four Americans just returned from Germany were introduced only as American patriots defending American interests. Four angry-looking men in close-cropped military style haircuts were acknowledged as leaders of militia units, ready to take up arms to protect their family and friends. The room also held a number of local government politicians and senior police officers, wearing plain clothes, but not introduced.

After a dinner of spicy baked chicken, black beans and rice accompanied by cold pitchers of beer, boxes of Cuban cigars were passed around at each table. A lifelong cigarette smoker, George discovered that he enjoyed cigars and posturing with them. He later bought several boxes to take home, silently promising to reward himself often with that newfound pleasure. He began combing his receding hair to resemble Reinhard Heydrich's and would soon almost never be seen without a trademark cigar that he jabbed with as a pointer to give emphasis to intimidating remarks.

With a fork and beer glass becoming an improvised bell, the room was quieted down. Several speakers took turns at the podium to thank their Cuban hosts, acknowledge the attendees for having come to Havana, and express low-keyed emotional pledges of loyalty to their "extended big family," which had joined together to take control and protect their common business interests. Using strong language peppered with four-letter words, several of the speakers warned of "do-gooders" at home, such as government liberals and their newspaper supporters. Others denounced meddling, money-lending Jews and negroes, who didn't "know their place," Former President Roosevelt, ex-Attorney General Francis Biddle, ex-FBI Director J. Edgar Hoover, were all mocked, cursed and wished well-gone. New York District Attorney, Thomas E. Dewey came in for especially caustic criticism for having sent Lucky Luciano to prison with one member of the audience suggesting to loud acclaim that "maybe this District Attorney needed to have an accident." According to one of the speakers, better days were ahead with reasonable, friendly men in office. Attorney General Eugene Talmadge was called "a team player, who knew how to take care his friends."

George was fascinated by the broad scope of the gathering and felt himself important for just being a part of it. KKK Grand Dragon Sam Green knew of George's reputation and his just-completed training in Germany. They had a friendly conversation during which George gave assurances of being ready with his organization to be entrusted with important assignments. His conversation with Dr. Green was interrupted by one of Green's assistants, who took him away to a separate discussion with another group led by a Mafia *consigliere,*[98] with connections in the Justice Department, on how to manipulate U.S. laws on free speech, publishing and voting.

---

[98] A legal counselor

15

GEORGE'S TRAIN RIDE

Suppose Nazi-led subversive treachery was launched in the U.S.?

The Alternative History . . .

Back home in Mobile, George was at the kitchen table, underlining passages in the book, *The Jewish World Plague,*[99] when he heard the newsboy's cautious, soft footsteps on his porch stairs. He went out and retrieved his copy of the *Register* from where the Black newsboy had placed it near the door, precisely following George's humiliating insistence, and carried it inside. He flipped through the first few pages, skimming some of the headlines and photos before turning to the classifieds on the paper's last pages. There, on Page 53, finally was the ad he had long been watching for, "Wanted to Purchase: Used Radiators for 1938-1940 Dodge and Plymouth." The ad asked prospective sellers to write to a contact address, "3262 18th Street, San Diego," for Railway Express shipping instructions. Excitedly, George read the ad twice, mentally subtracting "2" from each digit of the contact address, as he had been taught in Nürnberg, and immediately grasped the ad's exclusive message for him (George's codename: "Used Radiators"). He was to be on the 10:40am train from Mobile (codename "Dodge") with a ticket to Gulfport, Mississippi (codename "Plymouth") on the 16th, three

---

[99]English translation of *Die judische Weltpest*, by Hermann Esser, 1939

145

days away. All he needed to do was to be on the train and he would be contacted.

Remembering his Nürnberg training, George made a person-to-person collect call from a pay phone to a Virginia number, asking for Doctor Wallach. He heard the operator ask a woman on the other end for the doctor and heard the woman reply that Doctor Wallach was out of town till Friday but did the caller wish to speak with Doctor Townsend? Without waiting, George said that he "would ring again early Monday morning." The woman in Virginia acknowledged, "I'll leave a note for Doctor Wallach." George hung up, satisfied that he had successfully acknowledged the newspaper ad.

Expecting a need to move quickly in coming days, George phoned two fellow *Bund* members and ascertained that they were available for a meeting on the 16th and suggested they get together to shoot pool then. Those two each called two others and a meeting of seven planners was arranged. Already aware that his Gulfport meeting would be brief and that he would be home the same night, George said nothing to his wife, who never knew when to expect him anyway and had learned long ago not to inquire about his plans.

Trying to appear nonchalant, even though his pulse was elevated, George took an aisle seat in the rear of the last rail coach in the train, anxious to be contacted by the expected messenger. He had hoped to keep a watch on everyone in the car but the seatbacks were too high and his view was limited. Afraid of appearing "nosey" and calling attention to himself, he maintained his composure in his seat. He would never have worried about local law enforcement but now he was nervous about being alone and possibly watched or questioned by federal agents he didn't know. He regretted not bringing his trusted aide, Ray Lockman, as an extra pair of eyes but had followed his training to be alone. The train left on time and arrived and departed very close to schedule at the Pascagoula and Biloxi stations but no one even tried to make eye contact with George, not even the conductor. As the train slowed for arrival in Gulfport, George frantically retraced his decoding of the *Register* ad, fearful he had made a mistake and wished he had brought the newspaper along. He was desperately hoping to be contacted by someone on the platform.

Delaying his alighting from the coach so that he could watch other passengers passing his row, George finally got into a gap near the end of the file that was moving toward the exit. He stiffened but resisted the urge to turn around when a female voice, just behind him, softly asked, "Would you like to take a walk?"

On the platform, walking to the exit, Karen Goodman caught up to him, took his arm, and steered George out of the station and across 29th Avenue. "You look just like your handsome picture," she assured George. To George, however, Karen was the kind of unglamorous, large middle-aged matron he would never look at twice and he was disappointed. He particularly disliked her hair severely pulled back in a bun, her lack of makeup, and grandmotherly sensible shoes. She reminded him of the dumpy old math teacher, who used to embarrass him in front of the whole class. Later, he would rationalize that unremarkable Karen had been a good choice for their undercover meeting.

She led George through several streets not far from the train station and talked almost non-stop in a "take-charge" tone. On two occasions she stopped them in front of stores with big plate glass windows. In front of Madison's kitchen wares store, George had no idea why she was pointing out toasters to him but when they stopped in front of Reese's Hardware a few minutes later, he noticed that Karen was using the glass as a mirror to surveil people and cars in the street.

Karen had George memorize his instructions and repeat them back while they walked. She was emphatic about precise timing and an unstated warning that George was being counted upon to deliver. She offered no opportunity to ask questions. When they turned the corner at Diana Drive, Karen stopped in front of the window of Amy Sue's Beauty Parlour and asked George if he was sure he could handle all the details. Bravely, George replied that he could whereupon Karen said, simply, "I leave you here" and walked directly to the curb, getting into a waiting green Pontiac, which drove off immediately. Surprised at suddenly being alone on the street and suspecting that he might be watched, George walked slowly back toward the train station, cagily using Karen's store window mirror technique to see if anyone was following him. He knew he had almost two hours before the next train back to Mobile and decided he'd have lunch.

On 16th Street, across from the station, George entered the Savannah Coffee Shop and took a booth in a rear corner. When he sat down, he discovered he was sweaty all over. The assignments Karen had relayed to him  were bigger than any he had handled previously and he knew that their repercussions were going to be far more attention-getting than the more local KKK forays of his previous experience.

Numerous details raced through George's mind and were tangled with mixed emotions of the pride he felt in the trust he was given in so vast an undertaking versus his anxiety over the risks he would have to take. For the first time, he felt that he was exposed to great danger that could hurt him badly but his resolve was stiffened by the convictions he had confirmed during his Nürnberg visit and his assumption that others on his unseen team would also be performing their assigned tasks.

George's train got back to Mobile at 5:40pm and he made four calls from a pay phone in the train station. What sounded like a friendly chat was understood by his cohorts to be confirmation of the meeting that night in Edwards' barn off Winford Way, west of town. Ten plotters in four cars drove out to the Edwards farm at 8:00pm. One, Ray Lockman, was dropped at the farm's dirt road intersection with Winford Way to keep watch and two others stood guard outside the barn on opposite sides. The seven planners entered, confident of their privacy. All ten were members of both the *Bund* and the KKK; four were also members of the county or Mobile City police forces.

George set the stage by quickly summarizing the recent world events and then recounting the instructions he had been given via Karen but without mentioning her or his train ride to Gulfport. The soberly apprehensive group discussed objectives, individual assignments, timing, signaling and reporting, disguises and alibis, and security. When the meeting broke up and headed for the cars, George took his principal deputy's arm and held him back till they were alone in the barn. "I'm meeting the boys from Montgomery and Atlanta first thing in the morning, I'll probably be back by afternoon but you know what to do if things start. Don't wait on me; I'll be here soon's I can." George got into his car, picked up Ray, the off-duty cop waiting at Winford Way, and headed for his next meeting in Oxford, Alabama.

16

CONFIRMATION OF THE HOLOCAUST

Suppose Hitler's callous bragging about having slaughtered all of Europe's Jews triggered a massive, emotional response in the U.S.?

The Alternative History . . .

A jubilant Hitler was buoyed by the string of important successes coming so close together. Although his subjugation of Europe and acquisition of atomic weapons were satisfying means to ambitious ends, *der Führer* prized the destruction of European Jewry as the brightest feather in his cap. He reasoned that the time had come to claim his deserved credit and to sound the warning that his patience was not infinite but his punishments could be terrible.

During an introduction by Heinrich Himmler, Hitler was roundly saluted, wildly cheered and lengthily applauded at a festive outdoor New Year's Day rally in Nürnberg before three hundred thousand uniformed combat veterans in parade formation. At the podium, beaming over the hushed assembled troops and fluttering unit banners flawlessly assembled in brilliant sunshine and cold, crisp air, Hitler began with the same words he had spoken at the *Reichstag* in April, 1939:

> *"As I have said before, since the day I began my political life, I have had but one goal: winning back*

the freedom of the German nation, building the strength and power of our Reich, overcoming the domestic fragmentation of our people, removing the barriers abroad, and ensuring its economic and political independence."

By extending both arms over the crowd in a double *Nazi* salute, he silenced a roaring full-minute ovation as if he had pulled its electric plug. To rapt silence, Hitler continued, wide-eyed and gesticulating emphatically, "The German nation is again free; with German atomic weapons and Vengeance rockets, the *Reich* has risen to become the strongest, most powerful on earth; our people are no longer fragmented but are united and are purified by the final elimination of the Jews, who are never coming back."

Dramatically drawing an imaginary line swiftly from left-to-right above the podium with a gloved second finger, he repeated, "Never." Expecting a thunderous response to his "purification" announcement, he pressed two fists to his chest and raised his chin, awaiting the certain adulation. His words caused a collective gasp that quickly erupted into another prolonged, noisy acclamation.

When he quieted his audience again, he observed, "Our people need fear no one. No enemy can ever again match German power or erect barriers to German will." Hitler spoke for another ten minutes and briskly left the podium before the start of another noisy response.

151

An officer signaled to a rank of trumpeters for a loud fanfare and the parade commander ordered the troop formations to pass in review.

The Holocaust News Spreads

News accounts of Hitler's address to the Nürnberg rally traveled swiftly by mid-1940s standards. Relayed by radio and telephone to newspaper pressrooms and broadcasting studios, the self-congratulatory remarks were translated and widely circulated in the English-speaking world within 36 hours. Most of the bombast was "old news" but Hitler's "the Jews are never coming back" statement stimulated anxious questions that wouldn't go away. Assumptions of the worst scenarios gained credence over the next several days but even those with access to official *Nazi* information were unable to wheedle confirmations or denials beyond whispered rumors.

From the start, the Germans had ruthlessly dealt with anyone even suspected of spying, using a radio, or trying to smuggle-out a letter abroad, thereby effectively shutting-off flows of intelligence that might have given a glimpse of the holocaust's horror. It was, however, impractical to keep secret the rounding-up and rail shipment of large throngs and the *Nazis* used a cover-story for the duration of the holocaust that those being transported were collectively guilty of crimes against the *Reich*. The cover-story maintained that those transported were resettled in labor camps, where they would repay a debt to the German people. The joke included encouraging signs over death camp entrances, "*Arbeit Macht Frei.*"[100]

---

[100] "Work Brings Freedom" or "Work Makes You Free"

Especially in the U.S., a Jewish conclusion that millions had been murdered exploded onto newspaper front pages, savage political cartoons and was repeated in hourly radio news bulletins. In particular, Walter Winchell, broadcasting nationally on ABC, used

inflammatory language that glossed-over the rumors, subtly suggesting the validity of the genocide suspicions.

The Norman Thomas Administration, which had been briefed a year earlier by outgoing Roosevelt aides, hid secret intelligence that inevitably was leaked by conscience-stricken present and former civil servants of the State Department. Journalists began asking direct questions on the front pages of major newspapers and the covers weekly news magazines. The White House was forced into the release of a terse communiqué confirming reality of the Holocaust but lamely tried to blame the previous administration, adding an apologetic "nothing they could have done" disclaimer.

This staggering revelation unleashed a reaction that was first expressed across American Jewry as a common mournful wail, shortly morphing into an upwelling of outrage that spilled noisily into the streets of the U.S. and in England and the Vatican.

In an instant, the U.S. national face-off between the isolationist anti-war faction and the interventionists, whose majority were Jews and Communists, shifted dramatically from years of sometimes acrimonious but usually polite civil discourse to noisy, emotional clenched-fist accusations of anti-semitic complicity and blame for America's decline.

Protest marches in Washington were planned for the upcoming weekend but the first contingents from Baltimore and Silver Spring, Maryland, began assembling almost immediately on the

National Mall. The "wrong number," asking for Victor Bridgeman, called to George's house from a pay phone in rural Virginia, set Reinhard Heydrich's sinister plot laid in Canada into motion.

January 46 - George Strong Goes Into Action

Three Klansmen from George's Klavern, all Mobile County Deputy Sheriffs, drove up U.S. Route 31 to Montgomery in an unmarked car, keeping an ear on the CBS affiliate, WKRG, for the latest national news on the protest demonstrations in major American cities.

At the 'Bama Diner on Highland Avenue, two of the Mobile travelers joined two Montgomery police officers in civilian clothes they already knew, who were seated in a booth at the rear.

Earl, the third plain-clothes officer, who drove them, stayed in the parked car, keeping watch on the diner and its parking lot. Two other Klansmen from Montgomery were already seated in the booth just in front, making sure no one else could get close enough to listen-in.

Lee Bob, a local Klavern member behind the counter, was aware that the group was meeting in private and motioned to Heather Anne, the waitress, to leave them alone. Lee Bob put together a tray of coffees and glazed donuts, served them to both tables himself, and moved off without lingering. He told Heather Anne to take a cold Dr. Pepper out to Earl, sitting in the car, and he next started the jukebox playing the Andrews Sisters' *Rum and Coca-Cola* to make it even more difficult for anyone to eavesdrop.

The four conspirators plus Earl, were a team with Charlie Davidson, from Mobile, in the lead. He did most of the talking in a soft voice, relaying George's instructions and answering questions. Charlie and Bubba, his partner from Mobile, would stay in Montgomery to work with the team and be the communications link to George. In all, sixteen Montgomery men, all KKK and/or *Bund* members, were on standby for a message from Mobile that Charlie would receive on the unmarked squad car's radio. With the "waterfall" alerting procedure agreed, the group broke up.

The three from Mobile drove over to the fire house on Perry Street, where they were expected. The people of Montgomery had presented their firemen with one of the first TV sets in town and the visitors from Mobile were fascinated to be able to watch one for the first time. They and the Fire Department duty crew crowded close to the ten-inch black and white RCA set for the Joe Louis-Billy Conn heavyweight championship match.

Yelling loud encouragement rich with racial slurs at the fuzzy screen for Conn to defeat the Black champion, the Mobile men were briefly excited, when Conn landed several good blows but finally groaned in common disappointment at Louis' commanding eighth-round knockout. After thumbing through some magazines and listening to the radio news for any developments concerning the protest demonstrations, the out-of-towners went to sleep in three vacant beds, expecting that the dawn would bring a historic new day.

Protests and Riots

Listeners across North America were uniformly snapped to silent attention and stared as intently at their radios across the room as they would look at their TVs a decade later, when they heard the always ominous, *"We interrupt this program for an important news bulletin."* In big city newspaper offices, editors shouted in commanding tones to *"Stop the Presses"* and to get ready for an *"Extra."* Sketchy news flashes followed by amplifying details were flooding into newspaper offices and broadcast media studios.

Large protest marches had been conducted in New York and Washington for three days, mostly from morning to nearly midnight. With crowds periodically swelling to an estimated thirty to thirty-five thousand in Washington and to one hundred thousand in New York, shouting, banner-waving protesters were up against the White House fence on Pennsylvania Avenue and, in New York, had marched south out of Central Park to Times Square. The common theme of both marches protested the appeasement of the German genocide and occasionally interspersed softly-sung Yiddish dirges with shouted demands for "Revenge" and "Justice for Europe's Jews." Both marches were covered by news photographers on their fringes with mounted and motorcycle police buffering the marchers from counter demonstrators, who were equally as loud and as animated in shaking fists and waving signs that countered, *"War is Not the Answer,"* and *"Hell No! We Won't Go!"* Occasional belligerent forays by small groups from the sidewalks into the massed marchers had to be turned back by police batons.

To contain the New York demonstrations, Mayor Fiorello LaGuardia directed a police build-up and had assembled reserves that left some other areas unpatrolled. The exact times and sequence of unfolding events and inter-twined news bulletins have been lost to history but a frantic phone call from Pier

26 on Manhattan's west side is believed to mark the opening act of a very crowded day: "Operator! Get me the police!"

Desk Sergeant Clancey at the 10th Precinct needed to ask an agitated, incoherent male to repeat three times before he could understand: men had stormed up the gangway of the *Norddeutscher Lloyd* liner, *Friedrich der Grosse*,[101] and had set it on fire. And there was shooting!

MV Friedrich der Grosse

By the time Clancey had gotten word to the Precinct Dispatcher and to Engine 14 of the Fire Department, the 17th Precinct had received a report of a riot in Times Square between demonstrators and hecklers.

Because of the "Shots Fired" report, the Engine 14 firemen delayed boarding the ocean liner, already heavily shrouded in smoke. When finally cleared to go aboard by the police, the firemen discovered only scattered piles of burning blankets that had blackened the ship's white paint in spots but had not caused any serious damage. No damage from bullets was ever found on the ship. In the morning, a large red-brown splotch, later determined to be beef blood, and the phrase, "*Nazi* Jew Killers", were discovered painted on the ship's bow.

---

[101] Frederick the Great of the North German Lloyd Line

The Times Square activity was far less under control. With all vehicle traffic blocked by the thousands in the square, 17th Precinct cops in the first squad cars on the scene found gridlock in the cross-town streets and were forced to park over a block away. A sergeant radioed for heavy back-up before getting out of the car. Panicky pedestrians were running away from Times Square, colliding with the curious, going in the opposite direction and trying to get to the scene of the excitement. In Times Square, a rumbling, fluid melée of thousands undulated from sidewalk to sidewalk. To the cops, everyone seemed to be yelling, shoving and grasping for adversaries. Many fistfights were visible, protest signs had been converted to jabbing spears or swinging clubs, and occasional thrown bottles and other objects arced over the howling mob.

In minutes, additional black-and-white squad cars from the 17th and adjacent precincts were arriving and parking on the side-streets as close as they could get to Times Square. Uniformed officers began emerging from their cars with raised nightsticks, blowing whistles.

Robert Kaufman and Julius Reeder, *Bund* members from upstate New York, who were waiting on 40th Street with six accomplices for their chance, sprung into action.

Kaufman quickly moved to two parked squad cars and broke their side windows with a steel mallet he had pulled from his pocket. Two accomplices followed on his heels; one held two *Molotov* cocktails, the other a Zippo cigarette lighter. With practiced swiftness, they dropped two burning *Molotovs* into the cars, which instantly erupted with yellow flames that reached to the third floor windows of neighboring buildings. Kaufman's team returned to the sedan they had left parked on 39th Street, put four more *Molotov* cocktails into their coat pockets, and went in search of additional police cars. By night's end they had torched a total of seven black-and-whites and had painted red Stars of David on three more.

Reeder and four husky cohorts in long overcoats and brimmed hats spotted a lone policeman threading his way east on a 42nd Street sidewalk. Cleverly contriving what appeared at first to be a confused collision, the five managed to knock the cop down and fall on him in a tangled heap, exclaiming Yiddish oaths. In the six seconds it took for the officer to regain his feet, his gun was gone and the men who had pinned him had melted into the crowd. Reeder and his crew acquired four more police pistols in the next fifteen minutes. All the victimized police reported to their sergeants that Jews had disarmed them and the tactic was described in an *All Points Bulletin* that warned all police on the streets to watch out for gangs of Jews, who were assaulting cops and stealing their guns. Over the next few hours, jumpy cops shoved and night-sticked people in the crowd by whom they had been jostled innocently.

The burning squad cars caught the attention of rioters of both persuasions and also of the policemen on the scene. The pushing and shoving abruptly stopped as the mob, suddenly united as rubberneckers, divided and started moving toward the side-street fires. Staying close together, Reeder's men moved with the crowd into 40th Street, edging ever closer to a middle-aged protester carrying a sign, *"No More Jewish Deaths!"* Following Reeder's lead, the five *Bund* members surrounded the sign-carrier and nudged him out of the stream of pedestrians, up onto the sidewalk, and into the space between two storefront windows. In a flash, Reeder delivered a fatal blow with his mallet and one of the others put a police pistol into the dead man's hand. They then eased him down, making sure his body was atop the protest sign, and, splitting-up, rejoined with the crowd.

As the mob pressed as closely to the burning cars as the heat allowed, the sounds of approaching fire engines was heard. Shortly, fire trucks moving very slowly, gingerly forced paths through the crowds on four different side streets and firemen began unwinding their hoses. Before any of the fire companies could put water on the burning police vehicles, Reeder's men, standing between parked cars, took police revolvers from their pockets with gloved hands, and emptied them, rapid-firing above the crowd in the direction of the parked fire engines. A stampede away from the fires spontaneously ensued and the shooters simply dropped the guns where they were standing, between the parked cars, and joined the fleeing mob. Their night's work done, all the *Bund* members departed the area. From a pay phone, Reeder made his coded report.

FDR's Gravesite

In Hyde Park, New York the morning light revealed Franklin D. Roosevelt's tomb to have been vandalized overnight and defaced with anti-German slogans and slurs against the 32nd President.

Later, *Bund* leaders would shrug their shoulders when discussing who had been responsible, ultimately concluding they may have had some unexpected help from the Jews after all.

In Washington, three mixed *Bund* and KKK teams from West Virginia had already made their separate ways to their assignments. The first team distracted the two Metropolitan Police officers guarding the front of the German Embassy on Massachusetts Avenue by starting a roaring gasoline fire on the sidewalk across the street. It took Tommie Byrd just seven seconds to paint a red Star of David across the embassy's double front door and disappear before the cops resumed their posts. A prewarned German attaché made sure the fresh paint was preserved for the newsmen, who would be summoned.

The second team, using a similar ruse, enabled Louie Bannister to paint "Jew Killers" in large letters on the plate glass of *Norddeutscher Lloyd's* ticket office on K Street. Bannister, in a long black overcoat and hat pulled low, was seen defacing the window by passers-by and was accurately described, however, the description and report of Bannister's escape route toward 18th Street were of no help to the police or FBI. A partial can of red paint and a brush, both purchased in a Woolworth's store, were found in a trash can and saved as evidence.

The third KKK/*Bund* team of five joined a group of nearly ten thousand anti-German protesters crowded up close to the White House on Pennsylvania Avenue. Many carried signs critical of government inaction and the chants decidedly condemned letting Germany off the hook for the admitted holocaust. Billy Crowe, a burly garage mechanic from Martinsville, was carrying the sign he and Ed Burns had made, "*America is Painted with the Shame of Jewish Blood.*" Burns, an ex-high school football linesman, pressed his way forward through the crowd, closely followed by Crowe and the others.

As soon as they were up against the White House's iron fence, Crowe passed the sign between the bars of the fence and let it fall, just inside on the edge of the lawn. Immediately, Burns poked the pistol he was holding inside his cut-out coat pocket between two front buttons and through the fence, quickly firing two shots toward the left side of the building. As Burns dropped the gun inside the fence, the West Virginians began yelling, "Look out; he's got a gun!" and "Run!" and joined the mob, which instantly began scampering frantically to get away. The five split up when

they reached 15th Street, some turning the corner and the rest continuing east on Pennsylvania Avenue.

The Secret Service and Metropolitan Police, including two mounted patrolmen, had already been on the scene monitoring the demonstration and instinctively drew their sidearms, assuming defensive postures at the sound of shots.

In the noisy commotion of thousands of panicked protesters fleeing in three directions away from the White House and not knowing whether additional shots would be fired, the Secret Service and police crouched low in their saddles and watched the sidewalk in front of the White House empty of pedestrians, many of whom were running with and through the vehicle traffic, which continued to move east and west on Pennsylvania Avenue. The legs of both horses were repeatedly bumped by runners intent on escaping, some of whom stumbled and wound up on the pavement, under the skittering hooves.

The mounted policemen were distracted by having to rein-in their horses and lost their height advantage for watching the rapidly-dispersing mob. In less than a minute, there was no one left to stop and question. Many, who had fled, later came forward to give statements but the only good evidence available to the investigators were the recovered protest sign and gun dropped on the lawn, just inside the fence. Widely differing descriptions of the people believed to have been at the spot of the shooting were given both to the investigators and to news reporters. The highest numbers of eyewitness descriptions prompted the police to appeal for help from the public in identifying a man superficially resembling Ed Burns and a middle-aged woman wearing a grey coat and black hat, carrying a large black purse. Most news reports characterized the White House demonstration as "anti-German" and inadvertently fed a readers' inference that the demonstrators were primarily out-of-town Jews by quoting "unidentified witnesses" who thought the shooter had yelled something in Yiddish.

Inside, few of the White House staff actually heard the two shots that had been fired at the building but the word flashed throughout the mansion, causing reactions ranging from near-hysteria to cautious alarm. According to plan, the Secret Service locked-down the building and grounds, had all window curtains drawn, and detained everyone on the grounds inside the fence, pending searches and questioning. After an hour of quiet, small groups of White House employees were escorted outside and released to travel home.

The Secret Service asked the Metropolitan Police to barricade and patrol all the surrounding streets that offered a view of the White House to unofficial vehicle and pedestrian traffic. Within an hour, the first elements of the D.C. National Guard's 260th Military Police Group started manning the police barricades and ultimately had 110 guardsmen on the streets and surrounding rooftops.

Morning daylight revealed that four Sherman tanks of the 102d Cavalry and several jeeps mounting machine guns had been deployed from nearby Fort Meade in Maryland to keep order. Office buildings on surrounding streets were closed to their workers and not even press passes were honored inside the closed area.

Similar pre-planned steps were taken at the Capitol and other key federal buildings.

Events in Montgomery

In Montgomery, Alabama, Charlie Davidson received his coded "Go" instructions from George Strong in Mobile over his squad car's radio and called his team together in the bleachers of a softball field in Oak Park. Satisfied that everyone knew what to do and on what schedule, he sent them off in small teams. Three

Bund members in non-descript clothing infiltrated a crowd of about 300 demonstrators, standing on the marble steps going up to the Alabama Capitol on Dexter Avenue. A speaker in the back of a pick-up truck parked at the curb, wearing a blue-striped Jewish prayer shawl, was vehemently haranguing his listeners on the steps, criticizing the former Roosevelt and current Thomas Administrations in vitriolic language for having sold out the Jews of Europe and stripping the U.S. of a military capability for vengeance.

Two of the *Bund* members started a shoving match with protesters on an edge of the mob and the third fired a single pistol shot, breaking a window in the Capitol Building. The crowd including the *Bund* men scattered down the steps and across the lawn.

Alabama State Capitol

The perpetrators laughed later at the ungainly way the speaker jumped from the truck in panic, stumbling and falling on his face before scuttling away on all fours.

One of the *Bund* members, a Montgomery Police officer wearing a deceptive head bandage, later told a reporter for the Montgomery *Independent* that he had been struck over the head by a Jew carrying a protest sign when he tried to apprehend another Jew screaming something in Yiddish, who had fired the shot.

The next morning in daylight, police cars, several churches, and cemeteries were found to be defaced by painted Stars of David, anti-German, and anti-government slogans. A Black church was heavily damaged by arson and police and fire investigators reported finding Jewish protest literature, a map of the city with churches marked, and a *yarmulke* [102] complete with black hairs on the grounds. Similar events occurred overnight in numerous cities across the South and also in Chicago, St. Louis, Toledo, and Gary, Indiana.

Newspapers across the U.S. and interrupting news bulletins covered the riotous events in detail and Jewish responsibility was soon widely insinuated. The discovery of Murray Goldberg's body in the Ritz Camera storefront on New York's 40th Street, lying on a protest sign with a police revolver in his hand, was seized upon by many as *prima facie* evidence of Jewish guilt. Before any alternative scenarios could be explored, an anonymous telephoned tip to the New York *Daily News* openly suggested Jewish responsibility. The tip, from a "citizen who didn't want to get involved" offered the explanation that he and other protesters he didn't know saw a man with a gun and one of them hit him with a flashlight. According to the caller, Goldberg staggered out of the crowd and out of sight. The caller didn't think he'd been hit that hard. By afternoon, the term "Jewish uprising" was in increasing use.

Rabbis and prominent Jewish business leaders tried to mount a damage-control defense, insisting they could not be responsible for every hoodlum who had joined the demonstrations, failing to clearly make the case that such hoodlums were not necessarily Jews. Anti-Semites of various stripes came forward to refute the Jewish denials and many offered additional denunciations of Jewish anti-American behavior. After three days of newspaper and radio coverage, many in the nation concluded that angry Jews were indeed behind the riots and, taking the rabbis at their word, were convinced that the Jews were not and could not be restrained by their religious leadership. One prominent radio commentator observed that, "If you are demonstrating as a Jew, your real religion doesn't matter."

---

[102] Skullcap

The American *Kristallnacht* Riots Continue

Egged-on by the press and radio commentators, the Congress and several state legislatures were very quick to take up the matter with numerous calls for investigations. The Norman Thomas White House was happy to defer to the Congressional lead, although Vice President Lindbergh reminded the Cabinet that he had been warning about Jews with confused loyalties. Even before any Congressional investigations could start, several committees began discussing available measures for protecting government institutions and guaranteeing public safety. Gun control, the regulation and discouragement of protest demonstrations, plus restrictions on inflammatory and inciteful speech were passionately but uncharacteristically recommended by life-long liberal legislators in Washington and many of the states that were affected by the violence. A lawyer for the American Civil Liberties Union was improbably quoted as urging that First Amendment Freedoms needed to be moderated by individual responsibility and that "inciteful yellow journalism" was the equivalent of yelling, "Fire," in a crowded theater.

Replaying Germany's *Kristallnacht* of 1938, in the next twenty-four hours, *Bund* members in Mobile, Montgomery, and Dothan, Alabama had smashed the windows of every Jewish-owned shop that was on George Strong's list, had broken into and ransacked almost all the offices of Jewish doctors, dentists, lawyers, and insurance brokers, setting several ablaze. When hooded Klansmen carrying torches rammed the gate of Schneider's Lumber in Montgomery, two unarmed Black night watchmen coming to investigate were gunned down. In all three cities, newspaper offices, which had been critical of the Federal Government's appeasement of Germany or which had editorialized in favor of military intervention were heavily damaged. An over-exuberant Klansman worked his hands outside the sheet that covered him from head to toe and tossed a stick of dynamite into the office of the Dothan *Blade-News*. The building was a total loss and windows in a two-block area were shattered. Synagogs in several southern cities were set ablaze and, in each case, a few pistol shots were enough to make responding fire brigades hold back until the buildings could not be saved.

Bankers Targeted

Because of their secure construction and close association with moonlighting cops, bank buildings were not attacked but the homes of several Jewish bank executives were torched. In Montgomery, Sheldon Cohen, Vice President of the Farmers' Bank, emerged clumsily from his burning house with a hunting rifle and was shot dead on his lawn by two *Bund* members. In Mobile, the screaming accusations about *Nazi* hoodlums by Joel Blumenfeld of County Savings & Loan and his wife, Miriam were silenced by a fusillade of sixteen shots by a KKK and *Bund* team hidden in the bushes. The shooters slipped away in the dark while the Blumenfeld children collapsed in shock next to their parents' bodies while their house went up in flames.

The same script played out in Florida, Georgia, Arkansas and Mississippi but in none of these as ruthlessly and as viciously as in Alabama. Similar nighttime provocations were carried out across the South as far west as Texas and in many American cities, however, Alabama provided the greatest number and the most appalling examples. Everywhere, police reports commenting on the circumstances of the crimes suggested the partial responsibility of the Jewish victims for instigating and worsening the troubles. "Sources" for both the *Bund* and KKK claimed justifiable responsibility for the punitive *pogrom*, asserting a need to control warmongers who were more interested in war profiteering than preserving the peace.

An anonymous *Bund* leader was quoted, "If the Jews mean to have war, let it begin here!" Later coroners' inquests in the Montgomery and Mobile shootings found that the dead were unlawfully armed and their deaths to have been justifiable self-defense. The Mobile Coroner's report contained a veiled warning about taking the law in one's own hands and insurrection. No individuals were indicted for any of the break-ins, arsons, or shootings. The governors of all the states experiencing riots called out their National Guard units and most but not all the violence subsided.

Jewish leaders, who had sounded irresolute the day before about charges of a Jewish "uprising," vociferously demanded federal protection of Jewish interests and the investigation of those responsible for the anti-semitic reprisals. In Newark, Rabbi Joachim Prinz was interviewed at Temple B'nai Abraham by the New York *Times*. The rabbi, who had been forced from his native Germany by the *Nazis*, was quoted by the *Times* as "highly critical" of the Thomas-Lindbergh administration for cowering before German bluster and turning a blind eye to what he explicitly termed, the American *pogroms*. The *Times* interview was referenced in newspapers across the country and stimulated a great many emotional columns and letters to editors on both sides of the issue.

Jewish claims and demands were countered by KKK and *Bund* spokesmen, who insisted that the Nation needed vigilant protection from Jewish violence secretly contrived to drag the U.S. into an unwanted war with Germany and, probably, also with Japan.

To emphasize its position, the KKK held a parade, with a profusion of American flags, in downtown Washington on Pennsylvania Avenue, between the White House and the Capitol.

Horrified at even the merest suggestion of the prospect of having to fight a two-ocean war, it was the sense of both Houses of

Congress and the White House that the domestic disturbances must be quickly defused and brought under control.

In Washington and several state capitals, alarmed officials grappled ineffectively with the situation. All levels of the Federal Government were bombarded with demanding phone calls from governors, mayors, newsmen, labor union leaders, their constituents and from the German Embassy. The German Attaché for Trade and Tourism placed advertisements in leading newspapers announcing that, owing to "civil disorder," in the U.S., the liner, *Konig Albert*, en route from Bremerhaven to New York and Havana, would not call at New York. Passengers would disembark in Halifax, Nova Scotia. The cancellation was hailed as a victory by a yiddish-language newspaper published in Brooklyn, which called for all Germans visiting in the U.S. to go home.

MV Konig Albert

Leaders of the Jewish community in particular pounded the government with accusations of the bigoted, complicit sacrifice of slaughtered European Jewry and its craven readiness to do the same in America. Rabbis, who called for calm and a temporary "cooling-off" period without further marches, were attacked publicly for cowardice by some hard-line Jews but by a greater number of anonymous *Bund* members. Thousands of mimeographed forged flyers urging action against Germany and calling for renewed demonstrations were widely distributed to porches and mailboxes by neighborhood kids paid by undercover Klan and *Bund* members.

The Blacks Are Drawn In

In many of the cities and towns beset by the nighttime violence, the elongated commotion of breaking glass and the accompanying orchestra of burglar alarms awakened whole neighborhoods, bringing residents to their windows and out into the streets. Starting in the poorer sections of the rattled towns, opportunistic looting of the broken storefronts and offices began as soon as the KKK and *Bund* perpetrators were out of sight. Although whites as well as Blacks participated equally in the thefts, local photojournalists captured sensational images in segregated neighborhoods of Black men, women and children leaping from storefronts carrying merchandise. The Associated Press photo of gleeful Black teens, emerging from a liquor store on Decatur Avenue carrying bottles, made the front pages of morning editions nationwide and served to undercut same-page articles quoting the explanations of Black clergymen that poor people had understandably seized the opportunity to feed their hungry families.

According to plan, several KKK and *Bund* owners of sporting goods stores and pawn shops filed false police reports of forced entry and the theft of guns and ammunition. "Eye witnesses" described the mythical looters as "negroes." On cue, police and deputy sheriffs reported that their patrol cars had been fired upon by shooters inside "negro-owned" homes and churches of "negro congregations." Police in Little Rock and Chattanooga showed press photographers bullet-damage to police cars they had caused themselves.

Mixed-in with the malicious disinformation were scattered police reports of white schoolgirls being molested by "negro men" and the miraculous escape of two little white girls, who were "reported" to have been snatched off the street and into a car driven "by negroes." The lies were repeated often enough and from enough apparently "reliable" sources that they soon became believable. A generalized undercurrent buzzing across the U.S.

and abroad was that a violent uprising was in progress and that Jews and Blacks together were responsible.

The Klan's scripted response was an orgy of cross-burnings, lynchings, torched churches, and bullet-riddled homes and churches. Terrified Blacks across the south at first sought refuge in their houses of worship but the swiftly-spreading news of attacks on churches, including a drive-by shooting in Kentucky that killed a child seated in a pew, kept many at home behind drawn curtains.

In one night, seven Blacks were lynched from trees and lamp posts in Indiana, Kentucky, Maryland, Missouri and Ohio on trumped-up charges. Nineteen more were hanged, shot, or dragged to death behind pick-up trucks in rural Mississippi, Arkansas, Georgia, South Carolina, and Texas.

Neither police nor sheriffs deputies interceded in any of these atrocities except, in their aftermaths, to disperse gawking crowds.

The Skirmish at Sharpe Church

Well-intentioned parishioners of the Sharpe AME Church in Tupelo, Mississippi, played right into the KKK's hands. Having heard radio reports of church burnings, fourteen angry, defiant men stood outside the church with their hunting rifles and shotguns while the congregation sang spirituals inside. Determined to defend their new church, the small group ignored Pastor Jernigan's pleas to come inside or go home, instead forming a semi-circle around the white clapboard structure, ready to repel any sneaky arsonists who approached. The Tupelo police received a telephoned report of the armed guardians and began recalling off-duty cops to assemble a strong response team to

171

maintain order. However, many police could not be reached at their home telephones because they were already in their Klan robes and on their way to the rallying point.

One small KKK gang was on the scene first followed by the others just a few minutes later. Split into two squads of five gunmen each, the Klansmen advanced stealthily on the church down Mound Street and intersecting Magnolia Drive, using hedges, trees, and the few parked cars as cover. To the Klan, armed "negroes" even thinking about shooting at white people was provocation enough, regardless of their defensive intention, and the hooded gunmen had not come for negotiation. Byron James later claimed to have fired the first shot from half a city block away but not hitting any of the "negroes." On the church lawn, the defenders heard the shot before spotting any of the Klansmen and instinctively began to inch backwards toward the building. Details of the following general fusillade could only be surmised by later investigators but it seemed clear that both sides fired numerous rounds.

Ill fortune conspired against the amateur church defenders from the start. Their exposed position against a white building illuminated by street lamps made them easy targets to thugs with armed street-fighting experience and, lacking any organization or tactical plan themselves, the defenders panicked quickly, fired wildly, and were all shot.

Several minutes after all fourteen defenders were down, whooping Klansmen continued firing from behind trees and hedges until new shots from a house to the rear of the Mound Street squad sent them scrambling toward Magnolia Drive. Unsure of what was happening, the sight of sheet-covered figures scooting in their direction prompted all the Klansmen on Magnolia Drive to retire nervously towards their cars and flee the area.

Only two KKK members were superficially wounded by shotgun pellets fired from the church lawn and did not seek hospital treatment. Ten of the Black defenders were dead, several having received their fatal wounds while lying wounded on the ground. The remaining four were seriously wounded but all recovered to face a variety of criminal charges. The funerals of the ten killed in the gun battle drew numerous Black notables, who had to be escorted to the church by the National Guard.

The Mound Street shooter or shooters, who routed the Klan, was never identified and the Tupelo Police and local KKK Klavern brutally harassed all that neighborhood's residents. The bullet-ridden Sharpe AME church mysteriously burned down two weeks after the incident, which became nationally-known for the "Stand of the Tupelo Fourteen" and the "Skirmish at Sharpe Church," long after calm had been restored.

Within hours of the last Tupelo shots being fired, a synopsis of the national news characterized the apparently coordinated widespread region-wide incidents as a "Negro Revolt" and drew parallels with the so-called "Jewish Uprising." Leading questions were being posed about whether a Jewish-Black Revolution had broken-out.

The Situation in New York City

News of the spreading violence truly horrified many but secretly gratified an equal number of others. Out of genuinely patriotic motives, on Saturday, February 9th, the America First Committee organized a "Consolidated Anti-War Demonstration for Peace" in New York City. The event was very broadly advertised to potential attendees in the surrounding states and listed, as speakers, Vice President Lindbergh, Secretary of State, Gerald P. Nye, Father Charles Coughlin, and John T. Flynn.

Avoiding the Times Square venue of the earlier violence further downtown, 120,000 gathered at Grant's Tomb on 122nd Street, where John Flynn welcomed the assembly of "true American patriots" without calling attention to the scattered *Bund* uniforms. Ostensibly walking into Black tenement neighborhoods of

Grant's Tomb

Harlem to encourage responsible pacifist citizenship, the taunts aimed at onlookers by some of the more abrasive marchers were almost more than many observing Black youth could handle but cooler-headed adults hustled potential trouble-makers indoors before any violent clashes could start.

Father Charles Coughlin

Leaving the seething Black residents of Harlem behind, the marchers proceeded into the South Field football stadium on the Columbia campus to be addressed by the VIP speakers. Father Charles Coughlin offered an opening invocation to the respectfully silent gathering and then brought them to full voice, responding in agreement to his castigation of Jews whose lust for war profits was shown ready to send American boys to die and, worse, to the destruction of American cities, if Germany were forced to defend itself. Coughlin turned next to "negroes" demanding undeserved special treatment during a time of severe economic hardship.

Waving a copy of his newspaper, *The Cross and the Flag*, Father Coughlin urged steadfastness against America's true enemies, pronounced a blessing on the assembly, and turned the podium over to Secretary of State Nye. Nye made only very brief welcoming remarks before introducing the Vice President. Vice President Lindbergh began by reminding the crowd of America's historical greatness and unique ability to rise above difficult challenges. He told the crowd that President Thomas "felt the pain" of America's minorities who had unfairly suffered generations of discrimination and was prioritizing actions that would level the playing field for all. During this compelling work, Lindbergh "stood with the President in recognizing that the greatest obstacle to achieving lasting economic and social gains for all Americans lay in avoiding a war that would cost us dearly in blood and treasure."

He continued, thumping the rostrum with the heel of his hand for emphasis, "We must not permit our actions at home to bait other nations into disagreements with us so serious that armed conflict is even considered. In these trying economic times, every dollar diverted to guns and ammunition must be subtracted from what is available for addressing real social needs here at home. Those, who clamor for revenge for actions beyond our control, either because they were committed outside our jurisdictions or before we were born, must consider the enormous damage they may cause to innocent Americans and to future generations. The greater good must drive our thoughts and our actions and the way of peace must be allowed to prevail. Let's give peace a chance."

Although Lindbergh did not single-out any groups or factions by name, some reports of his remarks referred to "veiled criticisms" or "unspoken blame" of both Jews and Negroes who were endangering the peace.

The most direct attacks on the Vice President condemned his appearance onstage with the "Anti-Semite Father Coughlin" and Lindbergh's known connections with the *Nazis* in Germany. A political cartoon, drawn by Theodore Geisel, who signed as "Dr. Seuss," appeared in national newspapers mocking Lindbergh's earlier appeasement of German militarism and questionable loyalty.

Geisel's actual cartoon (1941) signed "Dr. Seuss"

17

AMERICA'S LOSS OF FREEDOMS

Suppose the Federal Government was confronted by a need to control widespread, damaging riots and to restore civil order?

The Alternative History . . .

President Norman Thomas agreed immediately with his Chief of Staff's recommendation for an emergency cabinet meeting on Monday, February 11th. It was the consensus of the cabinet that direct appeals by the President for calm would be respected and the national radio networks were asked to bring the necessary broadcasting equipment to the White House for a Presidential address to the nation at 8:00pm the next day. A draft of the President's talk was immediately started by a White House team augmented by key Congressional leaders and the governors of three states. The team worked late into the night and at mid-morning, was reviewing and editing the draft when Secretary of State Nye telephoned, requesting an immediate meeting with the President on a matter of great urgency.

In the Oval Office, a shaken Secretary Nye reported to President Thomas that he had been visited earlier by the German Ambassador, Hans Thomsen, who formally protested the unprovoked attacks on German property and interests. Thomsen transmitted Berlin's demands for guarantees that the U.S. Government would prosecute those behind the violence and protect against further occurrences.

Thomsen had emphasized that the *Führer* himself declared it absolutely essential that the U.S. Government clearly demonstrate its intentions so as not to be seen as signaling official hostility to Germany.

Quoting Hitler, Thomsen stressed that American failure to curb Jewish anti-German aggression would be interpreted as implicit official tolerance and a breach of the German-U.S. armistice agreements. As an aside, Thomsen added that he was aware that Hitler was already being advised that, if the U.S. was unable or unwilling to assure the safety of German interests, Germany reserved the right to take the appropriately strong protective and deterrent measures.

Nye would later recall that the President was visibly upset at receiving the German ultimatum and seemed unable to digest the recommendations that were pouring in from those trying to advise him. Nye advised Thomas that they needed to avoid being trapped by what might appear, at the moment, well-intentioned commitments they would not be able to repudiate later.

Gerald P. Nye

In his memoirs, Nye quoted Thomas as pacing the floor and repeatedly questioning, "What can we do?" Nye also admitted that neither he nor other advisors in the room were offering the President anything really helpful.

Vice President Lindbergh, who had left the discussion to make some phone calls from his office, rejoined the group and listened to a summation of the deliberations by the Chief of Staff, his palms pressed together and his pointing fingers holding the bridge of his nose. When the Chief of Staff had finished, Lindbergh spoke directly to the President in a somber tone, "I learned a short while ago that the German fleet may be crossing the Atlantic in our direction again. Our Naval Intelligence was monitoring fleet maneuver exercises that were predicted to have ended four days ago but Intelligence has now lost continuity on the major German ships plus the oilers and supply vessels that played in the exercise. They estimate that the Germans may have a major Atlantic deployment underway and are checking now to determine whether troop transports have sailed with the fleet. Intelligence is unwilling to guess at probable missions or destinations but suggests the German fleet could be off the East Coast in as little as four days."

"Mr. President, unless you want German gunboats in Chesapeake Bay and German paratroops patrolling their embassy on Massachusetts Avenue here in Washington, we had better show Berlin that we are in control here and we better show them fast," the VP warned. "We mustn't let the Germans force a showdown by making us try to block their ships after which they may escalate their threats to atomic rockets." Anxious discussion in the room shifted to whether the President should inform the nation of Hitler's demands and the naval threat. Secretary Nye worried aloud that word would surely get out about the German demands and the possibly renewed presence of the feared German fleet. Nye warned that damaging charges of a cover-up or of underestimating the risks would surely arise. Ultimately, Thomas accepted a majority view that the threats needed to be revealed as one driver of necessarily stern measures to restore order.

Thomas next asked Secretary of the Navy Henry Ford whether the U.S. Atlantic Fleet should be put on alert but, before Ford could respond, Jeanette Rankin, the Secretary of War, answered for him in a superior, mocking tone, wagging her finger like a school teacher. "Let's not be foolish in our haste. Just because the Germans challenge us to fight, it doesn't mean we have to behave like silly little boys and oblige them. All the big cities on the East Coast will be in range of German guns and rockets. Millions of Americans could be killed and our cities made to look like London after the *blitz*. Even if we sink their ships or finally drive them off, which I doubt we could do, the damage will be done and we won't be better-off than we are now. I say we not play soldier and concentrate instead on handling our own domestic problems ourselves."

Lindbergh jumped-in as soon as Rankin finished, "If we push the Germans to give us a demonstration of an atomic rocket attack, which city are you prepared to see hit?" The meeting ended with the President asking Secretary Nye and VP Lindbergh to use their German contacts to assure *Herr Hitler* that the U.S. intended no disrespect to German interests and was taking the necessary steps to control the disruptive behavior of the few hooligans in our midst.

At 8:00 pm Washington time, President Thomas spoke to the nation via radio and the full text of his remarks was printed across the U.S. in morning editions. Essentially, Thomas appealed for restraint and calm in the name of neighborliness and good citizenship.

He obliquely acknowledged Jewish grievances against genocidal Germany and the entitlements of the Black community to equality but tried, uncharacteristically, to come across as unyielding on the need for an immediate end to the violence. With what were meant to be heard as soothing references to the futility of trying to undo history and accepting things "we can't change," Thomas made a bid for convincing the aggrieved minorities to abandon or at least tone-down the protests. He reminded listening Americans that an armistice had been signed in good faith by former President Roosevelt and that the damaging anti-German attacks in American cities had provoked the Germans into threatening war. "Even now," Thomas warned, "German warships may be heading our way to emphasize their demands that we honor the terms of the armistice we signed and behave respectably."

The President also promised to begin addressing the root causes of discontent: high unemployment, inflation, commodity rationing, and racial equality but identified no immediate initiatives or new programs. He pledged to work closely with the Congress on these highest priority domestic issues. In the Capitol, Congressmen on both sides of the aisle grumped at not having been let off the hook. News commentators dismissed Thomas' radio address as offering "nothing new" and "short on specifics." Beyond Washington, the state and local governments of the most disturbed areas were also sharply divided by serious emotional conflicts and dithered at finger-pointing, taking no immediately useful measures.

Heavily infiltrated by the Klan, *Bund*, and politicians, who tolerated "lynch law" as an expedient necessary evil, some local officials, who were politically closer to the fascist outlaws than to the citizens they represented, sheltered the police from disparagement instead of protecting the victimized minorities. It fell to the highly reluctant U.S. Congress to reimpose order and prevent recurring strife. The Thomas Administration was blasted by most editorialists for its "failed leadership" in the face of America's worst crisis since the Civil War.

On February 17th, a *Kriegsmarine* destroyer heading west was spotted and reported to the U.S. Coast Guard by a weather patrol vessel 300 miles east of Cape Cod. Naval Intelligence estimated that the destroyer was probably German  and screening for other German vessels proceeding on a similar course. The intelligence report commented that, if the destroyer was part of the expected German fleet, the fleet could be right off the East Coast of the U.S. in less than fifteen hours.

The broadcast and print commentators divided, as expected, along ideological lines. The Administration received approving support for avoiding provocations that would force the German fleet to attack as well as rebukes for its failure to defend America. Other strongly-worded editorials called for the immediate resignations of Jeanette Rankin and Gerald Nye. Relentlessly prodded by commentators offering these extreme viewpoints, the debaters in Congress soon came to see, as an easier path to some form of claimed success and requiring far less backbone, the suppression of malcontents rather than try to reform all of society and its governance infrastructure.

The perceived need to respond to the steady barrage of stinging newspaper and radio criticism was seen by many in Congress as keeping a hot blowtorch pointed in their direction that they desperately wanted extinguished. The House and Senate leadership of both political parties, which had yearned intensely to fall-in behind a White House initiative that they could later claim credit for supporting or criticize as not having gone far enough, was unavoidably forced into action and opened its own Pandora's box of problems.

Both the House and Senate Judiciary Committees debated resurrecting the old Sedition Act, which had been quietly allowed to expire in 1801, instantly sparking a firestorm of press and broadcast opprobrium. Between the unremitting press criticism and the German fleet maneuvering off the East Coast and believed to be accompanied by submarines towing missile-launching platforms, the Congressional leadership felt itself in a thorny dilemma.

However, standing their ground, those in favor of renewing the Sedition Act argued for giving the President urgently-needed emergency power to suspend the First Amendment's guarantees of inciteful free speech and press, just as the 2nd President, John Adams, had.

John Adams

Citing an immediate need to halt the advocacy of violent insurrection as well as the jingoistic criticisms of the Federal Government seen as intended to force the Nation into war, a grudging committee consensus was reached and an emergency powers bill was drawn. On February 18th, German float planes, launched from *Kriegsmarine* battleships offshore, began flying reconnaissance along a line thirty miles from the mid-Atlantic coast. Although classified "RESTRICTED" by the U.S. Navy, news of the flights was slipped from the German embassy to senior American *Bund* officials in Maryland, who made certain that the Washington *Post* and Baltimore *Sun* were tipped-off. Front-page articles quoting "unnamed sources" led to intense questioning and, ultimately, government confirmation of the aggressive provocations by the German fleet offshore.

On February 20th, the threat from the sea dominated the Nation's news coverage and triggered a storm of demands for action by the White House and Congress. Hand-counting, in pre-computer days, suggested that an agitated 70% of the Nation favored the calming effects of the proposed emergency powers bill while 25% urged an honorable military response. Armed "militia groups" in Idaho and Washington State encamped on farms and proclaimed their readiness to defend their homes and families, if the government couldn't or wouldn't. A serious motion on the floor of the House of Representatives to rename the emergency powers bill "The German Navy Dismissal Act" was ruled "out of order" and allowed to die.

The bill, which came to be known as the National Emergency Powers Act, attracted significant approval by those anxious for any expedient that would quell the deadly disturbances and send the German fleet home. Civil libertarians, who ordinarily would have fought bitterly against any erosion of American freedoms whatsoever, were mollified by the triple fear of being blamed for a continuation of the deadly violence, provoking German naval intercession, and the possible eruption of a Civil War sparked by home-grown militia actions. Co-sponsors quickly came forward and offered additional powers, which were only to be used temporarily during national emergencies declared by the President and agreed by a majority of the Senate.

- Newspaper, magazine, and radio station operations could be suspended by presidential order for up to 90 days, if deemed inciteful of insurrection or civil disobedience or if found to be hindering or otherwise obstructing essential governmental services during emergencies. After 90 days, a federal court order would be necessary for indefinite continuation.

- To control unruly protests and demonstrations that were recently shown too easily to decay into riots, the President was to be given the power to suspend the First Amendment guarantee of peaceful assembly in designated counties or whole states for up to 90 days. Unlicensed demonstrations and marches were to be prohibited within three miles of designated federal buildings, military bases, naval yards, and other enumerated essential facilities. Demonstrations and marches were also prohibited from interfering with interstate commerce, even though the senators and representatives were well aware that local officials would very broadly interpret "interstate" to include any transitory urban vehicle traffic.

- The gun-control lobby actually favored repealing the Second Amendment altogether but jumped at the opportunity to immediately equip the President with the authority to suspend, for indefinite periods, the Second Amendment's right of the people to bear arms and to declare "gun-free" zones around selected government buildings and facilities. This addition satisfied a majority of reluctant lawmakers of both parties, who were upset by all the destabilizing gunfire that had emerged from protest demonstrations and scattered skirmishing.

- From a posture of piety and flushed with their success at getting gun advocates to roll over, the gun-control lobby made a strong case for keeping public order by going beyond simple firearms registration to the confiscation of all privately-owned weapons during a presidentially-declared emergency. They proposed inserting new language in the Fourth Amendment that permitted properly-constituted law enforcement agencies to enter and search any premises in their jurisdictions where it was reasonably suspected firearms or other weapons useful for insurrection might be kept. The accompanying protocol listed edged weapons longer than three inches, explosives of any sort, chemicals that could be weaponized, and all flammables not commonly used as engine fuel or for the heating of dwellings. It was passionately argued that "reasonable suspicion" outweighed the need for a warrant and that that particular provision of the Fourth Amendment could be suspended as well.

Vociferous opponents of this measure were concerned more over the seizure of firearms than they were for the loss of protections against unreasonable searches. They finally compromised on the demand for the addition of "reasonably suspected" (ultimately relenting when challenged, "you have to trust somebody") plus provisions to be codified permitting privately-owned guns to be signed-out from police custodians for brief hunting or target-shooting periods. The use of firearms was to be explicitly forbidden for personal or domicile protection.

- Senior members of the U.S. Justice Department argued passionately in favor of the responsible use of Presidential authority to suspend Constitutional guarantees of the right to *habeas corpus*. Southern Democrats very reluctantly agreed to resurrecting Abraham Lincoln's Civil War suspension of *habeas corpus* and making it available for the President's emergency use. These Constitutional scholars insisted that the Founding Fathers had clearly foreseen the current scenario and, quoting Article I, Section 9, maintained that the Constitution provides for suspension of "the writ of *habeas corpus* when in cases of rebellion or

185

invasion the public safety may require it." However, suspicious of corrupt police and sheriff's departments, the lawmakers gave the President the concomitant authority to declare Martial Law, thereby suspending the authority of state and local courts and giving police powers to the Army and the National Guard. The Martial Law and *habeas corpus* suspension powers were to be strictly limited to periods defined by a majority vote of the Senate.

- During any period for which the Emergency Powers were invoked, the President was authorized to delay or suspend federal elections or, in the President's judgment, to supervise federal, state, and/or local elections, using military or federalized Nation Guard troops. Legislation was drafted to delete that provision of the Twenty-fourth Amendment that prohibited the payment of taxes as a condition of voting in federal, state, and local elections. This latter measure was intended explicitly to prevent negative voting by large numbers of the unemployed.

Congressmen of both houses contented themselves by adding a 72-hour "sunset" provision on any Presidential invocation of emergency powers not ratified by a majority of the Senate. Similar bills passed both Houses with slim majorities and went to a Conference Committee. During a conference committee hearing, Senator Stanley Loomis of Kansas mused that one of the root causes of the recent violence was the continuing depression and economic hardships being experienced by the people. Citing the latest unemployment report at just over 15%, Loomis wondered aloud whether any available remedies might be implemented in concert with the emergency powers. Senator Frank McMakin of Texas declared that he had been having similar thoughts and there ensued a lengthy discussion that resulted in a the inclusion of a Presidential emergency power to temporarily suspend the "involuntary servitude" provision of the Thirteenth Amendment, which had abolished slavery in 1865.

The Conference Committee's consensus to add the partial Thirteenth Amendment suspension to the bill provoked raucous debate in both Houses and across the Nation that threatened to derail the bill seen as reintroducing slavery. Those in favor, however, dug in their heels and persuaded a majority of their colleagues that the emergency powers were absolutely essential in the current economic crisis and that amendments could always be made later. The "involuntary servitude" provision was allowed to stand in the bill that went to the White House.

Citing, as parallel examples, both former President Roosevelt's Works Progress Administration of 1935, which had put some of the depression's unemployed to work, and the current military conscription, the President was to have temporary emergency powers to "draft" unemployed Americans for work that would be beneficial for the Nation. Unemployed workers on a government dole could be conscripted for up to one year and sent at government expense to perform farm, forestry, road-building, or other essential occupations. Those conscripted would be provided shelter, meals, and medical care plus a small stipend. Any who refused induction under the program would be declared ineligible for continued unemployment payments. Drafted unemployed persons would be moved to the camps President Roosevelt had previously used to house the Japanese-American internees. Work teams would cut new roads to areas for additional camps and men with forestry and carpentry abilities would build barracks and other facilities.

Difficulties with the emergency conscription concept were tabled to be solved later. Questions about whether the draftees would be free to quit the program or to leave their camp areas and whether they would be guarded and by whom were set aside. There were no ready answers to how a conscripted laborer would be able to pay his homeward fare, if he wanted to leave and whether "quitters" would qualify for unemployment benefits. The problem of families with children was not satisfactorily resolved but the provision had high-powered advocates and remained in the bill.

Attorney General Talmadge, in particular, provided energetic support for the proposed emergency civilian "draft" that took President Thomas by surprise. Inherently disposed to complete labor freedom guaranteed by law, Thomas felt blind-sided by Talmadge's uncoordinated public support and the President was left with trying to salvage some minor points. He finally gave lukewarm agreement to the civilian draft after Secretary of Labor John L. Lewis nodded his own conditional assent, provided no draftees worked in mines, no work camps were located where they would compete with local union labor, and that all transportation of civilian draftees and associated freight was provided by unionized carriers.

A great number of editors, columnists and radio commentators were livid at the prospect of having to submit to censorship or suspension and raged against the whole proposed legislative package, soberly aware that their barbed criticisms might one day trigger the mechanisms that would silence them, if the hated bill were signed into law by the President. Both Norman Thomas and Robert La Follette had serious misgiving about the emergency powers but did not identify effective, preferable alternatives.

Worried about when the next riots might be incited, Thomas finally came to believe he could sign the bill during a walk in the woods with Vice President Lindbergh at the Camp Hoover presidential retreat in Shenandoah National Park.

Tossing stones into the Rapidan River, the VP convinced Thomas that merely having the law on the books actually changed nothing. The ultimate authority remained in his hands and it was the *invocation* of any or all of the emergency powers that

Camp Hoover

would have significance. If invocation were needed, it would be better to have the law on the books to deter irresponsible behavior than wishful thinking.

Although he couldn't contemplate ever implementing what he saw as such un-American draconian measures, Thomas accepted that, on balance, having the powers available for a *real* emergency had value as a deterrence to unacceptable behavior.

Back in Washington, the President was awakened at 2am and advised that the German fleet had suddenly approached to within thirty miles of the Maryland coast but had immediately withdrawn to its earlier station, forty miles out. Thomas thanked his aide on the phone but couldn't get back to sleep. He tossed and turned, silently struggling to find workable approaches to solving the sea of troubles he felt was drowning him. Although a committed pacifist, he wished that he had stood up to Hitler and kicked him out of Canada and Bermuda while there had been an even chance for success.

The President agonized over having disapproved the Navy's recommendations to force an April 1945 showdown with the German fleet well out in international waters, suspecting the admirals might have been right and wishing he could summon-up comparable personal courage to equal theirs. Thomas feared that history would characterize his actions in this crisis as weak and irresolute and that he would never be able to make his own case satisfactorily.

"Why did this damned military dilemma have to interrupt my reform programs? Why didn't I overrule Jeanette and Henry? But what if they resigned . . . ? Maybe *I* should resign? Would the Germans really shoot rockets at our cities? Suppose the Japanese invaded the West Coast? Where can we find the money for a proper defense? How much can we borrow in this damned depression? Why are the Jews making so much trouble *just now*?" Aware that his jaws were tightly clenched and that his tongue was firmly pressing the backs of his bottom teeth, he rolled over on his side, futilely willing sleep to come.

At just before 5:00am, the sounds of early-to-work vehicle traffic outside on Pennsylvania Avenue spurred him to swing out of bed and get up. As he shuffled to the bathroom, a pulsing headache began from temple to temple. Reaching for aspirin, the haggard, wrinkled, bloodshot-eyed old man looking back at him in the medicine chest mirror convinced Thomas that the job and its unending stream of tangled problems was ruining his health. His reflection convinced him he was beginning to resemble Franklin Roosevelt and experienced a flash of empathy for his predecessor's challenges.

Thomas knew instinctively that every well-intentioned measure in the Emergency Powers bill would be bitterly criticized by one faction or another more concerned with defending civil rights against the slightest erosion, even in the face of continued bloody rioting and the risk of war with an unmatched enemy that wouldn't hesitate to blast American cities with atomic rockets. Knowing that the decision to sign or veto was his alone stirred feelings of wandering loneliness. The President found it bitter to believe that he might have to sacrifice his core values of a lifetime to ransom peace. He took advantage of the early hour to soak in a very hot bath and finally reached his decision.

From the breakfast table, Thomas phoned his Congressional Liaison and asked him to advise the Speaker of the House that he would sign the National Emergency Powers Bill into law without delay. He asked the Vice President to carry the same message to the Senate. Later that day, Thomas insisted on signing the bill at small private Oval Office gathering at which only one Associated Press reporter was present. The President specifically wanted to avoid leaving behind any photographs for the history books.

His closest advisors saw an apologetic and visibly beaten Thomas, who explained to them and the lone AP reporter his unswerving commitment to civil rights and basic freedoms but saw a compelling need for the new law as a check on irresponsible excesses of the kind experienced in recent days. Directing his remarks to the rapidly-scribbling reporter, Thomas lectured the American People on the need for the personal control of emotions and the maintenance of civil discourse as essential for avoiding impressions of appearing provocative to Germany and Japan. "My most important task is keeping the United States out of war and keeping our people safe." He vowed to be ever mindful of his Presidential oath and to assure the transparency of any deliberations about exercising his authority to invoke the new emergency powers. Standing behind the President, Jeanette Rankin reassuringly squeezed his shoulder as the small group departed. Alone, at his Oval Office desk, Thomas counted the number of days left of his presidency on a calendar and yearned to escape to his promised seat on the Supreme Court.

At his kitchen table in Mobile, George Strong was savoring a smelly Havana cigar, whose end he had chewed to resemble a wet brown paintbrush. George was half-listening to Dinah Shore singing *Buttons and Bows* on the radio, half-skimming the *Register's* front-page news of the President's having signed the Emergency Powers Bill. Relishing the recollection of his own personal role, George glowed in deep satisfaction. The Page One article was continued on Page 36, just opposite the classified ads. As he unfolded the paper, he spotted the ad on Page 37, "Wanted to Purchase: Used Radiators."

18

BACK TO REALITY

The "Alternative History" invented in *At Least I Know I'm Free* ends here. The story's objective is to offer a plausible scenario in which Americans could lose their basic freedom and liberties and the story has reached the stage where the necessary mechanisms to allow that to happen have been put fictitiously in-place, ready for use. From this point, any number of continuations to various conclusions are possible and the reader is free to imagine them.

Perhaps the evil Reinhard Heydrich has ordered his distant cousin, George Strong, and George's cohorts to further actions that may force President Thomas' hand and an invocation of the "National Emergency Powers Act." Perhaps America is to be forced to some step that invites a German nuclear attack - small or large - followed by a subsequent overthrow of the U.S. Government and the ascendancy of a dictatorship protected by Hitler. Is there a larger role for Eugene Talmadge and what might his plans be for the likes of George Strong? The question to be answered is whether a lack of decisive statesmanship by the American leadership and a surrender to intense foreign and domestic pressures could have lasting disastrous consequences.

This point in the story also offers a lens for reëxamining the words of Lee Greenwood's popular song, *God Bless the USA*. Is it a fair question to ask how Americans, often undereducated in the details of American history, interpret the line, *"Where at least know I'm free?"* Has it become a common American interpretation that freedom is an automatic American birthright that comes without cost, without an acknowledgement of debt to earlier providers and defenders, or any obligation for self-imposed restraint?

Ronald Reagan

President Ronald Reagan reminded Americans often that freedom isn't free. President Reagan's reminders acknowledged that freedom, so easily taken for granted as a birthright and apparently available perpetually without cost or obligation, has been and is still being paid for by American citizens who step up to the most serious challenges.

Confronting difficult challenges by "doing the right thing" with courage and integrity are the unending installment payments that buy liberty and freedoms for yet a while longer until new challenges emerge to be handled, in turn, by succeeding generations of strong citizens. These payments fall heaviest on those who fight against armed enemies and criminals. Heavy payments are also made by those closest to the nation's defenders: the loved-ones who support and encourage members of the uniformed services, police, and first responders who go in harm's way. The nation's elected and appointed officials at all levels of government contribute substantially when they make or recommend the hard decisions to do the right thing made necessary by serious challenges.

President Reagan is also remembered for his vision of America as a "shining city upon a hill." Borrowing this vision from the 1630 words of Massachusetts Governor John Winthrop, Mr. Reagan saw the shining city as freedom's beacon light and his example has been often paraphrased. Perhaps another such paraphrase may be permitted here.

That shining city on a hill needed to be built up there by capable, willing hands. Going uphill always requires extra effort and, as hillsides always invite downward sliding, that extra effort can never end. To keep a shining city aloft in good repair, steady on that hill, a long line of new capable and willing hands is needed indefinitely. Finding and contributing the effort and discipline to keep the shining city "up" are challenges to American citizens that will always be greater than those lesser commitments and distractions that would allow the shining city to slide in descent. This should be one answer to what is meant by "At Least I Know I'm Free" in Lee Greenwood's song, *God Bless the USA*.

ANNEX A

THE FREEDOMS THAT COULD HAVE BEEN LOST

Lost Freedom	Guarantor of the Freedom	Fictional Cause of Loss
Freedom of speech in press and broadcasting	U.S. Constitution, 1st Amendment	Presidential invocation of the National Emergency Powers Act
Freedom of peaceful assembly		
Right to bear arms	U.S. Constitution, 2nd Amendment	
Freedom from unreasonable search and seizure	U.S. Constitution, 4th Amendment	
Right to *habeas corpus* and due process of law	U.S. Constitution, Art I, Section 9 (2) and the 5th Amendment	Presidential declaration of Martial Law and suspension *of habeas corpus*
Right to liberty and equal protection of the law	U.S. Constitution, 14th Amendment	Presidential invocation of the National Emergency Powers Act
Freedom from slavery and involuntary servitude	U.S. Constitution, 13th Amendment	
Right to vote and that right not contingent on payment of taxes	U.S. Constitution, 24th Amendment	Delay or suspension of federal elections or supervision of state and local elections by the President under the National Emergency Powers Act

History teaches that grave threats to liberty often come in times of urgency, when constitutional rights seem too extravagant to endure.

- Justice Thurgood Marshall (1989)

ANNEX B

WHAT IF EPILOGUE:

WHAT DIDN'T HAPPEN BECAUSE THE U.S. DIDN'T FIGHT

- The Axis powers, Germany, Japan, and Italy, were not defeated and extended their world domination into the 21st Century.

- Italy was never invaded by the Allies and enforced harsh occupations in Greece and North Africa. Benito Mussolini maintained warm relations with Hitler into his retirement and old age.

- Baseball did not come to Japan and no Japanese ballplayers made it to Major League Baseball.

- Soccer remained an obscure sport in the U.S. and never caught on with American kids.

- The UN wasn't formed.

- The USSR was humbled and diminished by the effects of Operation *Barbarossa*. Stalin was overthrown by Marshall Zhukov, who was succeeded by Nikita Khrushchev, however the country remained a third-world state. The USSR never developed nuclear weapons and was never permitted by Germany to export communism to the countries of eastern Europe, which remained under brutal *Nazi* occupation. Without Soviet support, Fidel Castro did not impose Communism on the Cuban people.

- NATO wasn't formed.

- China was savagely enslaved by Japan and subjected to Japanese-induced famines contrived to reduce China's population. Mao Zedung last appeared in history in a Chinese troop column withdrawing before a Japanese advance.

- Under Japanese occupation, China did not become communist and did not export communism to Korea or French Indo-China, all of which were occupied by Japan.

- The names of Ho Chi Minh, Vo Nguyen Giap, and other leading Vietnamese figures appear on Japanese POW rosters but later references are lost in time.

- The Korean and Vietnam Wars did not take place.

- Douglas MacArthur retired from the Army and ran unsuccessfully for political office. He wrote several books that tried to explain how the U.S. had missed opportunities to resist the Axis powers. George Patton resigned his Army commission after accusations of harsh recruit mistreatment; he spent his remaining years criticizing Army "softness."

- Following his retirement to Kansas, Dwight Eisenhower entered a successful business practice, never running for political office

- Most of the other key military and naval personalities had similar post-retirement experiences. The senior leadership of the Army finished-out their careers and quietly entered retirement.

- The Navy devolved to become a coastal defense force in which Admirals Nimitz and Halsey had little to offer; they both retired.

- Charles de Gaulle lived out his days in exile in Montreal, never returning to France.

- Bernard Law Montgomery retired from the British Army after the surrender at Dunkirk and later had a successful career as a County Councilman.

- The US Army retained responsibility for a drastically reduced aviation mission. The U.S. Air Force was not separated from the Army. Henry "Hap" Arnold reorganized the Army Air Forces and was acknowledged as having developed first-rate air defenses, which were never tested by German or Japanese air forces.

- Hitler's genocide was so thorough that there were no European Jews left to migrate to Palestine. British jurisdiction over Palestine was terminated by the Axis powers and Palestinians were not displaced from their homeland. The State of Israel was not established.

- Oil production and distribution from mid-East states was strictly regulated by Germany, which interfered, to varying degrees, in the foreign affairs of all the oil-producing Arab states. OPEC was not formed as Germany directed pricing structures that served its own interests.

- Without an Israel to unite against, the Arab League remained a toothless figurehead organization. Individual Arab nations prioritized tribal and Muslim sect relationships, preserving centuries-old internal squabbles and hatreds.

- No Arab state democratized. All remained monarchies or became dictatorships, following regicidal revolutions. The oil wealth of Arab states was concentrated in the hands of a privileged very few favored by Germany while general populations were impoverished and severely repressed. Arab women made no significant social, educational or professional gains, remaining under the tight control of husbands, fathers, and brothers.

- The British Commonwealth dissolved. Canada, India, Australia, and New Zealand all became independent. Japan displaced the British from Hong Kong when its occupation of China was complete. English did not become the world's most commonly-used language.

- Chiang Kai-shek and the remnants of the Chinese Army fled to Taiwan to escape capture by the Japanese. Upon Chiang's death, resistance faded and Japan occupied Taiwan after an unopposed invasion. The terrible bloody rampages inflicted on other populations subjugated by the Japanese army were experienced by the Taiwanese but especially so by the remnant mainland Chinese troops.

- Neither Germany nor Japan developed powerful North American consumer markets. No German or Japanese automobiles, cameras, or electronics competed well with rival American products and were rarely seen. Americans never developed a taste for *sushi* or German beers; *sauerkraut* became "brineslaw" and *wurst* was discontinued as a descriptor of specialty sausages. American women never favored Italian shoes or handbags and pizza remained a home-baked specialty only in Italian-American homes, never rising to the status of a briskly competed delivery product in every town in the U.S.

- Its heavy bomber market dried-up by the armistice limitations, U.S. aircraft manufacturers were eclipsed by their principal German rivals, Heinkel, Dornier, and Messerschmidt. The world's civil aviation fleets flew German aircraft and it was Messerschmidt AG that supplied the engines for the first commercial jets.

- The first men in space and on the moon were ex-*Luftwaffe* test pilots. It was a *swastika* and not the Stars & Stripes that was planted on the moon by astronauts.

- The British abandonment – in the face of *Luftwaffe* air attacks – of its interception of *Enigma*-enciphered radio traffic and of their decryption efforts at Bletchley Park, stalled man's development of computers. Rather than U.S. development of a giant computer industry, that supplied business and personal computers to the whole world, that role fell to the Japanese. Microsoft was never incorporated; Bill Gates became a successful insurance salesman and Steve Jobs had a career as a high school physics teacher.

- John Wayne never wore a World War II uniform in a movie. No great wartime epics, such as *12 O'Clock High*, *The Longest Day*, *Victory at Sea*, and *Saving Private Ryan* were filmed.

ANNEX C

END NOTES AND GROUND TRUTH

End Notes

The author welcomes comments, questions, and alternative views. Contact Bill Grayson at *SheffordPress@earthlink.net*.

Ground Truth

In the earth sciences, actual field checks to determine "Ground Truth" are performed at subject locations to confirm observations made via photography, radar, or other remote sensors. The term "Ground Truth" has been adapted routinely for use in military exercises to distinguish between what is real versus what has been written into a notional script. Thus, a military exercise scenario might include, as "Ground Truth," an actual road leading to an actual town, while the script might place "imaginary" enemy fortifications on either side of the road. The term "Ground Truth" is used in *At Least I Know I'm Free* to differentiate the factual record from the book's alternative history.

General Observation

At Least I Know I'm Free uses a fictitious story as a device for exploring how devastating change might have befallen the U.S. In the fictitious story, the putative cooperation of corrupt. law enforcement officers and agencies with the Ku Klux Klan and the German-American *Bund* is at the heart of the story's 1940s timeframe. It is emphasized here that, in the fictitious story's Ground Truth, organizations such as the KKK and the *Bund* committed heinous felonious acts but where any sworn law enforcement officers may have participated in those felonies, they were not carrying out official policies or direction from their agencies and were acting outside of their sworn oaths to serve and protect the citizens they represented.

A large body of published documentation alleges that some such unauthorized cooperation did occur in many parts of the U.S. during the period at issue and that some may even continue to the present day. As recently as June of 2006, U.S. Supreme Court Justice Antonin Scalia argued (in *Hudson v. Michigan*) that "police behavior is improved from earlier eras." Interested readers' research is simplified by *Googling* key terms such as: *police+KKK,; police+lynching; police+racism*, etc. Additionally, the website *http://www.fff.org/freedom/1093c.asp* documents the allegedly corrupt recent practices of many police departments in seizing out-of-state cars from innocent drivers on the probable-cause pretext of transporting illegal drugs. *Google* searches for: *police+corruption; police+extortion; police+abuse* will pull up many additional sources claiming to present factual information.

It is conceded that *At Least I Know I'm Free* exaggerates the actual historical record of the 1940s but suggests that the excesses described were plausible. Readers are reminded that the book's purpose is not to accuse or attack reputations. Its purpose is to describe a fictional but reasonable scenario in which failures to act responsibly and lawfully and failures to take risks while defending right could erode defenses of basic American freedoms and contribute to their loss. To the extent that the story's descriptions of failures are beyond plausibility, so then is the plausibility of the general scenario.

Ground Truth In the "Foreword"

FDR's "Four Freedoms" is a part of his State of the Union address of January 6, 1941, eleven months before the Pearl Harbor attack. In considering whether the U.S. went to war almost a year later only to protect American freedoms, consider FDR's choice of words, stressing in repetition, *"everywhere in the world."*

State of the Union Address - January 6:

"The American people began to visualize what the downfall of democratic nations might mean to our own democracy.

The first is freedom of speech and expression -- *everywhere in the world.*

The second is freedom of every person to worship God in his own way-- *everywhere in the world.*

The third is freedom from want, which, translated into world terms, means economic understandings which will secure to every nation a healthy peacetime life for its inhabitants -- *everywhere in the world.*

The fourth is freedom from fear, which, translated into world terms, means a world-wide reduction of armaments to such a point and in such a thorough fashion that no nation

will be in a position to commit an act of physical aggression against any neighbor --*anywhere in the world.*

[FDR continued] That is no vision of a distant millennium. It is a definite basis for a kind of world attainable in our own time and generation. That kind of world is the very antithesis of the so-called "new order" of tyranny which the dictators seek to create with the crash of a bomb."

[*http://www.libertynet.org/edcivic/fdr.html*].

Suggested additional reading for those interested in how the events and close calls of World War II can be spun: In *Rising Sun Victorious* ISBN 1-85367-446-X), Peter G. Tsouras has collected a number of short essays that present alternative histories of the principal Pacific engagements of the war.

A Legitimate Question: Was War between the U.S. and Germany Inevitable? In 1941?

Among the several actual villains in *At Least I Know I'm Free* are the members of the German-American *Bund*, who were ideologically allied with the isolationist "America First" organization, which numbered in excess of a million Americans. Throw the KKK and a politically-potent faction of Irish-Americans into the mix and a knotty tangle of motives and emotions complicates the roles of the players and the pressures they brought to bear on the Roosevelt Administration in the months before the attack on Pearl Harbor.

Ostensibly (but not completely), the America Firsters were fundamentally anti-war and sought to hold FDR to his solemn pledge to keep the U.S. out of foreign wars. The German-American *Bund* specifically favored *Nazi* Germany, approving Germany's European exploits without examining too closely the brutal tactics used against European populations. With links to and overlaps with the KKK, the *Bund* would never have stood in defense of Europe's Jewry against *Nazi* predations. And, behind the scenes, many Irish-Americans were strongly anti-British and would have been pleased to see the United Kingdom defeated, especially if Northern Ireland were to achieve its independence and reunite with the Irish Free State (Ireland), which had won its own independence from Britain in 1922. As a political bloc, Irish-Americans stood with the America Firsters, supporting isolationism.

Into this already-twisted set of relationships four additionally vexing ingredients must be blended into the swarm of troubles challenging Roosevelt. First, regardless of his promises to the American people, a pragmatic FDR was personally convinced that Hitler was a credibly dangerous threat to U.S. freedom and that the U.S. would have to neutralize this threat eventually, probably by force of arms. German U-Boat attacks on U.S. Navy vessels in 1941 solidified FDR's conviction but his hands were tied.

Second, what was probably a "German" map forged by the office of British Security Coordination (BSC) in New York convinced FDR that Hitler was planning to attack the U.S. after subduing and redrawing the borders of South and Central America. (See the review of William Boyd's book *Restless*, ISBN 0-679-31478-3 in the *Guardian* of August 17, 2006). On Navy Day, October 27, 1941, in a specific reference to the map provided by BSC, FDR actually claimed "This map makes clear the *Nazi* design not only against South America but against the United States as well."

The third ingredient was the daunting prospect of resisting Hitler from the U.S. homeland without European bases from which to stage. FDR's nightmare vision of a defeated Britain leaving the U.S. and Canada to stand alone caused him great anxiety and forced his clever use of loopholes in the neutrality laws to continue supplying the U.K.

Finally, after nearly completing two presidential terms, Roosevelt had a double dilemma: a decision to break with tradition and seek an unprecedented third term and then to win reëlection by an isolationist electorate while concealing his true attitude, expecting inevitable war with Germany.

The *Bund* and America Firsters quickly collapsed as a political force with the Japanese attack on Pearl Harbor. FDR specifically asked the Congress for a declaration of war only against Japan and an enraged Congress (with Jeanette Rankin[103] of Montana casting the lone "no" vote) swiftly delivered. FDR did not ask for and Congress did not declare war on *Nazi* Germany. Instead, ignoring

---

[103] Prior to being elected to the House of Representatives a second time, Rankin supported the 1938 "Ludlow Amendment," which would have mandated the approval of a majority of the states prior to any Congressional declaration of war. The amendment was defeated by a very small margin. Had the proposed amendment been approved and ratified, FDR's military response to Japan and Germany might have had different outcomes.

pleas from Herman Göring, Hitler declared war on the U.S.[104] Now released from his "no-war" promises and backed by an outraged nation, FDR was free to assume the mantle of wartime leader in his third new term.

But suppose Hitler had followed Göring's advice? What if Hitler decided to merely watch from Europe as the U.S. was distracted by war with Japan while he dealt with Britain and the Soviet Union? With Britain and the U.S.S.R. subdued, wouldn't the U-Boat problem in the Atlantic have resolved itself? Regardless of the outcome of the Pacific War, is it at all plausible that a totally victorious Hitler, ruling a completely undamaged Germany, might have developed atomic warheads for V2 and V3 rockets and then aggressively provoked the U.S.? Might those warheads have intimidated the U.S. into appeasement and renewed isolationism? Isn't the fictitious scenario of *At Least I Know I'm Free* plausible to some degree?

Ground Truth In Chapter 1, "Pearl Harbor and the Collapse of American Resolve"

- Actually, Vice Admiral Chuichi Nagumo, the Japanese task force commander for the Pearl Harbor operation, was unsure of the locations of the U.S. Navy Pacific Fleet aircraft carriers, which were not in port during the December 7th attack. He decided to cancel planned follow-up strikes and took the task force back to Japan. The chapter's account of continued Japanese strikes against the Hawaiian

---

[104] According to Kenneth W. Hechler, then a major assigned to the U.S. Army Europe Historical Division, Hermann Göring told him during a prison-cell interview that he believed the U.S. was potentially too powerful and warned Hitler, "I consider it a duty to prevent America going to war with us." (*World War II Magazine, September 2006*). The Hechler interview is the sole source for this claim by Göring. Detractors are unwilling to accept this single uncorroborated source and/or categorize Göring as a fabricating braggart.

Islands and the U.S. West Coast is mostly but not quite entirely fictitious. Shortly after the Pearl Harbor attack, a California oil refinery and the city of Hilo were shelled by surfaced Japanese submarines.

- The Hawaiian island of Kauai was not invaded by Japan and no Marine detachment was wiped out there. Japanese submarines actually did operate off the U.S. West Coast and did sink ships very close to the coast. Eleven Japanese submarines actually had been modified to carry floatplanes and Sub I-25 actually launched three *Kugisho* E14 "Glen" floatplane bombing raids on the U.S. West Coast. In the chapter, the fictitious account of two Eureka, California children being killed by Japanese bombs commemorates two Bedfordshire children, Monica R. and Edwin K. Phillips, senselessly killed in their farmhouse by the *Luftwaffe* one night in 1940.

Kugisho E14 "Glen"
Artwork by Artur Juszczak,
© Mushroom Model Publications

- Most World War II histories gloss over or completely eliminate consideration of the panicky levels of citizen morale and confidence in the U.S. in the immediate aftermath of the Pearl Harbor attack, when invasion and air raids were realistically expected. Details of the actual "Battle of Los Angeles" in February 1942 are little-remembered in the U.S. (Suggested additional reading: *http://www. sfmuseum.org/*

hist9/aaf2.html and *The Army Air Forces in World War II*, v.1, pp. 277-286, Washington, D.C. Office of Air Force History).

- Japan actually did invade and occupy the Aleutian islands of Attu and Kiska in June 1942 and did ship Aleut Eskimo natives to imprisonment in Japan. In August 1943, the islands were retaken at a cost of four thousand U.S. casualties. (Suggested additional reading: *http://www.worldwar2database.com/html/aleutians.htm*).

- Stations *Hypo* and *Cast* were actually U.S. Navy COMINT sites. On Oahu, Captain Joseph Rocheford was the OIC and Tom Dyer, Joe Finnegan, and Ham Wright were Japanese radio traffic analysts, who made invaluable contributions to the war in the Pacific. However, the Tokyo broadcast to submarines scenario is fictitious.

- Much of the credit for Japan's enormous success at surprising U.S. forces at Pearl Harbor is due to the Japanese Navy's highly disciplined adherence to an integrated communications security and communications deception plan. Implemented weeks before Vice Admiral Chuichi Nagumo's task force headed east into the Pacific, the plan lulled U.S. Navy COMINT into reporting to their principal intelligence customers in Hawaii and Washington that Japan's major strike assets - especially the aircraft carriers - remained in Japanese home waters. (Suggested additional reading: World War II Magazine, *Blinded by the Rising Sun: Japanese Radio Deception Before Pearl Harbor*, by R.J. Hanyok, December 2006).

- Chester Nimitz did succeed Admiral Husband Kimmel, who was relieved of command after the December 7th attack.

- The Station Hypo "intercept log" given in the chapter is completely fictitious but is a plausible facsimile of how such a log might have appeared, if the U.S. Navy had been monitoring Japanese broadcasts to deployed submarines. In the log:

    - "in here" is the intercept operator's notation indicating his start of collection of a particular target

    - "VAW" are the intercept operator's initials

    - "8285 and 7730" are the two frequencies the operator is monitoring

    - A series of "Vs" is commonly used to assist a distant listener fine-tune his radio receiver

    - Numbers with a "Z" suffix, such as "1336Z" are military times on a 24-hour clock, based on Greenwich Mean Time, referred to during World War II as "Zebra Time." 1336 hours = 1:36pm in Greenwich, England, which is 3:36am or 0336 hours, on the next calendar day, in Hawaii. In the current era, "Z" has been changed to "ZULU" in the phonetic alphabet and Greenwich Mean Time is often referred to as Coordinated Universal Time or "UTC" as translated from its French rendition.

- Faced with very difficult decisions, the U.S. Navy gallantly stepped up to engage Japan vigorously in the Pacific without waiting to repair or replace the Pearl Harbor losses.

- Actually, before the U.S. and Germany were at war, three U.S. Navy destroyers, USS *Greer, Kearney* and *Reuben James* were torpedoed by U-Boats in the

North Atlantic. Many Allied vessels were torpedoed or shelled by German commerce raiders off the East Coast of the U.S. before the U.S. entered the war.

- After the Pearl Harbor attack, FDR's decision to relocate and intern Japanese-Americans away from the West Coast was, in fact, based on valid Communications Intelligence. That intelligence informed that some among the Japanese-American population were already committing espionage for Japan and would conduct sabotage, in the event of a Japanese invasion. (Suggested additional reading: David J. Lowman, *Magic: The Untold Story*, ISBN 0-9602736-1-1).

Chapter 1 Photo Credits:

Japanese "Zero," seaplane on Japanese submarine and Joseph Stalin - Library of Congress Prints and Photographs Division.

Japanese "Glen" - Artwork by Artur Juszczak, © Mushroom Model Publications

Soviet "Sturmovik" -USSR TASS News Agency

Ground Truth In Chapter 2, "The Fighting Ends In Europe"

The chapter is totally fictitious. In a demonstration of legendary heroism, small boat owners, led by the Royal Navy (*Operation Dynamo*), did successfully evacuate 250,000 British soldiers from the beach at Dunkirk, whilst under the fire of German guns and aircraft. *Dynamo* prevented the Germans from having a quarter-million British POWs as negotiating bargaining chips. A nearly unknown assist to the Dunkirk rescue was provided by three British regiments under Brigadier Claude Nicholson, which held the left flank for three days, suffering heavy casualties. The men of those regiments had been told they could not be evacuated and all who survived became POWs.

The courage shown by the British people and all of British forces during a period of great sacrifice and bleakness stands as a model for emulation. Chicksands Priory, the site of the principal RAF Communications Intelligence listening post for collecting *Luftwaffe Enigma*-enciphered radio signals, was actually bombed twice during 1940 but the RAF and WAAF wireless operators stayed at their radios until the war ended in May 1945.

Kampfgruppe 55

Chicksands Priory was indeed damaged by bombs dropped from KG-55 He 111s and, although beautifully restored in the mid-1990s, some of the 1940 bomb damage remains visible to the practiced eye. (Suggested additional reading: *Chicksands: A Millennium of History,* ISBN 0-9633208-1-5).

The Soviets gave German forces in Operation *Barbarossa* no respite during the cold winter and there was no agreed truce line. The map is fictitious. The Soviets held at Stalingrad after which the Germans were steadily forced back out of the USSR, through Poland and to their last stand at home.

Chapter 2 Photo Credits:

"Chain Home" radar masts – RAF Museum, Hendon

Chicksands Priory – author

Jeannette Rankin – Library of Congress Prints and Photographs Division

Admiral Ernest King – U.S. Navy

Ground Truth In Chapter 3, "The 1942 Mid-Term Elections"

The scenario described and the election results are totally fictitious.

Chapter 3 Photo Credits:

Charles Lindbergh - Library of Congress Prints and Photographs Division (New York World-Telegram collection)

A lynching - Library of Congress Prints and Photographs Division

Ground Truth in Chapter 4, "1943 - The Armistice"

The chapter's scenario is almost totally fictitious with a few exceptions. Fort Miles on the Delaware coast actually did receive two 16-inch guns, which were installed in a new Battery Smith. Those two guns, however, were not salvaged from Pearl Harbor.

Chapter 4 Photo Credits:

Franklin D. Roosevelt - Library of Congress Prints and Photographs Division.

16-inch gun on Coast Artillery mount (on display at Aberdeen Proving Grounds' Artillery Museum) - author.

Ground Truth in Chapter 5, "The Axis Triumphant"

The chapter is fictitious but wrapped around some actual history.

"Japan's Asian Mastery"

- Japan's savage treatment of foreign soldiers and civilians under their control is well documented history.

- Admiral Isoroku Yamamoto, architect of the Pearl Harbor attack, was not elevated to the Japanese aristocracy and did not survive the war. A planning message detailing the itinerary of his inspection trip to Japanese-held Pacific islands in 1943 was intercepted and decoded by the U.S. Navy. Knowing where to find him, P-38s of the 339th Fighter Squadron, shot down Yamamoto's "Betty" bomber. Yamamoto died in the crash. As recently as May 2006, controversy remains over whether Captain Tom Lanphier or Lieutenant Rex Barber should be credited with the shoot-down.

"Axis Forces Press the Soviets"

Mostly but not entirely fictitious.

- "As the *Nazi* army galloped for Moscow, the Soviet Union was in pandemonium. Hitler's Operation *Barbarossa* aimed more than 3300 tanks, 7200 pieces of artillery, and 2800 aircraft not only at Mother Russia but also at her industrial capacity. Stalin moved factory production . . ." safely beyond the Ural Mountains. According to historian Pat McTaggart, "the Soviets had lost industrial potential during the first six months of the war and could not gear up until the summer of 1942 but during that time, the U.S. kept the Red Army going." Excerpted from the September/October 2005 issue of *History Channel Magazine*, in the article *Supply-Side Warfare*.

- The epic Soviet stand at Stalingrad (since renamed Volgograd) is aptly described in the chapter as having cost terrible losses on both sides and leaving the city in ruins. However, the Battle of Stalingrad really was a key turning point in the war, marking the German military's high-point from which it began its downward slide to defeat in 1945. Stalingrad was designated a "Hero City" (*Город Гэроя*) of the former USSR.

- The crippling labor strike and fearful suspension of the Atlantic convoys following losses to U-Boats are fictitious. At painful cost to lives and merchant ships, the U.S. kept the Soviet war effort alive by convoying essential supplies on the "Murmansk Run" from the U.S. East Coast to the Soviet Arctic. Alternate convoy routes via the Persian Gulf to Iran and then overland to the USSR or across the Pacific to Vladivostok across huge portions of the Pacific Ocean dominated by the Japanese Navy were less-preferred options. The North Atlantic convoys braved the U-Boat predations through the worst of it. Toward the end of 1942, U.S. naval and air forces began steadily pushing the U-Boats and *Kriegsmarine* surface vessels away from North America and merchant marine losses were significantly reduced.

- The USSR did not declare war against Japan until August 1945, right after the A-Bomb attack on Hiroshima. The Japanese neither blockaded the Soviet East Coast nor attacked Soviet shipping in the Sea of Okhost or the Sea of Japan.

- Japan did not bluff an invasion of Siberia and Stalin was not forced to withdraw forces from the western front in response. Finland was actually invaded by the Soviets in 1940 but only her eastern third was occupied. The IL-2 *Sturmovik* fighter-bomber actually was plagued by crippling maintenance problems but the emergency deployment to the Manchurian border and loss of the aircraft are fictitious. The Soviet Air Force was also equipped with U.S.-supplied P-39 *Aeracobra* fighters, delivered by the trans-Atlantic convoys.

"The Axis Dominant Across Europe and the Mid-East"

Totally fictitious. The fighting in Europe did not end in 1943 but actually continued until May 1945. There was no *"Z-E Day"* celebrated by Germany; the Allies celebrated V-E Day on May 8, 1945. The "guest worker" program for Soviets in Poland and Germany is fictitious but, while the war was still being fought, the Germans actually forced many thousands of conquered peoples into harsh forced labor that many were unable to survive.

"Latin America"

The scenario is factual; the *Nazi* thinking is fictitious.

"The Mid-East"

The Grand Mufti of Jerusalem is an actual historical figure who indeed raised an Islamic *Nazi* army, which was placed at Hitler's disposal. The photo shows him reviewing his troops, whose collar tabs read "SS."

- The Mufti sought and received Hitler's approval for anti-semitic crimes and a "final solution" for Jews in the Mid-East. However, the "death march" described in the story is fictitious.

- On March 15, 2007, the University of Leeds (UK) cancelled a planned history talk on the links between the *Nazis* and Islamic anti-semitism. *Daily Telegraph* (London), March 15, 2007.

"The Channel Islands and Bermuda"

The Germans actually did occupy the Channel Islands immediately after the fall of France in 1940 and staged bomber raids from the islands during the Battle of Britain. Bermuda was neither invaded nor occupied by Germany during World War II. Actually, the U.S. operated anti-submarine patrols from Bermuda to protect convoys from 1942 to 1945.

"A German Presence on the North American Doorstep"

- Sainte Pierre and Miquelon were not ceded to Germany after the fall of France in 1940, were not occupied or renamed, and remain French territories in North America today. No German radio intercept station operated from Sainte Pierre, however a station such as the fictitious "*VB-51*" could have collected and interpreted signals as described in the story. The choice of "*VB-51*" as a station designator commemorates the former "USA-51."

- In 1940, after the conquest of Denmark, the Germans actually established and operated weather stations in Greenland. FDR declared Greenland to be within the Western Hemisphere applicability of the Monroe Doctrine and proclaimed a vital U.S. interest in keeping Greenland free from German control. A British and Norwegian force destroyed the weather stations and captured Danish meteorologists in the pay of the Germans. A German ship was later captured by the Royal Navy transporting 50 Germans to Greenland.

- The Germans did not occupy Iceland but the British actually did. In May 1940, Iceland was "invaded" by the British Army. U.S. troops relieved the British in 1941. In July 2006, the U.S. advised the Icelandic government that military air and naval units based on the island would be withdrawn. When U.S. units have left, Iceland will be without military defenses as she was in 1940.

- During World War II, Churchill frequently signed his personal correspondence to President Roosevelt as "Former Naval Person."

- Churchill was actually hopeful that the U.S. would enter the war against Germany. Immediately after the Pearl Harbor attack, the U.S. declared war only on Japan, to Churchill's disappointment. However, Hitler then declared war on the U.S. and Churchill got his wish via an unimagined, strange path.

- *W3HUV* was actually FDR's callsign, used by the VC-54 *Sacred Cow* in the days before "Air Force One" was used, however, the Sacred Cow did not enter service until later than the chapter's fictitious meeting takes place. This callsign has been reassigned and is currently in use by another licensee. The COMINT traffic analysis described concerning the flight to Quebec is fictitious but plausible.

- Roosevelt actually did attend a wartime summit meeting in the Chateau Frontenac hotel with Prime Ministers McKenzie King and Winston Churchill. The meeting agenda, however, dealt with the much different European Theater strategy and did not address a German presence on Sainte Pierre and Miquelon, which did not exist. Sumner Welles did not go to Quebec with FDR.

Although an accomplished diplomat representing the U.S. in Latin America, Welles was a notorious homosexual in the era before acceptance and had been recommended for removal from sensitive duties as a security risk.

Pertinent to this alternative history is the reality of Sumner Welles' actual unseemly pre-war association with Herman Göring, which raised eyebrows in official Washington but led neither to Welles' censure or being disciplined. The photo, at right, shows the two men in 1940, discussing art at Göring's home.

Chapter 5 Photo Credits:

Emperor Hirohito, Admiral Yamamoto, Francisco Franco, J. Von Ribbentrop, Welles and Göring - Library of Congress Prints and Photographs Division
Ju. 88, Me. 109bf and VC-54 "Sacred Cow" - U .S. Air Force
Chateau Frontenac – Author
Grand Mufti - Library of Congress Prints and Photographs Division (New York World-Telegram collection)

Ground Truth In Chapter 6, "Post-Armistice America Swallows Her Pride and Reprioritizes"

Mostly fictitious; the West Point conference did not occur. The U.S. Interstate Highway system actually was originally described in the Congressionally-authorizing legislation as a national defense highway system. Also, shortly before the U.S. was drawn into the war, a program of strengthening coast artillery defenses had been started. Battery Smith at Fort Miles, Delaware, actually did receive and install two 16-inch guns, originally intended for Iowa-class battleships.

"Dawn of the Nuclear Age - Race for the Bomb"

- Secretary of War Stimson did not meet Albert Einstein at Princeton. However, Leo Szilard, a colleague of Einstein's, persuaded him to write to FDR, alerting him of German atomic capabilities.

- Neils Bohr is an actual historical character. He was indeed a leading nuclear researcher, who stayed in Denmark during the German occupation. Aware of his imminent arrest by the *Gestapo*, he escaped to Sweden and eventually was helped to reach the U.S. where he became a part of the U.S. Manhattan Project. The story's account of an RAF pilot playing it safe and abandoning Bohr to the *Gestapo* is fictitious. Bohr provided no support to the German atomic bomb effort although asked to do so by the German nuclear physicist, Werner Heisenberg. The play, *Copenhagen*, by Michael Frayn is an Alternative History of how the World War II outcome might have been different, if the Germans had obtained Bohr's help.

- In truth, there were members of the Manhattan Project with confused loyalties but not about helping Germany; some of the leading researchers gave atomic secrets to communist agents for relay to the Soviet Union. The most notorious spies were Julius and Ethel Rosenberg, whose guilt was confirmed by intercepted messages not decoded until after the war. (Suggested additional reading: *Google* "Venona Papers").

- In Chapter 5, the deliberate sabotage of the Manhattan Project by researchers sympathetic to Germany is fictitious. The historical record does not suggest any such motives or attempts, however, some of the key scientists regretted having provided the U.S. with an atomic weapon.

"German Missiles and the Fall of the British Empire"

- Generals von Halder and von Falkenhorst are actual World War II historical figures but their involvement in planning attacks on Britain are fictitious.

- Some of the *Sealion* personalities and the scenario for the German invasion of Britain are fictitious as are the estimates of invasion troop strengths.

- The chapter's descriptions of German invasion sealift problems are offered as plausible fiction. However, the missile statistics are actual: 9521 V1 "Buzz Bombs" and then 1150 V2 rockets were actually launched from sites in Northern Europe at targets in Southern England. The V2 range, with a one-ton high explosive warhead, was actually 200 miles with a Circular Error Probable of 11 miles - grossly inaccurate.

- In the chapter, Herman Göring is portrayed as promising whatever *Luftwaffe* air support may be needed without consulting any documentation. This portrayal is consistent with Göring's casual, overconfident assurances of the *Luftwaffe's* easy neutralization of the Royal Air Force and establishment of air superiority over Britain. Actually, the legendary defense of British skies by the RAF's "Few" forced the cancellation of the *Sealion* invasion.

- At war's end, the Germans were actually working on extending the V2's range to 350 miles by increasing the capacity of its fuel tanks and were actually experimenting with launches from submarine-launched floating platforms. Radio newscaster Edward R. Murrow actually did report from wartime London and the Chapter 6 remarks attributed to him are a close paraphrase of his actual admonition to his U.S. listeners.

- Baron Oshima, the Japanese Ambassador to Berlin, was actually a priceless source of U.S. intelligence. The Baron was a close confidante of Hitler and his messages back to Tokyo were actually intercepted and decrypted by U.S. COMINT. More on the Baron's correspondence in the notes for Chapter 12, below.

- The chapter's suggestion that the British successfully created the deception that coastal waters could be set afire to repel invasion from the sea is factual. Part of this deception included the deployment of dummy facilities and equipment in the North Sea village of Shingle Street, Suffolk. Continuing to the present day, myth and countermyth accounts concern an attempted German invasion on a rocky (shingle) beach in Suffolk by a large number of troops wearing British Army uniforms stripped from the dead at Dunkirk in June 1940. Adding to the intrigue is an assertion that the Shingle Street action remains classified under the U.K. Official Secrets Act and will remain so until 2021.

  [Read *www.shford.fslife.co.uk/ShingleSt/fullstory.htm*, and also *www.bbc.co.uk/suffolk/dont_miss/codename/bodies_ on_the_beach1.shtml*, and other sites found via Google].

Chapter 6 Photo Credits:

Henry L. Stimson, Albert Einstein, and Sir Winston Churchill - Library of Congress Prints and Photographs Division (New York World-Telegram collection)

Niels Bohr - Library of Congress Prints and Photographs

V2 rocket – National Archives

General Leslie Groves – U.S. Army

Ground Truth in Chapter 7, "A New Direction for America"

"Roosevelt Steps Down"

- The chapter is totally fictitious. FDR did not step down but won a fourth term in 1944. However, he actually did die of a cerebral hemorrhage on April 12, 1945.

- The account of the Norman Thomas Administration is fictitious. The major figures in the account: Charles Lindbergh, Gerald Nye, Jeanette Rankin, Henry Ford, Eugene Talmadge, John L. Lewis, Robert La Folette Jr. and Norman Thomas, himself, played other roles during the period described but were not members of any Presidential Administration. Stanley Loomis and Frank McMakin are fictitious. Nonetheless, many of the characters selected for roles in the fictitious Thomas Administration actually held isolationist, anti-war views that could be interpreted as pro-German. In January 1941, Lindbergh was a prominent vocal opponent of FDR's proposed "Lend-Lease" bill. [See *http://www.humanitas-international.org/showcase/ chronography/timebase/1941tbse.*htm]. Henry Ford and Eugene Talmadge actually held notoriously racist positions. Gerald Nye and Jeanette Rankin were leaders of the anti-war movement.

- About the chapter's having military uniforms disappearing from the White House scene, it is to be remembered that during the Bill Clinton administration (1993-2001), military personnel detailed to presidential duties were shabbily and disrespectfully treated. Early in that administration, Clinton's daughter, Chelsea, was quoted as having sniffed, "We don't talk to the military."

"Germany the First Nuclear Superpower"

Although the Germans were working on an atomic bomb, they were defeated before one was developed. While the story is totally fictitious, it is sobering to recall that a German nuclear physicist, who had been working on the Nazi bomb, was secretly recorded after V-E Day as saying privately, "If they [the U.S.] were able to finish it [an atomic bomb] by summer '45, then with a bit of luck, we could have been ready in winter '44-'45." The physicist, C.F. von Weizsaecker, ultimately became a dedicated pacifist. (Obituary: *Washington Times*, April 29, 2007).

In this fictitious telling, the Germans have chosen codenames for their first two atomic bombs that were actually used by the U.S. "Little Boy" ("*Kleiner Junge*" in German) was the first atomic bomb, dropped on Hiroshima, and "Fat Man" ("*Fettman*" in German) was the second, dropped on Nagasaki.

It is of interest that, according to J. Martin, writing in the *Daily Telegraph* (London) on the 60th anniversary of the Hiroshima attack, "Even Japanese survivors at Hiroshima have said, 'If Japan had the bomb, it might have used it in a worse way.'"

Chapter 7 Photo Credits:

Norman Thomas, Robert LaFolette, Eugene Talmadge, Speer and Hitler - tanker ship - Library of Congress Prints and Photographs Division

Ground Truth in Chapter 8, "The Canada Visit"

The chapter is totally fictitious.

The use of a phonograph repetitiously playing the first movement of Beethoven's Fifth Symphony commemorates the actual use of this music to prevent outdoor eavesdropping among the classroom buildings of a USAF classified training school at Goodfellow AFB, Texas in 1959.

Chapter 8 Photo Credits:

Trawler NS-88 and Black Lab "Shadow" – author

Buick – Courtesy of John MacDonald

Ground Truth in Chapter 9, "*Endlösung,* The Final Solution Achieved"

The chapter is totally fictitious. The *Nazi*s were only able to murder six million people before the end of the war in 1945.

In 1940, Vice Consul Hiram Bingham IV in Marseilles was actually ordered by Washington to deny exit visas to Jewish refugees.

Bingham defied those orders and, instead, issued documents that allowed well over one thousand Jews to escape. His "constructive dissent" was acknowledged by the U.S. State Department in 2002.

Hiram Bingham IV

Chapter 9 Photo Credit:

Enigma cipher machine (exhibited by the Nationalo Cryptologic Museum) - author

Hiram Bingham IV- Library of Congress Prints and Photographs Division

Ground Truth in Chapter 10, "Provocative Cruise of the Iron Fleet"

The chapter is totally fictitious, no such cruise took place and the cruise map of the U.S. mid-Atlantic coast is also fictitious.

Actual fates of the named German ships:

Ship	Actual Fate
Battleship Bismarck	Sunk in the North Atlantic in 1940 by Royal Navy warships and carrier-based aircraft. Admiral Lütjens went down with her.
Battleship *Tirpitz*	Sunk by the Royal Air Force in Tromsø Fjord, Norway in 1944 with 5.4 ton "Tallboy" bombs.
Battlecruiser *Graf Spee*	Trapped in Uruguay harbor, where she had gone to make repairs, scuttled by her crew off the coast in 1939 to avoid capture.
Battlecruiser *Deutschland*	Sunk by the Royal Air Force off Swinemunde by 5.4 ton Tallboy bombs in April 1945
Battlecruiser *Scharnhorst*	Sunk in the North Atlantic by Royal Navy warships in 1943.
Battlecruiser *Prinz Eugen*	Survived World War II; surrendered to the Allies in Copenhagen in 1945.
Battlecruiser *Gniesenau*	Struck a mine and was undergoing repairs in Kiel when sunk by the Royal Air Force in 1942.
Destroyer Z17 *von Roeder*	Sunk at Narvik in 1941.
Destroyer Z16 *Friedrich Eckhold*	Sunk in 1942
Yacht *Sachsenhausen*	Fictitious

- In the fictitious story, Lütjens was authorized to resort to arms if American warships tried to prevent the fleet from exercising their right of way in international waters.

Actually, before Germany declared war on the U.S. in December 1941, *Kriegsmarine* Admiral Rader actually said that German naval forces would ". . . if need be, resort to arms if American warships should try" to prevent them from exercising their right" to sink enemy merchant ships." Rader also complained about the American patrol system and hinted that American communication to the British of the positions of German naval units might be treated as an act of war. [*http://www.nationarchive.com/Summaries/v152i0022_03.htm*].

- *Korvettenkäpitan* Reinhard Hardegen was actually the skipper of U-123 and, in 1942, actually did surface the sub close enough to New York City to permit his crew to come up on deck to see the city's lights.

- Colonel Henry K. Roscoe, a member of the Delaware National Guard, was actually the Commanding Officer of the 21st Coast Artillery at Fort Miles, Delaware during World War II. Fort Miles actually did have two 16-inch guns in its Battery Smith but they were diverted from cancelled pre-war battleship construction plans. Fort Miles' 16-inch gun crews were actually at a very low level of operational readiness and quite possibly might not have been able to fight without help from experienced Coast Artillery cannoneers stationed elsewhere.

- Main gun armaments actually were salvaged from battleships sunk at Pearl Harbor. USS *Arizona's* 14-inch guns were actually removed and transferred to the Coast Artillery in Hawaii. In the fictitious story, 16-inch guns from the damaged USS *West Virginia* went to Fort Miles but the *West Virginia* was actually refloated, repaired and rejoined the fleet.

- Fort Miles actually did have eleven fire control towers near water's edge that afforded visibility limited to no further than a 14.1 statute mile horizon. All eleven remain standing and may be visited in Cape Henlopen State Park. The fort's tallest tower, 70 feet of concrete sitting atop a 40 foot hill, would have needed to be 233 feet taller (fully 343 feet above sea level) to give coast artillery spotters a 25 statute mile view that would match the range of the 16-inch guns. Actually, Fort Miles' 16-inch guns were limited to only 56% of their effective firing range because the artillery spotters could only see out to 14.1 statute miles. (Suggested additional reading: *Delaware's Ghost Towers*, ISBN 1-42084691).

Chapter 10 Photo Credits:

Battleship Bismarck, Admiral Lütjens, Reinhard Hardegen - U.S. Navy

"Sunderland" aircraft - RAF Museum, Hendon

Airship "K-11" - U.S. Navy, "K-11" marking added

Searchlight crew, Colonel Henry K. Roscoe, Ar-196 aircraft - U.S. Army

Fort Miles fire control tower – author

Ground Truth in Chapter 11, "The *Outfielder* Incident"

The chapter is totally fictitious. Readers will recognize the names of actual historical figures in this wholly fictitious account. The lesser characters, including the named RCAF officers, are all fictitious.

- During World War II Goodfellow Field, near San Angelo, Texas was actually a B-25 training base. Luke Field, Langley Field, Presque Isle, Lowery Field, Bolling Field, Hamilton Field, and Great Falls were all real Army Air Forces bases during World War II. The use of the unit numbers 6950th and 2167th are, for World War II, fictitious

Air Force units but commemorates two real USAF units based at RAF Chicksands, England, during the Cold War.

- As they remained in Allied hands, no U.S. raids on the islands off Newfoundland or Bermuda were actually planned or rehearsed. The radio interception and analysis ascribed to the Japanese in Mexico, to the Germans on the island of Saint Peter and to a German intelligence officer in Tokyo are fictitious but fully plausible.

- Eddie Allen was actually the Boeing Director of Flight and Research. Of course, the XB-29 program was successfully completed.

Chapter 11 Photo Credits:

Curtis Le May, James Doolittle, Henry "Hap" Arnold, B-17C, and -25H – U.S. Air Force

Hitler and the Grand Mufti - Library of Congress Prints and Photographs Division (New York World-Telegram collection).

Ground Truth in Chapter 12, "Pretext for the U.S. *Kristallnacht*"

The chapter's scenario is totally fictitious. The names of all the minor characters are fictitious and any resemblance to real persons, organizations and events are unintended coincidences.

Chapter 12 Photo Credits:

Cruiser *Baltimore* – U.S. Navy

Hitler and Benito Mussolini - Library of Congress Prints and Photographs Division (New York World-Telegram collection)

Ground Truth in Chapter 13, "George Strong"

- Gerd Strohminger, aka George Strong, is a fictitious character. The July 30, 1916 sabotage at Jersey City's Black Tom dockyard is an actual historical event that has been proven to have been committed by German agents. The U.S. was neutral in 1916 and the munitions were actually awaiting shipment to Czarist Russia.

- Although some placenames and streets in Alabama and Mississippi are real, all of the persons, organizations and events in the story are fictitious and any resemblance to real persons, organizations and events are unintended coincidences. The use of the State of Alabama in the story is a convenience not intended to single-out Alabama for criticism. However, during the writing of *At Least I Know I'm Free* in 2006, 15 Alabama churches were coincidentally set on fire in a four-month period. The State Fire Marshall's office declined to comment on any possible racial motivations on the part of the arsonists.

- The complicity of law enforcement officers and/or departments in the events depicted in the story is fictitious and is not intended to suggest or imply that current-day law enforcement officers and/or departments engage in or would engage in activities similar to those in the story. The story relies heavily on published past accounts of corrupt law enforcement officers and/or departments having provided support to the KKK and the German-American *Bund*. As recently as January 24, 2007, a former Mississippi sherrif's deputy, who had also been a member of the KKK, was charged in the 1964 deaths of civil rights activists.

- The problem of police complicity in criminal activities is not confined to the U.S. An investigation into police corruption, carried out during January 2007 by Scotland Yard, found "inappropriate relationships or criminal associations" among Metropolitan (i.e., London) Police officers and civilian staff. (Daily Telegraph, February 11, 2007).

Chapter 13 Photo Credits:

Freighter – author

"Black Tom" dockyard, longshoremen's demonstration, Woodrow Wilson – Library of Congress Prints and Photographs Division

"Ship" Café - author

Barn - author

Pistol – REME Museum, Reading UK

Two photos of *Bund* rallies, Woodrow Wilson – Library of Congress

Ground Truth in Chapter 14, "At the Olympic Games"

- Totally fictitious. There were no Olympic Games in Germany in 1946. At the time of this writing in 2006, a new German stage production, *My Ball - A German Dream*, in which Hitler conceives an international soccer tournament as a last-minute ploy for snatching victory, had triggered national outrage.

- On May 17, 1942, the Czech assassins did not lose their nerve and actually did kill Reinhard Heydrich as his open car passed them on the street. The little town of Lidice was actually leveled and all its male inhabitants slaughtered by the SS as reprisal for Heydrich's death.

- Heydrich was actually awarded the German Order by Hitler but posthumously after he was assassinated in 1942.

- The text of the oath George Strong took in the story is the actual oath that was taken by *Nazi* SS personnel.

"An Unholy Alliance [Cuba]"

- Many of the named principal characters are real but all the events and actions attributed to them are fictitious. In the 1940s and 50s, the Government of Cuba accommodated organized crime based in the U.S. and permitted its operations. This accommodation was ended when Fidel Castro seized power. The Havana meeting described in the story did not occur.

- Links between the KKK and German-American *Bund* are suggested by many publications to have been very strong. Links between U.S. Organized Crime and the KKK and German-American *Bund* are less certain. Interestingly, in October 2006, the FBI was investigating suspected cooperation by organized criminal groups in the U.S. with Al Qaeda, according to the Associated Press.

Chapter 14 Photo Credits:

Reinhard Heydrich and Adolph Eichman - Library of Congress Prints and Photographs Division

Fulgencio Batista - Library of Congress Prints and Photographs Division (LOOK Magazine collection)

Nürnberg Castle - author

Ground Truth in Chapter 15, "George's Train Ride"

The account is totally fictitious. The Gulfport street names are actual but all of the named characters and businesses are fictitious.

Chapter 15 Photo Credit:

Train station - Library of Congress Prints and Photographs Division

Ground Truth in Chapter 16, "Confirmation of the Holocaust"

- In the chapter, the text of the speech attributed to Hitler before revealing the Holocaust does begin with the same words he had actually spoken at the *Reichstag* in April, 1939:

  "As I have said before, since the day I began my political life, I have had but one goal: winning back the freedom of the German nation, building the strength and power of our Reich, overcoming the domestic fragmentation of our people, removing the barriers abroad, and ensuring its economic and political independence."

  [Note that Hitler claims to have had "but one goal" and then goes on to list five].

- The *Nazis* never officially confirmed the Holocaust. Details emerged during the post-war Nürnberg tribunal and from unending research that continues to the present day. Denial of the Holocaust has become a current debating weapon used to enrage and distract opponents and unhappily, in 2006, a Democrat candidate for Attorney General of Alabama (of all places) - the state's chief law enforcement office - included denial of the Holocaust as a part of his campaign. (*Washington Times*, May 13, 2006). The accepted estimate of the number killed in the *Endlösung* is six million. Although fictitious in this chapter, the probability that the *Nazis* would have continued toward completion of their "final solution," if not militarily defeated by the Allies, is a near-certainty.

- In the chapter, the limitations on available Communications Intelligence about the Holocaust and the reasons for the limitations are true. [Suggested additional reading: Robert J. Hanyok, *Eavesdropping on Hell*, published by the National Security Agency's Center for Cryptologic History, 2005].

- Director Dani Levy was inspired by Charlie Chaplin's film, *The Great Dictator,* and was keen to make a "German version" of the comic take on Hitler, *My Fuhrer: The Really Truest Truth About Adolf Hitler.* However, Chaplin had said he would not have made his film had he known the true extent of Hitler's extermination programme. [Daily Telegraph, London, Mar 7, 2006].

"Göring Warns; Hitler Threatens"

Hans Thomsen actually was the German *Chargé d'Affaires* in Washington before Germany's declaration of war in December 1941 but did not become Germany's ambassador.

Of course, Charles Lindbergh was not Vice President and received no friendly warnings from Herman Göring. But, during a 1938 visit to Germany, Göring actually did decorate Lindbergh with the Service Cross of the German Eagle for his services to aviation. Lindbergh's refusal to return the medal after the *Kristallnacht* pogrom only three weeks later seriously damaged Lindbergh's image. [*http://www.things.org/music/al_ stewart/history /Lindbergh. html*] In the run-up to the U.S. entry into World War II, Lindbergh was strongly criticized for his prominent isolationist position and for what was interpreted as pro-German views.

The political cartoon drawn by Dreiser (Dr. Seuss) is real and was actually published in U.S. newspapers. Lindbergh, who had been a pilot in the Reserves, redeemed himself by flying combat missions against the Japanese in the Pacific and was ultimately promoted to Air Force Reserve Brigadier General in the 1950s.

"George Goes Into Action"

The account is totally fictitious.

"Protests and Riots"

- Historical fact: New Orleans Mayor Ray Nagin ordered all firearms to be confiscated in the aftermath of Hurricane Katrina (2005). In July 2006, Senator David Vitter (R-LA) had proposed an amendment to the Homeland Security Appropriations Bill that would prohibit the confiscation of legally owned firearms during an emergency or major disaster. This bill attracted firm opposition and did not become law.

- The 2001 United Nations document: *Programme of Action to Prevent, Combat and Eradicate the Illicit Trade in Small Arms and Light Weapons* calls for gun control, worldwide tracking and national gun registries. The *Programme of Action* was adopted at the United Nations Conference on the Illicit Trade in Small Arms and Light Weapons in All Its Aspects from 9-20 July 2001. [UN DOCUMENT A/CONF.192/15].

- The incidence of lynching by mobs in the U.S. was by no means confined to the American South. By *Googling* "lynching," researchers will be able to access a heartbreaking history of lynching in the most improbable of states, far removed from the American South. The historical record lists over 4700 lynchings in the U.S. The degree of complicity and/or inaction by sworn law enforcement officials in that total can never be accurately known.

"In Montgomery"

The account is totally fictitious.

"The American *Kristallnacht* Riots Continue"

The account is totally fictitious. The names of all the minor characters are fictitious and any resemblance to real persons, organizations and events are unintended coincidences.

Chapter 16 Photo Credits:

Hitler addressing rally, Walter Winchell, TV set and added Louis-Conn fight scene, MV *Friedrich der Grosse* and MV *Konig Albert,* Times Square crowd, cross burning, Grant's Tomb, Father Coughlin, police car, KKK parade, and T. Geisel cartoon – Library of Congress Prints and Photographs Division.

FDR gravesite and White House - author

Sherman Tank – U.S. Army

Alabama State Capitol - Jeffrey S. Tobias

White church – Holly Mann and James Grayson

Ground Truth in Chapter 17, "America's Loss of Freedoms"

- The chapter is totally fictitious but is suggested as a prompt for thinking critically about the value of American Freedoms and how they could be lost through many kinds of failures on the parts of leaders and citizens.

- Concerning the basic civil rights protection of *habeas corpus*, during a hearing before the Senate Judiciary Committee on January 23, 2007, Senator Arlen Spector observed that the right of *habeas corpus* may not be suspended unless there is an invasion or rebellion while

U.S. Attorney General Alberto R. Gonzales suggested, during his testimony that, while the Constitution prohibits taking away a citizen's right to *habeas corpus* protections, ". . . there is no expressed grant of *habeas* in the Constitution." *(http://www.washingtonpost.com/wp-dyn /content/article/ 2007 /01/22/AR2007012201152. html?sub=AR).*

- Just as *At Least I Know I'm Free* was going to press, the popular Fox Broadcasting TV series "24" explored the issue of suspending *habeas corpus* during an acute national emergency. In its February 5, 2007 episode, fictitious U.S. President Wayne Palmer considers but rejects staff recommendations to suspend *habeas corpus* in the face of devastating terrorist nuclear strikes on American cities. The producers of "24" (Imagine Television) could easily have written a presidential decision for suspension into the script. The plausibility of a loss of American freedoms through an Executive Order by a President Wayne Palmer or a President Norman Thomas provokes serious thinking about terrible decision points that may materialize in the War on Terror.

- On February 27, 2007, the *New York Times* editorialized, That the United States responded to the horror of the Sept. 11 terrorist attacks with policies that went much too far in curtailing basic rights and civil liberties in the name of public safety.

Chapter 17 Photo Credits:

Gerald Nye, family at radio, German destroyer, and John Adams - Library of Congress Prints and Photographs Division

Camp Hoover - author

ABOUT THE AUTHOR:

WILLIAM C. GRAYSON

Bill Grayson is formally trained as a USAF Intelligence Officer. He served as Commander and as Operations Officer of various Air Force Signals Intelligence, Counterintelligence, and Operations Security units in Europe and South Vietnam and in the U.S. After completing his Air Force career, Bill joined the U.S. Department of Commerce as a Telecommunications Specialist team chief securing the computers and communications of whole federal civil agencies across the U.S. and in Latin America. Since 1981, he has been a Senior Security Consultant with a leading aerospace defense contractor and a Homeland Security analyst in Washington, DC. In those latter capacities, he has been an information systems security architect of very large networked computers of NASA, and the Defense, Treasury, Justice, and Transportation Departments and performed special activities for the White House, Air Force One, the Joint Chiefs of Staff, NATO and the Nuclear Regulatory Commission. In support of Homeland Security, Mr. Grayson supported U.S. Coast Guard port vulnerability studies on all three coasts. He holds BA and MS degrees, is a graduate of the Air Force Command and Staff College, and is a student of six foreign languages. He is a Certified Computer Systems Security Professional, an Operations Security Certified Professional, and an experienced Communications Security Professional. Bill is a member of the American Legion, Veterans of Foreign Wars, the Freedom Through Vigilance Association, the Tan Son Nhut Association, RAF Chicksands Alumni, Military Officers Association, and the Fort Miles Historical Association.